THE THIRD CROSSING

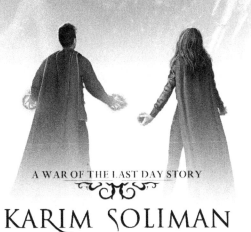

A WAR OF THE LAST DAY STORY

KARIM SOLIMAN

THE THIRD CROSSING

Copyright © 2022 by Karim Soliman

Edited by Yasmin Amin
Cover art & design by MiblArt

ISBN-13: 979-8-835177-325

In a moment of mental blankness, instead of deleting a paragraph, I deleted the entire manuscript.

To Warren Teitelman, the man who invented the Undo command.

Map of Koya

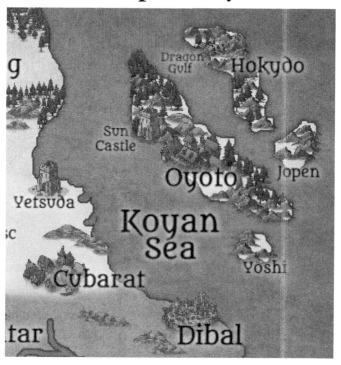

1. NATSU

Seventeen years before the War of the Last Day events,

Coastguards. They always showed up when you needed them the least. As though Natsu needed anything other than them keeping their noses out of her business.

"About time we turned the engines on, boss," Pantu suggested, looking from Natsu to the Turtle Ship closing in on their own vessel from the island of Jopen in the east. "We can make it to Yoshi before they know it."

Yoshi Island was already on their route. "Let them come," said Natsu, trying to appear composed in front of her men. They should never think she was weaker than Botan the Squid, her late husband. "They will find nothing."

"Natsu." Pantu stared at her. "This is not going to be a regular inspection. Coastguards do not ambush a ship unless they are looking for something."

Pantu was the only person on this vessel who had witnessed all of Botan's operations—a seasoned man she shouldn't take his advice lightly at all. "You know we never reveal the Wraith unless it's an emergency."

"*This* is an emergency, Natsu." Pantu gnashed his teeth, inspecting the dragon head adorning the bow of the Turtle, the iron spikes atop its closed deck making it impossible to raid. "We will be executed in a public square if the coastguards find the strings."

Selling those enhanced bowstrings to the Mankols on the other side of the Koyan Sea had earned her late husband a fortune. Shame the Emperor banned that kind of trade for the sake of his mages. "Then let's pray to the Light they won't find anything." She peered at Pantu. "You know what to do to keep their 'visit' short enough."

Her veteran right-hand man nodded and scurried toward the cabin.

Natsu inhaled the cool air deeply, allowing the addictive briny scent to sink deep down in her lungs. *The Wraith must remain a myth. Nobody must know what she looks like,* she recalled Botan's words, her oarsmen abiding by the coastguards' orders to halt. A dangerous game she was playing; she was aware of that, but she didn't want to risk losing the very asset that put her on top of the underground trading business (The Imperial officers would use the word 'smuggling' to label her activity, but why would she care? They would steal what they could from her, and still they would call it *taxes*).

The Turtle Ship anchored side by side with Natsu's ship. When a coastguard jumped into the Wraith, she gave Jirou a warning look before her brawny man might commit a deathworthy act. The only thing that rivaled his arms in their thickness was his head. And his black mustache.

THE THIRD CROSSING

Only four soldiers clad in the lamellar armor followed their slender leader who sauntered around in his embroidered silk tunic. Apparently, he was confident that his pink cloak would demand Natsu's crew's respect. *They sent a guardmage*, she thought, and strangely enough, she found that somehow flattering. Though the pale cloak he donned implied that he was not powerful enough to deserve the red mantle of the Emperor's mages, a guardmage could singlehandedly slay Natsu's twenty-three men.

Natsu looked up at the crow's nest, signaling to Sogeki-hei to stand down, and at once, he hid his crossbow. Calling for the services of her sharpshooter against coastguards should be a last resort. For now.

The guardmage stood right before Natsu, looking her up and down, his lip curled in disdain. "You seem to be the one in charge here. Am I right?"

Being the *woman* in charge could be a crime to these bastards, but now was the time to evade their handcuffs and get rich, not to make a stand. "How can I be of help, Officer Mage?"

The dubious mage scanned her face. "I need to see your trading permit."

Natsu turned to Pantu, who had fetched the document she knew the coastguards would ask for first. The mage almost tore the permit when he snatched it from Pantu's hand, and after a moment of scrutinizing the parchment, he asked, "Which part of Hokydo you come from, you say?"

"Sharks Gulf."

"And your destination is…?"

"The port of Dibal." Natsu folded her arms, nodding pointedly toward the permit she had paid in Mankol gold to obtain. "I'm an authorized importer of red mercury." But that didn't mean it was necessarily the *only* commodity she imported.

The guardmage squinted at her. "Why would a merchant from Hokydo be given such a permit? Don't we have enough merchants in Oyoto?"

"You have an army there, I presume. But are they *enough*?" She shrugged. "That I cannot answer."

The guardmage nodded, a wry smile slipping from his face. "Search the vessel," he ordered his soldiers.

Natsu kept her face a mask, sensing the doubt in the stares her men gave her as one soldier went into the cabin, the other three inspecting the deck crammed with supplies crates. Doubting her leadership in her first encounter with the coastguards was something that surely irked her, but she might understand that. What mattered now was the mood of this blasted mage who ambled on deck, his eyes scanning everybody and everything around him. The bastard wouldn't leave empty-handed if he sensed her men's nervousness.

"So, Dibal then," he began, his hands clasped behind his back. "A big ship for a few boxes of red mercury, don't you think?"

Regardless of what he was trying to fish, she wouldn't fall into this trap. "We trade in bulky goods quite often."

"What bulky goods?"

"Cattle, horses, oil, coal." She shrugged. "Anything we can buy or sell at a good price."

The guardmage grinned, revealing his yellow teeth. "I hear the Mankols treat gold the way we treat rice."

"The more coin we bring, the more taxes we pay," Natsu hurriedly said. "We are fulfilling our duty toward the Empire."

"I'm quite certain His Radiance is pleased with you," the guardmage said derisively.

THE THIRD CROSSING

A coastguard came to his superior. "The cargo hold is locked," he announced, glancing at Natsu.

When the mage shot her an inquisitive look, she said, "Let me handle this." She took one step toward the mage to call to her man standing behind him. "Jirou! The keys!"

For a second, the mage stole a glance behind him. A second that was enough for Natsu to snatch the tunjesten cuffs from her pocket and trap the mage's wrist in it. "Slaughter them!" she barked.

Jirou, who was certainly awaiting such an order, picked the nearest coastguard, smashed his nose and jaw with a massive punch, then tore his belly open with a dagger. Alarmed, the soldier standing in front of Natsu gripped the pommel of his sheathed sword, but before he could draw it, a bolt pierced through the back of his head, courtesy of Sogeki-hei from his nest.

"Hells and demons! What on Earth is this?" the mage yelled, clenching his fingers in a desperate attempt to draw anerjy from his surroundings.

"We could be some simple folks from Hokydo, Officer Mage," she gloated, her oarsmen finishing off the last two soldiers with the daggers and falchions they had been hiding under their shirts. "But we know one thing or two about anerjy."

The uproar on her ship drew the attention of more soldiers from the Turtle Ship. Most of them fell the moment they emerged thanks to Sogeki-hei's bolts, the rest slain by Jirou, Pantu, and the oarsmen.

"You know what Hokydoans are more familiar with, though?" Natsu drew her dagger and pointed it at the helpless mage, the sharp tip almost scratching his neck. "Blades."

"Please," the mage whimpered. "I have a child."

"So do I." Swiftly, Natsu slit his throat. The gurgling mage was down on his knees, holding his neck with both hands, but nothing could stop the surge of blood.

Pantu and Jirou stood at the edge of the Wraith facing the Turtle, waiting for more coastguards to show up, but all who came shortly after were the unarmed oarsmen of the Turtle, hands up in the air. When Pantu turned to Natsu, she said, "They are welcome to join our crew if they want."

Pantu wrinkled his forehead in disapproval as he approached her. "Too many mouths to feed, Natsu."

"We have a bigger prize now." She nodded her chin toward the Turtle. "I know a Rusakian lord who will pay a fortune for this beauty."

Pantu's jaw dropped, his eyes darting from her to the Turtle and back. "You didn't escape from the coastguards' ambush because…because…Blast! Why didn't you tell me this was your plan from the beginning?"

"Because you would think I'm insane." And maybe she was. Would anyone right in the head ambush the most formidable unit in the Koyan navy?

2. AKIRA

With a silk handkerchief, Akira wiped the beads of sweat from his forehead, making his way through the narrow, thronged streets of Oyoto. The shadows of the tall building blocks were surely a relief on this humid day, but what he needed right now was a cool, refreshing bath. And the day was just starting.

The people he stalked past were certainly not happy, but nobody dared to protest once they caught a glimpse of his pink mantle. Yes, all Koyans answered to the Emperor, but the mages in particular belonged to him. *We are his own people.* And the people of His Radiance were not to be delayed or even bothered.

Kim seemed to be struggling to keep up with him. "You are walking too fast, cousin," she said.

"We must catch that one before someone else does." He pointed to the stagecoach coming down the main road, a line of passengers waiting for their turn at the station.

"You are not asking me to run, are you?" Kim scoffed from behind him.

Akira doubled his pace as he strode beside the waiting line. "*Hells and demons! A mage,*" he heard an old woman mumbling, but he ignored her. If she wanted to complain, then she should address His Radiance who honored the laws his holy predecessors had issued.

The thirtyish man and his wife at the front of the waiting line pretended they hadn't noticed the mage coming through, and opened the door of the stagecoach that had just arrived at the station. Holding the reins of his two horses, the coachman wagged a firm finger at the couple, then pointed at Akira who was right behind them. "You know the rules. Wait for the next ride," the coachman instructed the man and his wife.

"But he was not here when you arrived!" the lady protested, but her *wise* husband held her hand, whispered into her ear, and gently pulled her away. Now the way was clear for Akira to hop on, but he had to wait for Kim to join him. *Come on, cousin,* he wanted to urge her. *We have an angry waiting line here.*

Giving the disgruntled folks a quick apologetic smile, Kim strode past them until Akira let her into the stagecoach first. "Sun Castle," he said to the coachman before he closed the door and seated himself opposite Kim.

His cousin groaned, stretching her tired legs. "Father had better find us a house closer to the station."

"Your father could have made our journey much easier if he wanted."

"You know him." She curled her tiny nose, a smile spreading over her small mouth. "He would never let me use his carriage until I earn it."

THE THIRD CROSSING

That rigid bald head. Wasn't being the Archmage's daughter enough to earn a stupid carriage? "We *will* earn it," Akira said confidently.

"Speak for yourself." She sighed. "I don't think I will pass the last trial."

Akira was aware of Kim's struggle with herbs and potions. Her estimates were never accurate. *A clumsy girl, she always has been.* "Even if you don't, I believe you deserve another chance. It wasn't fair to try you in your first six months. It took me two years to get the quantities right."

Folding her arms, Kim shook her head, a smile of contempt across her face. "You don't know, do you?"

Not sure what she was talking about, he asked, "Know what?"

"What those rushed trials were all about," Kim said, and then she bit her lower lip, as if she regretted saying too much. "I presumed that tutors would share more details with their senior students."

Though Kim was only one year younger than him, Akira was four years her senior at Sun Castle. "What details, Kim?"

Cornered in this carriage for at least a couple of hours, Kim should realize that it was too late now to keep hiding what she knew.

"All right," she finally said after a moment of awkward silence. "Father didn't tell me everything, but before heading to Sun Castle three days ago, he said something about a very big meeting there. A meeting to which every mage in Koya will be summoned."

Wait a minute. That was not what he thought the letter he had received from his tutor was about. "I thought we were urgently called to Sun Castle to hear our results."

Kim leaned forward toward him, her voice low when she said, "His Radiance himself is going to be there, Akira. We are summoned for something graver than the announcement of our results."

The Emperor? He rarely went outside the walls of his magnificent palace in the heart of Oyoto, his capital. The only people who had the honor of seeing him were the members of his court, his Imperial mages, and the guards of the… "Blast!" he exclaimed, feeling a smile tugging at his lips. "Do you know what it means if what you say is true?"

Kim shook her head, eyeing him inquisitively.

"We are going to see the Emperor, Kim," Akira went on. "Today, we are donning our red mantles."

* * *

From a mile away, both Akira and Kim could see the torchlit walls and towers of the colossal fort perched on a crag in the hills facing the western coast of Koya. As the two cousins came closer to Sun Castle, their coachman had to slow down as they encountered more stagecoaches and carriages on the road paved through the woods. Half a mile away from their destination, the path uphill was so packed they were forced to halt.

"Why aren't they moving?" Kim wondered.

Akira craned his neck outside the window of the stagecoach. Supervised by three Imperial Mages, dozens of soldiers clad in lamellar armors were inspecting everybody and everything passing through the gate of the mighty castle. "Exaggerated security measures for the sake of the important visitor." He turned to Kim. "Would you mind a little walk?"

THE THIRD CROSSING

Kim clambered out of the stagecoach and gave the coachman a handful of clinking dragons. Grateful, the coachman inclined his head toward the sweet girl, and then he wheeled his horses to go the other way downhill.

"You didn't have to do that," Akira rebuked his cousin, both of them walking uphill past the line of coaches.

"Being exempted from paying him doesn't mean that I'm not allowed to reward the poor fellow for his services."

"You and your soft heart," he scoffed, shaking his head. "Mother used to say that soft hearts only attract the darkest souls to prey on in this world."

Kim raised her eyebrows, as if she was shocked that her 'heartless' aunt actually said something like that.

Two soldiers stopped them when they reached the gate. "Name," one of them hissed demandingly, the other holding a book in his hand. *This must be the roster of attendees.*

"That's the Archmage's daughter," one of the Red Cloaks answered on Akira and Kim's behalf. "And that's my student Akira. Let them pass."

Akira approached his beefy tutor and bowed to him. "Jihoon Sen."

Jihoon was the hugest mage in Sun Castle, and arguably the nicest. He should have been Kim's tutor instead of the dreadful Tashihara. "A good day to show up on time," Jihoon said, not in his usual warm tone, though. *It must be the blasted big meeting.* Surely, it loomed large in the minds of all Sun Castle's folks.

"Has His Radiance arrived yet?" Akira asked his tutor, almost whispering.

"Just go to the courtyard and wait," Jihoon urged both Akira and his cousin, then left them behind to resume his supervisory duty.

The courtyard was bustling with activity when Akira and Kim arrived. A dais was set, atop which a magnificent seat was placed, the top of its back chiseled into a golden dragon's head, the armrests into two massive wings. Down the right side of the dais was a row of chairs lined in an angle that would face both the Emperor—no doubt, that seat was his—and the audience that already thronged the courtyard. Most of the attendees wore the pink cloak, but Akira was aware that pink wasn't always the label of a novice. Mages with a limited capacity of channeling anerjy would don the pink cloak until they died.

Most of the mages sat on the ground, waiting for the big meeting to begin. Upon seeing Kim, a few fellow Pink Cloaks pushed to their feet and went to ask her if she knew anything about this gathering. Certainly, she disappointed them with her useless answers. It was hard to imagine how secretive the Archmage could be, even with his own daughter.

"Stop this hubbub right now," a slim, dark-haired Red Cloak commanded, and at once, Kim's friends dispersed and returned to their places in silence. Akira had never had a conversation with that mage before, but he knew him very well. Who in Sun Castle hadn't heard about Minjun Sen, the youngest mage ever to put on the red mantle?

Minjun Sen stood right before Kim, his hands clasped behind his back when he said, "Your father must be proud of you today."

Kim grinned, obviously not understanding what Minjun was implying. *She was not pretending to be reticent with her friends; she is really that clueless*, Akira wanted to tell him, but he wouldn't expose his silly cousin.

"You know? I was your age when I was declared an Imperial Mage," Minjun continued. Now Akira felt like an idiot.

"I'm eighteen. I heard you were even younger than that when they raised you," Kim said to Minjun. *I'm invisible now.*

"Eighteen?" Minjun furrowed his brow. "You say you joined Sun Castle two years later than you should?"

Kim shrugged. "Father didn't believe I was ready for this place then." *She wasn't indeed.* The Archmage's daughter had failed her final academic tests of the Foundation School two years in a row.

"You had better be ready now." Minjun barely smiled, his voice flat as he added, "Our lives won't be the same after that seer has gone to Gorania."

"What seer?" Akira asked, unable to tame his curiosity.

Only now did Minjun notice that Akira existed. "Who are you?"

Hearing this question after spending four years in Sun Castle did hurt Akira's pride.

"That's my cousin Akira." Kim spared him the trouble of introducing himself, breaking this brief moment of awkward silence. "His mother, my aunt, is Chiaki Sen. One of the renowned tutors at the Foundation School."

"Akira, yes; I remember the name." Minjun nodded, managing a smile at Akira. "Jihoon Sen raves about your potion-making skills. But don't tell him I told you that."

The Red Cloak's praise took Akira by surprise, and it did make him feel better, but only a little bit. *Is he complimenting me only because I'm the Archmage's nephew?*

Akira harrumphed. "I'm honored that Jihoon Sen—"

"If you excuse me," Minjun interrupted him, and hurried to answer the call of one of the senior Red Cloaks. Could

Akira's first conversation with Minjun Sen have gone any worse?

"Did you hear what he said?" Kim asked Akira in a low voice.

"I don't mean to brag, but Jihoon's praise didn't surprise me." Come to think of it, Akira found it disappointing that Minjun mentioned nothing about the rest of his capabilities. *Potion-making skills?* His mother was a *Seijo*—a person who lacked the ability to channel anerjy—and yet, she could even craft more potent potions if she just studied and practiced as hard as he did.

"I'm talking about the seer, Akira." Kim leaned forward toward him. "That doesn't bode well."

"Why do you say so? What if that seer has brought good news at last? Isn't that what we have been waiting for?"

"Speak for yourself." Kim scowled. "Blood and ruin is not something I have been looking forward to."

Akira looked around to make sure nobody was paying attention to the mumblings of his silly cousin. "Even your father's position won't protect you if someone hears this nonsense." Actually, her father's position itself would be in jeopardy. How would the Emperor react if he learned that the daughter of his Archmage didn't approve of the War of the Last Day? The holy war all Koyans had been preparing for to reclaim the homeland they had lost to the so-called Goranians?

A bunch of Red Cloaks spread themselves across the courtyard, commanding everybody to line up. Guards and Imperial Mages secured the perimeter of the meeting venue, and shortly after, members of the Imperial Court entered, sauntering in their bright, light-blue cloaks save for Hanu Sen. The short, gray-haired lady, who had been in charge of the Imperial Court for a decade, wore the only dark-blue cloak in Koya. None of the members assumed their seats down the dais until she claimed hers first.

Yes, colors did matter in Koya.

Kim stood on her tiptoes, fretting. "I can't see Father."

"He will come, don't worry." The Archmage always had a seat at the Imperial Court, and that made him the only person in Koya who had two cloaks of different colors. "Perhaps he is going to attend this meeting as an Imperial Mage, not as a member of the court. After all, this gathering is held at his own playground."

The bald fiftyish man didn't disappoint Akira, and indeed, he came in, clad in the Imperial Mages' red cloak. Instead of joining the members of the court, he lingered near the steps of the dais until the Imperial Guards emerged from the main building of Sun Castle. Wearing their distinctive purple cloaks, they advanced toward the courtyard, surrounding the holiest human being on this Earth.

His Radiance, the Emperor of Koya.

For many Pink Cloaks here, if not for all of them, it was their first time to lay their eyes on the Light's chosen man to lead this nation. *He is younger than I imagined.* Akira contemplated the Emperor's lean frame and clean-shaven face that made him look about Minjun Sen's age. There was grace in his strides, elegance in his glossy, embroidered, black and purple, silk robe. Judging by His Radiance's shiny head, Akira understood why bald heads were so popular among Red Cloaks and members of the court.

The Emperor ascended the dais, his Imperial Guards ringing him till he assumed his magnificent seat. After that, they split themselves up into two groups; one forming a line behind the Emperor, the other down the dais facing the audience. All members of the court, as well as every mage in the courtyard, were kneeling until His Radiance gave them his gracious permission to be at ease.

"My sixteenth great-grandfather built this stronghold, but not only to deter the Goranians from invading our western coasts," the Emperor began, his voice deep yet loud and clear. "This place was meant to be a beacon for every Koyan, to instill hope in their hearts, to assure them that we never forgot, and we will never forget, the glorious mission awaiting us." He paused for a moment, then continued, "In other circumstances, I would say 'Awaiting us *and* our descendants.' But with the news that I recently received, I have come here to confirm to you all that it is only *our* mission. Our descendants will be born there, in the homeland our ancestors were forced to abandon centuries ago!"

That was quite a huge announcement. An announcement worthy of the presence of His Radiance himself. The War of the Last Day was a big topic the likes of Akira's mother had been teaching to Koyan younglings for hundreds of years. If the Emperor really meant what he said—of course, he meant it; he was the Light's voice on Earth, mind you—then from now on, the Last Day would finally come to exist outside the books and scrolls of tutors and scholars.

"Lately, my meetings with the Imperial Court were centered around nothing but our preparations for the Last Day," the Emperor continued, his voice firm. "It was disappointing to learn that, as we speak now, we are still not ready to achieve a crucial victory against the Goranians. While that has been our status for long, it won't be acceptable anymore. We must deal with the fact that the Goranians could be amassing their armies for a Third Crossing soon."

THE THIRD CROSSING

Alright. The beginning of the Emperor's speech misguided Akira somehow. *A Third Crossing?* That would be a nightmare if it happened.

"Starting from this moment, we are at war," His Radiance declared. "The Third Crossing will happen, but this time it will be different. It will be *us* crossing to the Goranian continent."

The Emperor knew when to pause; Akira would give him that. Because right after His Radiance finished the last sentence, a storm of applause shook the courtyard. *He has just turned the label of our most humiliating defeat into our own war banner. Brilliant.*

The Emperor waited until his crowd quieted down again. "For this war, I will need a fully dedicated court to accelerate our preparations before it is too late. By the power vested in me by the Light Himself, I hereby announce Kungwan Sen as the Head of the Imperial Court."

"Your father." Akira turned to Kim, hoping nobody heard his low voice. Speaking in the presence of His Radiance without his permission was not a deed to be taken lightly, but Akira couldn't simply keep his lips sealed. The news he had just heard was not only great for Kim and her father; it was an unprecedented event in Koya's recorded history. Kungwan Sen would be the first Archmage to lead the Imperial Court.

The Emperor signaled Kim's father to come and stand next to him to address the audience. The new head of the court started with a diplomatic introduction, thanking His Radiance for entrusting him with such a huge responsibility, acknowledging Hanu Sen for her wise leadership during her tenure. After he was done with the formalities, he addressed his 'people.' "Putting me in the highest position a Koyan citizen could ever reach is not just an honor for mages; it's a reminder to all of us of the great mission we are destined to fulfill. Starting from this day, and until we celebrate our victory in the War of the Last Day, nothing less than perfection will be expected from each and every one of us. Whether you are called to fight at the frontline, or organize the books in the library here, you will do it in the best way possible."

Kungwan Sen motioned for one of his cloaked assistants to hand him a scroll. "You all heard what His Radiance just said; we don't have what it takes to defeat the Goranians for good. And that urged us to make the trials sooner this year. For the upcoming war, we need as many Red Cloaks as possible, and we need to prepare them fast. That's why we were so meticulous about choosing our new Imperial Mages. We wanted to ensure that their merciless training would enhance them, not break them."

Akira's stomach was in knots as the Archmage opened the scroll to read the names of the new Red Cloaks. "We chose nine candidates based on their performance in the last trials. We also took into consideration their tutors' evaluation reports during their entire tenure at Sun Castle."

Come on. Say the blasted names. Akira bit his lower lip, waiting for the Archmage to announce the first new Red Cloak. Why was it taking too long? Was it Akira's anxiety that rendered him impatient?

You will be our salvation, I know that, Akira recalled his mother's words to him the first day he donned the pink cloak.

"Fumiko Kaito," the Archmage began.

You will be the one who abolishes the disgrace your father has brought to this family.

"Keisuki Itachi."

No one will even remember that this sinner even existed...

"Aira Kija."

…after you become the holy scourge of the Light to the eternally-damned Goranians.

"Lan Wei."

Trust the seer's vision, Akira.

"Shu Tao."

The War of the Last Day is sooner than we think.

"Asa Ada."

And you can't be just part of it.

"Dal Moon."

You must be one of its heroes.

"Chikao Souta."

Hearing the name of the eighth candidate catapulted Akira back to the current moment. To the courtyard. Where the Archmage was about to announce the last mage to join the *heroes* of the Last Day. Akira's mother would never forgive her son if he didn't…

"And Kim Kungwan."

3. NATSU

She laid a soft kiss on the forehead of her five-year-old boy lest she wake him. The sleeping brat could be a handful sometimes, and old Sakura deserved a break.

Natsu tiptoed out of Riku's room, Sakura waiting for her outside, hands on her waist. "Not ready to talk now either?" the old lady asked, her judging tone not bothering Natsu anymore. Another lecture was coming, and Natsu had no time for this endless back and forth.

"Later, Mother," Natsu said, stalking past the old lady to pick up the cloak she had left on the nearest chair to the door of the house.

"Isn't losing his father enough?" Sakura snapped.

Natsu inhaled deeply, hoping the fragrant scent of incense would soothe her nerves. "You are going to wake him up this way." She put on the cloak and headed to the door.

"We never needed your husband's coin, and we never will." Sakura followed her as she held the doorknob. "All the coin in the world will be of no use if that little child loses his mother."

"You are wrong, Mother. We have always needed that coin." Natsu glared at Sakura. "It's just you who have forgotten how life outside this house looks like. You want me to quit and do what? Work on Father's pathetic boat to earn a handful of copper coins every day for what I fish? No, Mother! I won't let my son be raised in a smelly hovel on some mud-laden alley packed with drunkards. Are we clear now?"

Her mother looked down without uttering a word.

"Good." Natsu heaved a sigh. "Because I'm done talking about this every day."

Natsu slammed the door shut behind her and joined Pantu and Jirou, who had been waiting for her down the street—the only paved street in Hokydo, mind you. When Pantu ushered her to the cart, she said, "This shall draw too much attention." Horses were rare animals to encounter across the islands of Koya, especially in its poorest parts.

"It's a long walk to the meeting venue," said Pantu. "We shouldn't keep Qianfan waiting too long."

The name of Qianfan could be intimidating to many people in Hokydo, but not to Natsu. She should heed Pantu's advice, though. "The cart, it is." She grinned. "We need to save our strength for the meeting."

Natsu clambered onto the cart, Pantu joining her at the back, Jirou assuming the coachman's seat. "*Save our strength*," Pantu echoed dubiously as the cart moved. "Another plan you are not sharing with me?"

Natsu took a moment till she understood what he was hinting at. "Still unable to forgive me since the Turtle job?" she teased her deputy.

"It's a mere question." Pantu cast her a studying look. "I'm not fond of surprises, you know. Especially, with the likes of Qianfan."

Qianfan was the one who had benefited the most from her husband's death. Having no rival in the underground business for some time, the way was paved for him to undertake as many jobs as he could. *Me taking over Botan's business must have disappointed him.*

"The likes of Qianfan must know that they are not alone in the market any longer," she said to her deputy.

"Still, you didn't answer my question, Natsu. What are you up to?"

"He is the one who called for this meeting," she reminded her deputy. "Why don't you ask him?"

Pantu stared at her accusingly. "Sogeki-hei told me you had sent him to do a task this morning."

Indeed. Her sharpshooter must have arrived at the meeting venue already. "Nothing more than a precautionary measure. I will feel safer, knowing that he is watching my back."

Pantu didn't seem convinced. What should she do to win back his trust?

"We got away with the Turtle," he said. "But any reckless acts today will have serious implications. To the coastguards, we are ghosts; they can't follow our tracks. But Qianfan? The man knows more than enough to hurt us."

"Don't we know enough about him as well?" Natsu peered at her deputy, the man who had his own network of spies all over Hokydo and even Oyoto. Thanks to his eyes, she had become aware of the location of the Turtle ship and the fact that a Pink Cloak had been in charge of its crew.

"Natsu, the man wants to talk. Let's hear him out first, and whatever he asks, don't give him a final say right away. Just tell him you will think about it and leave."

So, her deputy wanted her to behave. Well, she couldn't promise him. It might be hard for her to abide by his piece of wisdom if she heard something she didn't like.

The meeting venue was near the Sharks Gulf. To go there, Jirou had to take them through the Old Village (Not that there was a New Village; it was nothing more than a name. Every place in Hokydo was in the same miserable condition), and that was today's main event for the simple folks inhabiting these slums. Everybody, mostly children, gathered in the muddy streets and the small windows of their cracked shacks, gaping in awe at the horse passing by. *Too young, too fragile to join their fathers at the docks in the west or the mines in the east,* Natsu thought, the sight of the little ones reminding her of her childhood in this very place.

The childhood she wanted to protect her son from.

The venue was an abandoned warehouse on the outskirts of the Old Village. Studying every rooftop around her, Natsu still couldn't spot Sogeki-hei anywhere. *If I can't find him, then Qianfan won't,* she thought, staring at the two lookouts posted at the door of the warehouse.

"I don't like this, boss. There could be more men inside," Jirou said in his hoarse voice. "We will be badly outnumbered inside this trap."

"Not with you on our side, Jirou." Natsu winked at her burly man. "It will be us trapping them."

The shorter lookout held the door ajar and apparently, he notified whoever was inside the warehouse of Natsu's arrival. The taller fellow kept his eyes fixed on the cart approaching the warehouse until Jirou pulled on the reins of the horse to halt it.

Natsu and Pantu clambered down from the cart and waited for Jirou, who found a wooden sign to tie the horse to. As the three of them went to the door, the lookouts gestured for them to stop. "No weapons." The tall lookout pointed to the falchion hanging from Jirou's belt.

"I'm sure your boss is abiding by this rule." Natsu sneered.

The tall man tilted his head.

"*Let them in, boys*," came Qianfan's voice from inside. "*After all, we are here to* talk."

Not feeling comfortable about Qianfan's tone, Natsu exchanged a quick look with Jirou. "Just be ready," she mouthed to him before Qianfan's men opened the door for their master's visitors to come in.

The warehouse was not 'too abandoned' inside, considering the dozen men Qianfan had brought with him to the meeting. Half of them formed a circle around their black-bearded boss who stood at the center of the warehouse, the remaining six covering the windows and the only exit of the place. And they were all armed, Natsu observed. For someone who was here to *talk*, the bastard had brought too many men. Was it a trap like Jirou expected?

Without looking at Pantu and Jirou, Natsu signaled them to calm down as the men standing in front of Qianfan made way only for her. "I never thought a woman could scare you that much." Natsu smiled lopsidedly at Qianfan.

"You mean the woman who captured a Turtle Ship?" Qianfan arched an eyebrow. "Some security measures won't harm."

"If this is a joke, then it's a bad one." Natsu wore a stern face. No way would she admit her responsibility for that…

brilliant piece of work. "You think anyone with a sane mind might even think of facing a Turtle Ship?"

"Taking over a Turtle requires a brilliant mind, not just a sane one." Qianfan leaned forward toward her. "And I think you are brilliant enough to realize that such a job is not only a grave act against the coastguards; it's a violation of the deal your husband and I struck years ago."

The Mankol market was for Botan while the Rusakian was totally Qianfan's; Natsu was aware of that. "That deal died with Botan. You need to strike a new one with me."

"Listen. Everybody in this business knows that Rusakia is mine." Qianfan nodded his chin pointedly toward Pantu, who was standing behind her. "Right, boy?"

That 'boy' was actually Qianfan's age, if not older. "You only talk to me, Qianfan. If there is something I don't have an answer for, I will be the one addressing my men." Natsu straightened her back as she glared at the bearded man. "Is that clear?"

Qianfan stared at her. "The guts you have, Natsu." He laughed, then said, "I can't believe you have been lurking in the shadows all of Botan's life."

Natsu feigned a smile. "I guess we have an understanding, then."

"Very well," Qianfan muttered thoughtfully, his hands on his waist as he ambled inside the ring his minions had formed around him. "A new deal with the old conditions. The Mankol market will exclusively be yours while the Rusakian remains mine."

That was easier than she had thought. "Deal. And the Light is our witness."

"What about the Turtle?" Qianfan looked her in the eye. "I was told it brought you an unbelievably huge amount of coin."

Alright. The duel was not over yet. *I celebrated a little bit too early.* "The Turtle you would have never dared to capture, you mean?"

That didn't seem to offend Qianfan, who said nonchalantly: "The Turtle you sold to one of *my* customers."

Natsu grinned scornfully. "Shame we didn't have a deal back then."

"Right." Qianfan smacked his lips. "That's why I only demand one-third of your trophy as a fair compensation."

May he burn in hell before he takes a single coin from me. "This is not how you strike a deal."

"Don't be greedy, Botan's widow," he warned. "Two-thirds are more than enough."

"You did *nothing* to earn that damned third," Natsu snarled.

"And you wouldn't have been able to turn your Turtle into gold were it not for my Rusakian lord."

This negotiation was worse than useless. "We are done here, I believe." Natsu turned, motioning for Pantu and Jirou to follow her to the door of the warehouse. The latter didn't stop looking around until they reached the exit, none of Qianfan's goons intercepting them.

"One quarter, Natsu," Qianfan called from behind her. When she stopped, he continued, "That's my final proposal."

It wasn't about the coin, Natsu reflected. That bastard would claim anything just to affirm his authority over her in front of her men. *We won't be rivals if I pay him a single dragon.*

"If you are really keen about our deal, then you should withdraw your humiliating proposal," Natsu said firmly. "Take three days to reassess the entire situation. I will patiently wait for your answer."

Natsu and her men exited the warehouse. Hurriedly, Jirou untied the horse while his boss and Pantu were climbing back onto the cart. Qianfan's lookouts followed them with their eyes as Jirou spurred the horse to a canter. Truth be told, Natsu felt a sort of relief when the blasted warehouse was out of sight.

"You don't think he will reassess a thing, do you?" Pantu asked her.

"You tell me," Natsu said to her veteran deputy, who was more familiar with Qianfan than she was. "Because I believe we have just started a war."

4. AKIRA

The knocks on the door of his room awakened him. What was wrong with the people of this tavern? Couldn't they mind their own business and leave him in peace?

Akira closed his eyes and tried to resume his sleep, but the knocks sounded again on his door insistingly. "Get lost!" Akira cried.

"*Open, Akira.*"

The female commanding voice startled him. *Can't be.* At once, he pushed the blanket away, jumped out of bed, and scurried to the door to open it for the last person he wanted to see right now. "Mother? How did you find me?"

The fortyish lady wearing the *Seijo* tutors' yellow cloak peered at him, one hand on her waist. "We are not going to have this conversation in the corridor, are we?"

For a week, he hadn't returned home to avoid this very conversation. Reluctantly, he let his mother into his room and closed the door behind her.

The lady in the yellow cloak sat on the edge of the bed, looking judgingly at the small wardrobe and the mirror next to it. "What are you doing in this rathole?"

Only Kim knew he was in this 'rathole.' "Didn't you ask the one who revealed my whereabouts to you?"

"I want to hear the answer from you, son."

Akira puffed, groping for the answer his mother never wanted to hear. "I failed you, Mother. I will never be a Red Cloak."

"That's what I heard," Akira's mother pointed out impassively. "So, what are you going to do next? Spend the rest of your life hiding in this hole with your shame?"

My shame? His mother's words sank deep into his heart. Her *support* was not something he needed for the time being. Should he bother to defend his hurt pride?

"Say something," his mother demanded. "Don't tell me I gave birth to a boy who grew up to become as helpless as his father."

Akira was unable to take any more of her nonsense. "You know what? I'm sick of you bringing him up whenever something wrong happens. Why do I have to carry the burden of his despicable deeds?"

"Why did I?" his mother snapped. "My entire life was ruined because of someone else's *despicable deeds*! After more than two decades of service in the Foundation School, they tried to relieve me of my duty, claiming that I wasn't qualified to teach anymore. Do you know why? Because an adulterer's wife could never be a role model for younger generations!"

Akira was too young when his father was publicly executed for his sin. His mother had never told him about her troubles with the school. "Who were *they*?" he asked. "The school supervisors?"

"Them, fellow tutors, *and* pupils' parents," she said bitterly. "I struggled to defend my position there, and I barely kept it. But they made it clear to me that this was the farthest I would get. The orange cloak was something I had to forget about, because I was blamed for a sin I never committed."

The orange cloak was the highest tier any *Seijo* outside the Imperial Court could ever dream of. It meant for his mother what the red cloak meant for him.

"Nobody has the right to judge anybody except the Light Himself," Akira said.

"We are nothing but sinners who judge other sinners." His mother grimaced. "It's not right, but that's the reality that we have to deal with." She rose to her feet, approached Akira, and held his cheeks with both hands. "I had to fight to earn my place, Akira. So, instead of fretting about the reason why your life has become like this, ask yourself what you must do to change it to the life you deserve."

The prestige of the red cloak; Akira was aware that many mothers in Koya—other than the one holding his face right now—were obsessed with the idea of seeing their sons and daughters wearing this distinguished attire. The attire of the Light's soldiers in the holy war to liberate their occupied homeland. But in Akira's mother's case, it wasn't all about the honor of fighting the Goranians.

It was *never* about the Light's holy war, he would dare say.

"I did whatever it took to *earn my place* too, Mother." Akira gently took his mother's hands down, away from his face. "I worked really hard, read every book, studied every potion and jumun, implemented everything I had learned in the trials. What else was I supposed to do?"

"A few more things. For a starter: Did you talk to your tutor or anybody at Sun Castle to understand why you were not raised to a Red Cloak? Did you ask them when the next trials are? What do you need to improve to pass them?"

His mother's presence of mind was not bad. "You stated every step I should consider except going directly to my uncle. Don't you want me to talk to him?" He leaned toward her. "Don't you want to talk to your *brother*?"

"My brother," she echoed in contempt. "He was never there for his sister. He always looked down upon me because I was a *Seijo*, not a *Mahono* like him. I'm not going to beg him after all these years."

Mages were only wed to mages; a law the emperors had enforced to ensure that sorcery would never perish. But that didn't prevent Akira's *Mahono* grandparents from giving birth to a *Seijo* daughter. *Mother was their malformed child.*

"Your brother happens to also be the Archmage, who has the upper hand in every decision made at Sun Castle," Akira reminded his mother. "Doesn't that make you believe that returning to that place to question my results would be futile?"

His mother wagged a firm finger. "Don't you dare tell me it's futile before you fight the fight. What worse could happen to you, boy?"

"Nothing, most probably." He shrugged. "But I know for sure that nothing good would happen either."

"So, this is your next big move?" His mother curled her nose, gesturing at the cracked walls of his small room. "Don't you understand that they will definitely expel you from Sun Castle if you disappear like that without notice? Do you think this will pass without repercussions for you?

For *me*?" Fidgeting, she returned to the edge of the bed and sat down, her eyes fixated on the floor. "I won't only be the adulterer's widow; I will also be the reject's mother."

His mother wouldn't relent until he did as she asked; Akira should know better. *She will blame me forever for her misery*, he thought. *Silencing her is worth it.*

"Fine." Akira rubbed his face with both hands, then forced a smile. "I will go back to Sun Castle and see what went wrong."

Without asking, his mother opened the wardrobe, took the pink cloak out of it, and put it in Akira's hands. "You are going now."

* * *

Akira had never loathed his pink cloak as he did today. *Wrong. I hated it the most the day Kungwan Sen, my dear uncle, announced the names of the new Red Cloaks.*

The tavern he had been staying in was in the heart of the capital. Finding a coach here implied skipping a long waiting line of irked travelers—longer than the one at the station near Kim's house. Except that they were not so angry today. Actually, they urged him to go ahead. *I lock myself up for one week, and I find a different country on my first day out.*

To Akira's surprise, the smiles on the travelers' faces vexed him—they just didn't seem right. What happened to the angry murmurs and the eyes shooting daggers at him; his usual routine whenever he went to seek a ride at a station?

The first woman in the line made way for the young mage to take her turn. When the stagecoach arrived, Akira turned to the first four people. "There is plenty of room." He motioned for them to get inside as he clambered to sit next to the coachman.

"I will be flogged for this, Master Mage," said the coachman politely.

"If any guard stops us, I will tell him I asked for it." He looked at the travelers who had already assumed their seats. "And take them to their destinations first. My stop is the farthest anyway."

The hesitant coachman took some time to decide. *This simpleton must be wondering if I'm testing him,* Akira reckoned. "It's alright, good man," he reassured the coachman. "Let's go."

The coachman drove through the packed streets of the Craftsmen's Quarters, which was arguably the noisiest district in Oyoto, if not across the entire Koyan Empire. But cramming all smithies and carpentry workshops into the same neighborhood was a move the restless capital needed; it might have granted the majority of this populous city some peace. *May the Light help the folks who live here.*

The coachman had dropped two passengers at their destinations when he surprised Akira and asked him, "So, when will it happen?"

"*What* will happen?"

The coachman's eyes widened in excitement when he said, "The Third Crossing. Come on, Master Mage. You can't pretend you know nothing about it."

When had the rumors leaked outside the walls of Sun Castle? "Perhaps I do," Akira scoffed. "You seem glad about it, though."

"You have no idea, Master Mage." The coachman smacked his lips. "It is relieving to know that all these centuries of suffering will soon be over."

"You live in the capital and talk about suffering? What would the folks from Hokydo say, then?"

The coachman cast Akira a judging look. "Forgive me, young Master, but you're a mage. You know nothing about prices and taxes because you never need to pay. You know nothing about the good folks who move from this city every day because of its ever-increasing cost of living."

Taxes were a big problem in Oyoto, Akira knew, but it wasn't necessary to brag about his knowledge right now. Because as the coachman had just said; the likes of Akira never went through the struggle of affording anything. *That's why they hated us. We have been privileged for doing nothing.*

But that wouldn't be the case with the *Third Crossing*. Now Akira understood what those smiling faces at the waiting line were for. *We are their saviors.*

Except that he wasn't. Those ignorant folks couldn't imagine how huge the difference between the Pink Cloaks and the real saviors of the Koyan nation was.

"Wars come at a cost." Akira borrowed this piece of wisdom from some book whose title he didn't remember.

"Our people have already been paying its cost in vain. About time we reaped something."

The stagecoach halted to drop the last two passengers. The coachman gestured toward the empty seats behind Akira, but the young mage insisted on resuming the journey next to him. After a week of seclusion, Akira could certainly use some company.

"What makes so you sure you will reap anything good from that war?" Akira asked.

"We may not be well educated like you, Master Mage, but our grandparents told us the tales they had heard from their grandparents about our *Old Koya*; our real homeland, which was *twenty* times bigger than the wretched islands we have been trapped on for centuries. Don't tell me our life won't be better there!"

The difference in areas between their current homeland and Old Koya—the continent its people now called Gorania—was not accurate, yet not much exaggerated. Those vast, rich lands across the Koyan Sea were enough to change the Koyans' lives forever. Seijo *mothers will be allowed to give birth to siblings, to say the least.*

"I was talking about our chances of beating the Goranians," said Akira. "What makes you believe that our victory is guaranteed."

"We have mages, the Goranians don't. In fact, I wonder why we have waited for too long to wage war on them."

"Because our emperors wanted to avoid a fate similar to the one we suffered in the Second Crossing." It was clear that some Koyans had forgotten what their ancestors had narrated about their previous two wars against the Goranians. After a failed first attempt to invade the Koyans' continent, the Goranians had learned their lesson and crushed the Koyans in their second campaign, forcing them to abandon their homeland until this day. *Although we had mages back then, too.*

"You say we are not ready yet, Master Mage?" the coachman asked warily, making Akira wish he could take all his questions back. *I just wanted to understand, not to make you question the Emperor's decision.* Questioning anything His Radiance did or said was a grave action that would never pass without a befitting sanction.

"Of course, we are, but I have my reasons to be certain of that." Akira didn't flinch. "I was just curious to hear yours."

For the sake of safety, Akira steered the conversation toward the humid weather and the mosquitos infesting the western coast of the island, particularly Sun Castle, and the trick worked. After that, he let the coachman blabber on about his persistent great-grandfather who had made a bold move and left his parents in Hokydo to start on his own in the great city of Oyoto. For the rest of the journey, Akira didn't pay much attention to the coachman's prattle.

Akira did his best to avoid any familiar faces as he entered the castle. While his attempt wasn't a complete success, he managed to evade any long conversations with the few colleagues he ran into by not falling into the trap of stopping to greet them. They might judge him for that, they might understand later. Either way, he didn't care.

His mentor, Jihoon Sen, was reading a book in his office when Akira reached it. "Took you too long to show up." Jihoon placed the book on the desk he was sitting behind, the faint smile on his puffy face not concealing the rebuking tone of his voice.

"I...I..." Akira should have prepared himself better than this for his meeting with Jihoon. "I just needed some alone time to reflect."

"Good." Jihoon nodded approvingly. "And what did you conclude from this reflecting?"

Aware that would seem rude, Akira couldn't help smiling mockingly. "That I did everything right to earn the damned red cloak."

Jihoon glared at him, probably for the first time since Akira knew him. "I should punish you for your insolence, young man. The only thing that holds me from doing so is my understanding of your frustration."

Akira was lucky that his mentor was someone soft like Jihoon. If he acted the same way with the dreadful Tashihara, she would expel him at once. *She promoted Kim, though.* "With all due respect, Jihoon Sen; you can never imagine how frustrated I am."

"I said 'I understand your frustration,' but that doesn't mean I *accept* it." Jihoon pointed a firm finger at the chair on the opposite side of the desk. "Sit."

What Akira needed now was an explanation for his result, not a lecture about good behavior, but he shouldn't test Jihoon's patience more than that. Without objecting to his mentor's last statement, Akira did as Jihoon asked, and waited for him to speak.

The beefy tutor heaved a sigh. "Do you know how we lost in the Second Crossing?"

Seriously? The question sounded so basic Akira felt offended. A student in the Foundation School could give a lecture about the old wars between the ancestors and the Goranians. *Is he testing me now?* "Was my score in the history test this low, Jihoon Sen?"

The beefy tutor tilted his head, waiting for Akira's answer.

"Alright." Akira couldn't believe he was doing this. "The Goranians flanked our army and launched a suicide attack at our mages. They lost half of their army in that charge, but still, they outnumbered our soldiers who had lost the protection our mages had been providing for them."

"That's a passage from a history book, not the answer to my question." Jihoon didn't seem impressed at all. "Can't you infer why we lost?"

What was the trick Akira was missing? Jihoon's question couldn't be as straightforward as it seemed. "The Goranians were too many."

"Our mages got exhausted before they could defeat the Goranian horde." Jihoon leaned forward toward Akira. "Because that's what we do, Akira. Our stamina is not infinite."

Akira didn't like the direction the conversation was headed to. "We were talking about my *frustration*. What does this brief history lesson have to do with it?"

"In your last trial, you did extremely well in most of the aspects. Your performance in the potions' test in particular was the best I had ever seen from a student in a while."

A slap on the face was coming after all this praise, Akira knew. "But?"

"Your jumuns were far below the expected level, son." Jihoon pressed his lips together. "I'm sorry to be the one telling you this, but you can never become a Red Cloak. It's not your fault, but it's something you can't do anything about."

Akira had come to Sun Castle, expecting to hear some lame excuses about the results of his trial. But a clear statement like the one he had just heard from his mentor? That was really devastating.

"Is that because of my parents?" It was rare for *Seijo* parents to give birth to a mage. And even if it happened by chance, their child wouldn't be as powerful as the offspring of two *Mahono* parents. That was why it was forbidden for a *Mahono* to wed a *Seijo*. And that was why two *Mahono* parents were allowed to give birth to siblings. *Because Koya needs as many powerful mages as possible.*

"We only assess our candidates for their capabilities, not for their parents."

"Are you sure you did, Jihoon Sen? Because I remember very well that I wielded every jumun you and the other respectable assessors asked me to." Telekinesis, telekinetic slapping, binding with air to create fire and wind, binding with water to freeze it; he hadn't failed in a single one.

"Wielding jumuns is what makes a mage, Akira. *How* you wield them decides who gets the red mantle and who keeps the pink one."

Nonsense, Akira almost blustered. *Nothing but meaningless, empty words.* "Those who passed the trials; how differently did they wield their jumuns, may I ask?"

"Their jumuns were more efficient than yours," Jihoon said flatly. "You understand what this means? They swiftly wielded more powerful jumuns while channeling less anerjy than you did. Is it clear now why we chose them over *you*?"

Akira was at a loss for words. All that crossed his mind right now was all those years of studying and practicing in this damned castle. In his dreams, they were supposed to lead him to a moment totally different from this one. How would you feel when you realize that you have wasted your life chasing a mirage?

Jihoon sighed, his voice warmer as he went on, "I know how badly you want to have a significant role in the Last Day." He paused to demand Akira's attention, and he did. "Trust me, Akira; you can. Even if you are not a Red Cloak. You don't need to be one in the first place."

Akira was sick of Jihoon's blather. "Jihoon Sen, your reconciliation is not what I have come for today. I'm here, so that you tell me what I should do to—"

"I don't have to reconcile you or anybody else, Akira," Jihoon cut him off, a gentle smile on his round face though. "I'm just a tutor who is impressed with your deep understanding of chemistry together with your unparalleled potion-making skills. Kungwan Sen himself read your essay about the potions that could be produced from herbs and plants that grow here on Koya, and he did approve of your work."

Akira was now confused. Yes, he believed in the brilliance of his work, but seriously, what was the significant role a potion maker could play in the War of the Last Day? "I remember the speech Kungwan Sen gave last week. It was all about Red Cloaks…not the likes of me."

"It seems that you've learned nothing from the 'brief history lesson' you loathe." Jihoon leaned back in his seat and took a deep breath. "The Third Crossing will fail if we don't improve the potions our Red Cloaks use to boost their stamina in battle. It is one of our main priorities now; developing more potent potions that do not damage our bodies." He rested his head on the hands clasped behind the nape of his neck. "That's why we need your brilliant mind more than we need your jumuns."

Despite all Jihoon was saying, Akira still believed that the stamina issue and the *dire* need of new potions were a bit exaggerated. "You once said in a lecture that one Red Cloak could defeat a thousand men on his own," he reminded his tutor. "How many more should a mage defeat in order to win this war?"

Jihoon unclasped his hands and leaned his elbows on the desk, looking down for a moment. "You don't understand, Akira." He sighed for the third time. "When the Third Crossing happens, we will have to worry about beings that are way more dangerous than mortal humans."

5. NATSU

After this long walk through the abandoned southern territory of Hokydo, the bag slung across her shoulder started to bother her. But not as much as the linen mask that made her want to scratch her nose. "Is this necessary?" Natsu asked Pantu, who seemed comfortable with the mask covering his face except for his eyes.

"Listen. If we are going to follow your wild ideas, then at least, listen to me and follow my precautions." Pantu led the way as they ascended the forested hill facing the Dragon Sea.

"My wild ideas?" Natsu repeated warily. "Are you implying something?"

Her deputy glanced over his shoulder, his forehead wrinkled. "No ill intentions meant. Doing business with the mages directly is a bold move that might prove beneficial to us. But you can't deny that we are risking everything with such a move."

Natsu didn't stop ascending the hill as she said, "It's a risk we need to take for the time being." Three days had passed, and yet Natsu hadn't heard from Qianfan since their last meeting. Only a fool wouldn't see the impending conflict between them. "Unless you want to wait for Qianfan to strike first."

Pantu smiled nervously. "I was the one who advised you to seek allies. But I was talking about other players in our field, not the folks we all fear the most."

"Those other players will not guarantee a crucial victory over Qianfan." *Besides, they may turn on us after we are done with our common enemy,* Natsu thought, her eyes on the uneven ground she was stepping on lest she slip downhill and crush her bones. "The folks we fear the most will."

Nobody was at the hilltop when they reached it. Pantu walked across the cherry blossom trees to the opposite edge to see if their mysterious contact was coming from the other side of the hill. *He had better show up soon,* Natsu thought, gazing at the reddish horizon in the west, where the sun would set in less than an hour. She would have to spend the night here if darkness fell. Descending this hill under moonlight would be a sure way to die.

The cool breeze at the hilltop kissed her cheeks as she ambled by the western edge, surveying the abandoned foot of the hill in frustration. "Are you sure we are on the right hill?" she asked Pantu, looking at the other hills in this deserted area.

Pantu produced a map from his pocket. Spreading it out with both hands, he kept looking from the hills around them to the map and back. "We are in the right place." He folded the map up and returned it to his pocket. "Let's get some rest."

THE THIRD CROSSING

Natsu unstrapped the bag, put it on the ground, and grabbed a waterskin from it. "What is so particular about this hill?" she wondered after she wetted her parched throat. "Why on a hill in the first place? By hells and demons, this is Hokydo! We are not short of locations for secret meetings!"

Pantu sat on his haunches and drank from his waterskin. "My eyes in Oyoto tell me that they are extremely alert these days because of the Third Crossing announcement."

Natsu needed to digest the last part she heard. *The Third Crossing?* How did Pantu mention it so casually? Didn't he understand what he was talking about?

"The Goranians are back?" she muttered, still in shock. "Why would they invade our small islands? Don't they have enough lands in the continent they have stolen from us ages ago?"

Pantu chuckled. "It's us who will 'cross' the sea this time."

"You sure about that?" Natsu had never thought she would live that long to witness this moment. "*The Third Crossing.*" She tittered. "Who came up with this stupid name? It's not a good omen." The Second Crossing was the darkest moment in Koyan history. The moment that had started a new age of suffering for generations of Koyans on these wretched islands. "Our defeat will be even more devastating this time." The Goranians now were far more advanced than the barbarians who had vanquished the Koyans' finest mages centuries ago.

"I'm afraid you are right." Pantu smacked his lips. "There is a rumor that a seer betrayed us and went to the Goranians to reveal our secrets to them."

"Our secrets," Natsu scoffed. "If we had any good ones, we would have attacked the Goranians a long time ago."

A crack startled both her and Pantu, the latter jumping to his feet when a small glowing oval appeared between them. The shimmering oval grew until it became big enough to hide Pantu behind it; a sight that urged Natsu to instinctively draw her dagger. "What on Earth is this?" she growled.

"I'm damned if I know!" Pantu was holding his sword when he slowly circled the baffling oval until he stood next to Natsu facing the evil thing.

And then, a robed figure came out of it, a crimson mask covering his whole face. *Is this a portal?* Natsu wondered, because she had never seen one for herself.

"If one of you is Pantu, then there is no need for these blades." The masked mage pointed his finger at Natsu's and Pantu's weapons, his voice commanding yet calm, as if these blades were not much of a threat to him. *I doubt we are a threat at all. If anybody here is going to be hurt by these blades, it will be us.*

Natsu nodded to her deputy as they both exchanged a quick look and sheathed their weapons. She tried to appear as composed as possible, to give the masked mage an impression that his theatrical entrance did not daunt her, that meeting the likes of him was nothing more than a daily routine for her. Unfortunately, she couldn't do the same for her deputy.

Swallowing, Pantu spoke on Natsu's behalf as they both had previously agreed. "Did our common friend tell you why I wanted to meet?" *You should do better than this, Pantu. We rehearsed this conversation a dozen times.*

"You had a business deal to discuss, he said," the mysterious mage said flatly.

"It's about red mercury." Pantu's answer should demand the mage's attention.

"What about it?"

"I hear it hurts your coffers. And since the nation is going to war soon, I presume your mages will need lots of red mercury in the coming period."

"You haven't told me anything I don't know of yet," the mage stated in the same cold tone.

"Alright. You want to hear my business proposal, of course." Pantu cleared his throat for no reason. *Don't let him intimidate you, you fool.* "I'm offering you six months of free red mercury shipments."

The mage narrowed his eyes, Natsu observed. *He is giving it a thought.* "How many shipments can you bring us during the said period? How big is your shipment, to begin with?"

"Well," Pantu tilted his head, "it depends on—"

"How much do you need?" Unable to tolerate her deputy's hesitance, Natsu interrupted, peering at the robed mage. Though his mask only showed his eyes, Natsu could tell the mage was smiling now.

"I can't name our price before I hear my end of the deal," said the mage.

They sent us the right mage to talk business with. "Your friendship." She grinned.

"What benefits do you expect from our friendship?"

"Exemption from taxes and protection against rivals." Natsu shrugged. "That's all."

"You ask for too much."

"I'm offering too much, don't you forget."

"Taxes are the major, if not the *only*, source of income for the Empire. Nobody gets a total exemption for any reason. *Reduced* taxes is something we can discuss, though."

That's why lawful trading is not worth it. "What about my second request?"

"It depends on the kind of protection you want from us."

The mage's response to her first request wasn't promising, but she hadn't journeyed all that way south for nothing; she would name her demands loud and clear. "The kind of protection that guarantees that my rivals never bother me. I want to conduct my business without worrying about my safety."

"You want us to guard you or what?" The contempt in his voice was not lost on her.

"Yes," Natsu said firmly. "And eliminate those who pose threats to me if necessary."

The mage stared at her, obviously not amused anymore. "It seems you have contacted the wrong person. We are mages, not mercenaries."

What was the point of embracing virtue now? Everybody in this great empire was corrupt at a certain level. "Aren't our righteous mages interested in ridding our nation of some evil folks?"

"You are lucky I'm not. Otherwise, I would start with you two."

Natsu had to admit that the mage's rhetorical menace did unsettle her. *Damn it, Natsu! Keep it together! Don't let him notice!* But the pretense of nonchalance was becoming an arduous task now. As for the deal she had come to strike with him; she was not interested any longer. All she wanted right now was to get out of here.

"Don't worry. We might need the services of the likes of you in the near future." The mage brushed the fallen cherry blossom flowers off his shoulder, then turned, heading back to the portal which was still open. Shortly after he stepped into it, the shimmering oval shrank until it totally vanished.

Natsu sighed in relief that the intimidating mage was gone. But as she mulled over the whole conversation, she started to feel infuriated. "Those arrogant bastards," she muttered. "Who do they think they are?"

"Calm down, Natsu." Pantu gestured to her nervously with both hands, as if afraid that the mage might hear her. "This could have gone worse."

That lackwit didn't understand. She hadn't just failed in forging an alliance with the mages; she had ended up under their thumb. *We might need the services of the likes you*, she recalled the humiliating promise. For certain, that mage knew what she did for a living. She and her gang would be the mage's errand boys. And if she refused; well, the 'righteous mages' would be interested in ridding the nation of some evil folks.

Maybe she had gone too far with this 'bold move'—as Pantu politely described it.

Despite her deputy's warning, Natsu insisted on descending the hill in the dim light of sunset, even refusing to stop to make a fire and light a torch. "We don't have time for this," she said, her eyes on the ground as she went down the hill. "If we hurry up, we might make it to the foot of the hill before it's pitch black."

This time, she was the one leading the way, Pantu behind her watching every step he made. Midway downhill, he doubled his pace until he caught up with her.

"So, without the mages on our side," Pantu began, "what is our alternative plan?"

"Contact the right people this time," she said, her rage growing by the minute. "We will hire mercenaries."

6. AKIRA

The hubbub outside in the corridor demanded the attention of everybody in the potions chamber.

Akira, whose working space was the closest to the door, was the first to exit the room. Two men wearing the red mantle were carrying another mage, a bunch of newly-promoted Red Cloaks following them across the hallway.

"Kim, wait!" Akira hurried after his cousin, who was among the junior Red Cloaks group. "What's wrong?" he asked the alarmed girl who covered her mouth with both hands.

"Lan collapsed," she said, her voice barely audible.

"Why? What happened to him?"

Kim heaved a deep sigh, folding her arms across her chest as she closed her eyes. "It must be all the jumuns he wielded in today's long session. He exhausted himself until his heart almost halted."

THE THIRD CROSSING

Our stamina is not infinite, Akira recalled Jihoon's words. He had also learned from his mentor that one of the main differences—if not *the* main one—between a seasoned Red Cloak and a novice was the ability to channel as much anerjy as possible with the least stamina.

"Calm down." Akira briefly held her shoulders. "What matters now is that you are—"

"I don't want to see anybody in the corridor!" a firm feminine voice rang in the palace. *The dreadful Tashihara,* Akira thought, looking at the short, slim, dark-haired lady who stood in the way of the junior Red Cloaks at the end of the corridor. "Your friend is stable now. His body just needs rest to recover from the shock. Now back to your chambers!"

Without saying a word, Kim exchanged a look with Akira and shook her head, as if telling him that she was not ready to resume her baleful session for the time being. Taking her by the hand, Akira ushered his cousin to the potions room. Luckily, no senior mage was supervising him and his peers today.

Akira motioned for her to pick a seat at the corner of the hall as he dragged forth a chair and seated himself opposite her. "Who was in charge of your session?" he asked Kim.

"Tashihara was the most senior mage in the room. But it was Minjun who was doing most of the work."

Of course, who else other than the prodigy of Sun Castle? "How did he let Lan reach that level of exhaustion? That's a crime! Your father must punish him as well as his senior." Akira could wager that Tashihara's students would celebrate such an event.

"He will," Kim winced, "if their students are not ready soon."

Akira had to admit; he had been jealous the moment he had heard the Archmage name Kim as the last newly-promoted Red Cloak. Now he felt worried about her. "How are you faring so far?" he asked her warmly.

"I'm doing the best I can, Akira." She sighed again. "The thing is that I'm not..." She hesitated, and then she continued, "I don't know if I will ever be in the level a Red Cloak is expected to reach." Her lips curved into a smile of contempt as she added, "I was just lucky in today's session that Lan's turn was before mine."

Should Akira consider himself lucky as well? "This can't be right. There must be another way."

"You have any idea what the likes of me will be supposed to handle?" She paused for effect, but Akira knew already.

"Demons." Akira surprised her with his answer. "You are supposed to contain them until the summoners command them, right?"

Kim peered at him. "I see you are well-versed in the process."

"It's not a secret anyway." Not for someone who had dedicated his entire life to earning the honor of donning the red cloak.

"It's not that simple either. Taming one demon requires channeling too much anerjy."

Akira shrugged. "Shouldn't be a problem when you have a summoner on your side."

"So I hear," she scoffed.

There was something strange about his sweet cousin today. At first glance, Akira would attribute that to Lan's incident that might be looming large in her mind, but he hadn't forgotten what she had said the day the Emperor had visited this castle. *Blood and ruin is not something I have been looking forward to,* had been Kim's words about the Last Day. What could be her problem with the Light's holy plan?

"Sometimes I don't understand you, Kim." Akira lowered his voice. "Right now, you seem suspicious of the effectiveness of His Radiance's plan. Earlier, you questioned the entire notion of the Third Crossing." He leaned forward toward her. "What is your concern exactly?"

"What is yours, Akira?" she countered. "Don't you have any?"

"Why should I? It's the Light's will. That's what we are fated to do."

"What if we are *not?*" Kim gnashed her teeth. "Because I don't believe the Light would ever glorify the extermination of hundreds of thousands of innocent people."

Despite her low voice, Akira couldn't help looking around to make sure nobody was eavesdropping on them. "We are not in the place to judge His commands, Kim. We just comply."

"What if they are not His commands, Akira?" Kim looked him in the eye. "Didn't this possibility cross your mind?"

His cousin's issue was more serious than he had imagined. "Don't let such intrusive thoughts get the better of you, Kim." He held her shoulders, not so gently. "You are stronger than this."

Kim shoved his hands away. "Do you know about *The Tree of Amagesdon*? They are working on it as we speak! They will make it real, Akira! The Light would never be pleased with such atrocity!"

This was a first. When it came to knowledge, Akira was always the stronger one. "What is that tree you are talking about?"

Kim pushed to her feet when Kyong Sen, the tutor of potions and chemistry, entered the hall. "It's an old weapon," she said to Akira in a low voice. "Soon, they will involve you all in it."

Akira's cousin strode to the door, giving the senior mage an apologetic bow before she left the chamber. *I must do something before she says something stupid*, Akira thought, hoping his foolish cousin hadn't divulged her ideas to someone else. Even her father shouldn't hear this nonsense; he would be the one issuing the order of expelling her from Sun Castle.

"You." Kyong Sen was brushing his black beard when he called to Akira. "Is everything alright?"

The bearded tutor was not as nice as Jihoon, but definitely not as menacing as Tashihara. "My apologies, Kyong Sen." Knowing that leaving unfinished assignments was not an option, Akira rose to his feet and returned to his workspace.

"Let what happened today be a reminder to all of us of the great role we must play in the Third Crossing." Kyong Sen addressed the entire class. "Without our help, our brothers and sisters on the frontline will never be able to win the War of the Last Day."

One of Akira's peers raised her hand. With Kyong Sen's permission, she said, "Speaking of the frontline; when the time comes, will we cross the Koyan Sea alongside the Red Cloaks?"

"Most of you won't have to, if I understand correctly," Kyong Sen replied. "But I assure you; all the potions and weapons you craft will be there in your stead. That's how you will all claim your glory."

"Weapons, Kyong Sen?" Akira dared to ask.

The bearded tutor grinned. "We will get to that in our next chemistry class."

THE THIRD CROSSING

* * *

There was an hour to spare before the obligatory sleep time in Sun Castle.

Akira found his legs taking him to the healers' hall, where Lan was being taken care of. Not because Akira was worried about him—Lan was never one of his close friends. Was it curiosity? Perhaps.

Lan's eyes were shut when Akira tiptoed toward his bed, but the young mage who had almost died today was breathing now, his chest slowly rising and falling. *The potions worked*, Akira thought, glancing at the colored vials cramming the small table at the corner.

"I knew you would come."

Minjun's voice startled Akira, who took a few seconds to process that the slim dark-haired mage had been assuming a seat at the corner of the dimly-lit chamber before he entered.

Akira greeted the Red Cloak, and then he asked, "Why did you think I would, Minjun Sen?"

Minjun rose to his feet and slowly approached Akira, his hands clasped behind his back as he cast a long look at the unconscious young mage. "Maybe you wanted to see for yourself an upside for not being selected as a Red Cloak." He turned to Akira, a strange smile on his face. "Or maybe I'm wrong."

"I was never afraid of being placed at the frontline," Akira blurted, unable to hide the tension in his voice. "All my tutors and peers know that."

The right side of Minjun's mouth quirked upward. "Do you know why the upcoming war was called *the Last Day*?"

What was this basic question for? "Because it will be the last day for the Goranians in our homeland."

"Right," Minjun Sen scoffed. "But if we are not taking good care of our measures, it may become the last day for the whole of mankind." He glanced at Akira, surely taking note of his astonishment. "You never knew how grave the risks would be, but you shouldn't be blamed for that. None of you were told how the Last Day would *really* be like."

Akira was confused for a moment. Was that a mere warning for the sake of enlightenment? Because after giving what he heard a second thought, Akira sensed an implied criticism of the plan of the Last Day. *Have you lost your mind?* Akira thought to himself. *Only a fool like Kim would blatantly condemn our holy mission.* A relatively young mage like Minjun would never acquire his fame if he was too clueless to understand what to say and what to keep for himself.

"If dealing with demons is that dangerous; why do we bother?" Akira began. "Aren't our mages enough to vanquish the Goranians?"

"We have learned our lesson a long time ago, young man." Minjun's annoying smile vanished at last. "In the First Crossing, our ancestors thought that fending off a barbarian horde was enough to keep their borders safe. Even in the Second Crossing, we still underestimated our foes, who had managed to sneak past our defenses and attack us in the heart of our homeland. We were badly outnumbered, but we never doubted our inevitable victory. You know why?" He leaned forward toward Akira. "Because we blindly believed in our mages as you do now."

Blindly? Hearing that from a Red Cloak was shocking, Akira had to say. "If I understand you right, Minjun Sen; we are far from ready for this war."

"Then you understand nothing." Minjun cast him a hard look. "This war is not about defeating the Goranians; it's about *annihilating* them. And bearing in mind that they have become more numerous and more advanced than the barbarians who defeated us in the past, we have no room for mistakes this time. The Third Crossing must be a perfect victory."

Because we can't allow the Goranians to rally, Akira reflected. There wouldn't be wounds to licks. Only dead bodies.

Millions of them.

Akira noticed the concerned look on Minjun's face as the latter was staring at Lan. "Something wrong?" Akira asked, the mage laying his left hand on Lan's chest.

"His pulse is gone!" Minjun pointed at the vials on the table. "Ephedra! Quickly!"

Only now did Akira realize that Lan's chest had stopped moving. Alarmed, he pushed to his feet and hurried to the table, the panic confusing him for a moment. "The green one!" Minjun urged, and at once, Akira snatched it and handed it to the Red Cloak who was keeping his left palm on Lan's chest. From the tension in Minjun's wrist, Akira could tell the mage was channeling his anerjy to revive Lan.

"Raise his head!" Minjun instructed, and right after Akira complied, Minjun emptied the vial into Lan's mouth, tossed it aside, put his right hand on the left, and now he was channeling his anerjy with both hands. "No, no, no! Wake up!" he blustered, as if Lan might simply obey his command, but the lad didn't move a muscle.

"Should I call for help?" Akira asked nervously, but Minjun Sen ignored him, still trying to revive Lan's heart with his anerjy. While Akira was now certain that the lad wouldn't come back, the Red Cloak needed another minute before giving up. Leaning over the edge of the bed, he murmured a prayer for the first victim of a war that hadn't even started yet.

7. NATSU

Clear sky, warm sun, and dry air. Was there a place with better weather than Mankola at this time of the year?

Natsu had another reason to prefer Mankola over Rusakia—the only two Goranian kingdoms she had ever set foot in. Aside from Rusakia's dreadful winter, the Mankols didn't loathe the Koyans—not as much as the other Goranian factions did, to say the least. "We are distant cousins after all," a Mankol merchant had told her once, referring to the old, unpopular myth of the *Mongrels*; the descendants of the Goranian invaders who had wedded the few Koyan survivors of the Second Crossing.

Natsu disembarked the Wraith with Pantu and Jirou, leaving Sogeki-hei with the rest of the crew to secure her precious ship docked at the port of Dibal. In Natsu's reception was a balding man who escorted her and her small retinue to the tavern near the entrance of the bustling port. The balding man, who probably didn't know a single Koyan word, didn't speak to his guests—something that didn't bother Natsu at all. "Thank you," she said in a thick Goranian accent to the mute man who pushed the door of the tavern open for her. The only response she got in return was a hollow look.

Silence fell over the place when Natsu and her men stepped inside. The tavern customers stared at them, and then they turned to the table in the center, particularly to the man wearing the dark woolen deel robe, his beard pointed, his dyed mustache brown and long. Bilguun was his name, and he was Natsu's biggest distributor in Dibal. Even if you hadn't met him before, you could easily tell that he was the man in charge here.

Bilguun clapped, and at once, everybody rose to their feet, leaving their unfinished plates and mazers on the tables. In a minute, the tavern was empty. Having no need for his protection at the moment, Natsu motioned for Jirou to wait for her outside.

With a wide smile and open arms, Bilguun greeted Natsu and Pantu, inviting them to join his table. "Bring my guests your finest mutton," the Mankol ordered the tavern keeper, the only one who had stayed despite *the clap*.

"Generous as always, Bilguun," Natsu spoke in the Goranian tongue she was still learning from Pantu.

Bilguun gave a throaty laugh. "You are improving!" He turned to the busy tavern keeper. "A new pitcher and two clean mazers here!"

While the tavern keeper was attending to Bilguun's demands, Pantu began in fluent Goranian, "We heard some news coming from Inabol."

Bilguun guffawed, wagging his finger at Pantu. "You and your eyes! How did the news fly so fast from the far west to

58

the far east?" He gulped down the last of his ale. "Well, the news is true, if that's what you're asking about."

Pantu waited until the tavern keeper was gone after placing the two mazers and the pitcher on the table. "A seer from Koya?" he asked in a low voice, leaning his arm on the table.

"And that's not even the best part." Bilguun took the responsibility of filling Natsu's and Pantu's mazers with ale. "He did a demonstration in front of the rulers of the six Goranians kingdoms; *the Demon in the Cage*." When he noticed the clueless expression on his guests' faces, he chuckled. "What were you told, then? He brought a possessed lady and shot her with a thousand arrows, but the evil creature possessing her body revived her every time she died."

Pantu's spies had informed him about the seer's warning, but his demonstration? This was news to him, and consequently to Natsu.

"What does this have to do with the Last Day?" she asked the Mankol merchant.

"You sure you are Koyan?" Bilguun sneered.

"We are from Hokydo," she scoffed, exchanging a quick look with Pantu. "We never cared about the plots they weave in the capital." *Because they never cared about us.*

"Fair enough." Bilguun laughed while pouring from the new pitcher into his mazer. "That possessed lady was supposed to be a demonstration of how your soldiers would look like in battle; an army of undead men." He took one big gulp from his drink, then wiped his mouth and beard with the back of his hand. "Except that your seer showed the Goranians how to kill a possessed soldier."

Pantu furrowed his brow. "Our soldiers will be possessed? They will let the demons—"

"We don't say their name here," Bilguun interrupted, glaring at Pantu. "And yes, they will let those cursed beings occupy your soldiers." The Mankol's face relaxed a little. "The thing is that your soldiers won't be Koyans, my friend. Another faction will play that role."

Natsu wasn't sure about her deputy's opinion, but she found the whole conversation somehow amusing. "So," she said to Bilguun, "you tell me that my people are planning to invade your lands with an army of immortals, and that doesn't bother you?"

Bilguun shrugged. "I told you the news that came from Inabol, not what we believe."

"We?" Natsu echoed quizzically.

"Our Kaan disapproved of that farce in front of every king and queen in Gorania, and we, his people, believe he is right." The Mankol merchant emptied his mazer with one final gulp and belched in his arm. "It was brilliantly played, I must admit. A breath-taking display of sorcery to support a meticulously detailed story so that all kings and queens sign a treaty that grants a neighboring kingdom one of our territories," he shook his head, smacking his lips, "we must bow in respect to the mastermind behind such a scheme."

Natsu's main distributor in Mankola didn't believe in the Last Day, and it was all that mattered right now. "Our business is good, then." She raised her mazer and took a sip from her drink. Yes, it was heavier than the Koyan ale, but she would survive it.

"You should expect some repercussions, though," said Bilguun, his smile fading. "Sooner or later, the three Goranian kingdoms that have signed the Treaty of Inabol will start producing the immortals-killing weapon. Guess what its main component is; red mercury."

A growing demand for red mercury in Gorania would increase its price and consequently, hurt Natsu's margins. "You surely have a way to sell all your red mercury stock," she scoffed.

"One month later, you will thank me."

"Even if I want to, I don't have the coin for this unmissable deal."

Bilguun's thick eyebrows rose. "You squandered the fortune you have earned from the Turtle job this soon?"

Natsu did her best to conceal her smile. "I'm not sure I know what you are talking about."

"Really?" Bilguun leaned his arms on the table, his hands clasped together. "So, that man called Qianfan is waging war against you for nothing?"

According to the old agreement between her late husband and his rival, no Mankol merchant should be familiar with Qianfan's name. "Did you do business with him?" she asked curtly.

"Only after Botan died." Bilguun gestured with both palms. "At that time, I didn't know you would take his place."

Natsu would let that slide for now. "Qianfan's war; what do you know about it?"

Bilguun let out a deep breath. "That he is recruiting an army to fight you."

"That's funny," she sneered, "because I'm here for the same reason."

Bilguun jerked his head backward, looking from Natsu to Pantu. "I thought you were here to sell me bowstrings."

Natsu drank half of her mazer before she put it on the table. "This time, I'm taking my price in mercenaries, not in gold."

"Mercenaries from here?" Bilguun narrowed his eyes. "To fight in Koya? I thought no Goranian was allowed to set foot on your islands."

"I'm not allowed to sell you our enhanced bowstrings either," she countered. "But we do what we have to do."

Pantu cleared his throat. "There is no need to worry, Master Bilguun. Smuggling people into Hokydo will be less complicated than into Oyoto."

Bilguun leaned back in his seat, his arms folded across his chest as he smiled crookedly. "Why us? I have always heard about the fearless folks of your island Hokydo. Can't you find the soldiers you need there?"

"I need more than fearless folks, Bilguun," Natsu stated. "I need the battle-hardened warriors I have always heard about."

"Your street fights do not require our cavalry archers. Our warriors will be of more use on open field battles."

"Whose warriors should I hire then? The Rusakians?"

Bilguun raised his thick eyebrows as he played with his pointed beard. "You are determined to hire mercenaries from outside Koya, aren't you?"

Natsu folded her arms as she leaned back in her seat, waiting for the Mankol merchant to say more. Because plainly, he had more to offer.

"I might need some time." The look on Bilguun's face intrigued her. "How long can you hold up?"

Natsu looked him in the eye. "What do you have for me?"

"The most ferocious footmen the world has ever seen." Bilguun smiled crookedly. "They don't call themselves the Sons of Giants for nothing."

* * *

Even among smugglers, starting a voyage in the dark was a bad omen.

Most of Natsu's crew showed their indifference about the timing of the return journey to Hokydo, but one person in particular seemed genuinely enthusiastic. Mushi was her name, and steering the Wraith across the Koyan Sea was what she was doing right now.

"The light rose from behind the mountains of Yoshi." The superstitious, tall lady was telling Natsu about her dream last night. While Natsu was pretending she was interested and listening, she stared at the stars in an attempt to memorize the constellations. Truth be told, it wasn't as easy as the shrewd helmswoman made it look.

"You saw *the Light* Himself?" Natsu asked her, playing along.

"No." Mushi chuckled. "I mean like the sunlight." Holding the helm with one hand, she continued, "But trust me; a mountain in a dream is a good omen."

Natsu never believed in Mushi's gibberish, but she hoped the helmswoman was right nonetheless. Under the current circumstances, she was in dire need of good tidings.

"You are dozing," Mushi remarked. "I'm sure your cabin is more comfortable than the mast you are leaning on."

Only now did Natsu realize she was doing so. "I will stay here to make sure you don't fall asleep."

"I have been doing this for decades, boss," Mushi scoffed. "And don't worry. It's almost dawn now. Sogeki-hei will wake up and join me anytime soon."

Practically, they were still in the Mankol waters; the hard part of the voyage was yet to come. Natsu had better seize the moment and steal a few hours of sleep before it was too late.

Her cabin was so cold she couldn't sleep without her coat. She wasn't even sure she slept in the first place. The only thing she did right was shut her eyes, but the sight of Qianfan's face roused her, gasping.

The sunlight streaming through the window of her cabin made her realize that she had indeed slept for a few hours. But did she feel better now? Thanks to Mushi's advice, Natsu was even more fatigued than she had been last night.

It was right after sunrise when Natsu went outside her cabin. The wind was gentle, yet colder than yesterday, forcing her to pull her coat about her shoulders as she gazed at the Koyan Sea from the bow of her ship. The mist didn't curtain the mountainous island of Yoshi on the horizon, which meant that they were now closer to Oyoto, the Koyan capital, than to Dibal. From this moment, she and her crew should be on the alert for coastguards. What gave her some relief was the sight of Sogeki-hei atop the crow's nest. If all human beings were allowed to be distracted for once—at least—in their lives, Natsu's sharpshooter never enjoyed such a luxury.

The sun was rising when Pantu joined her on deck. "Did you sleep well?" he asked her.

Natsu had had better nights before. "Would you blame me if I didn't? We were supposed to return to Hokydo with more men on board."

Pantu didn't seem as concerned as she was. Was it because he had just woken up? "The men we have recruited so far are enough, Natsu."

"I hope so." The men he was referring to belonged to small gangs from across Hokydo. Yes, they were bold, familiar with this kind of fights, and *probably*, they would be enough as Pantu hoped. But Natsu was not like her deputy. Leaving this upcoming clash to chance was not an option she would accept. She wouldn't just fight the fight; she would win it. "Because we don't have the luxury to wait for the damned Skandivians." The Sons of Giants, as they called themselves, would need ten days, at least, to receive Bilguun's messenger. And if they agreed to work for Natsu at once, they might take three weeks to travel to Dibal—they were not as fast riders as the Mankols. And then a few days of sailing across the Koyan Sea to reach Hokydo. "A lot can happen during a month of waiting for their arrival."

Pantu sighed, holding the taffrail as he stared at the sea. "That's why I told you that hiring a bunch of Skandivians would be a waste of coin." He glanced at her over his shoulder. "But when did you ever listen to me?"

Ignoring his rhetorical question, she said, "We will make use of their services either way. If they are not the soldiers who win a war for us, they shall help us avoid another one."

The wind became warmer as the Wraith sailed by the eastern rocky coast of Yoshi. At this pace, they would pass by the main island of Oyoto before noon and make it to Jopen by nightfall. Under the cover of darkness, they would turn around that small island to avoid the coastguards, and after that, they could head straight to Hokydo, where Natsu's real problems awaited her. *I barely have one day to figure this out,* she thought, hoping she was wrong about doubting Pantu's judgment on their situation in the upcoming clash with Qianfan. *Maybe I am underestimating our…*

"Natsu!" Sogeki-hei yelled from his nest. "We are being followed!"

Both Natsu and Pantu scurried toward the bow of the ship. It wasn't easy to see through the mist, but after a minute of squinting, she thought she might have spotted the shadow of a vessel. "Can't you discern what it could be?" she asked her sharpshooter.

"The mist is not helping," he replied. Even the incomparable Sogeki-hei was a human after all.

"Set course to the northwest toward the shore," she commanded Pantu. "Let's see if we are still being followed then."

Pantu left her hurriedly to see to her order, but before it was put into action, Sogeki-hei bellowed, "TURTLE!"

Natsu couldn't see the Turtle ship for herself, but she would always believe Sogeki-hei's eyes and question her own. "Stay away from the shore!" she demanded as she sprinted toward Mushi, who was about to respond to her earlier instructions from Pantu. "Keep our course straight!"

The tall helmswoman looked from Pantu to her. "I was told you wanted to go—"

"Forget what you were told and do as I say now!" she cut Mushi off, and turned to Pantu. "Tell the men to abandon the oars. We are turning the engines on."

In a similar situation, her deputy would be the one begging her to unleash the Wraith, but for some reason, he didn't show any enthusiasm toward her decision. Maybe she had just surprised him?

"Did you hear me, Pantu?" She glowered at her dumbfounded deputy. "I need you to oversee them yourself."

Pantu gestured with his palm to calm her down. "I'm just trying to figure out your plan to capture the Turtle this time."

Hells and demons! "We are not capturing any Turtles this time, Pantu!" Actually, the Wraith was the prey today. The Turtle at their heels now hadn't just come across them during some regular patrol; it had been lurking by the southern coast of Yoshi to ambush them. "Now go, because

66

I feel this is not the only Turtle we are going to encounter today."

Finally, Pantu realized that his boss did want to flee. While he was urging her crew to hurry downstairs to the engines room below deck, she kept her eyes fixated on the coast on her left. If the coastguards were serious about ambushing her, they would be lurking at the northeastern gulf as well. *A couple of minutes, and we shall know for certain.*

But thanks to Sogeki-hei, it didn't take that long.

Natsu couldn't see what her sharpshooter was pointing at when he yelled, but she knew better—again—whose eyes to trust. Now she had to deal with the fact that *two* more Turtle ships were coming from the very gulf Natsu had been worried about. "You heard him?" She turned again to Mushi. "Head northeast! Get us away from them!" *And why is Pantu taking so long?* Handling coal was laborious, she knew, but that was why she sent *all* her oarsmen down below deck. *We are sitting ducks.* That damned engine had better work now before…

BOOM!

The last sound Natsu would like to hear startled her. Not the thundering cannonball coming from the Turtle behind her ship; it was the splash of the missile that missed the Wraith's hull by only a few feet. *Blast! The next one will surely hit us.* "Change our angle again!" she bellowed at Mushi. A desperate measure for a vessel stuck between three Turtle ships closing in. Fortunately, the Wraith's huge rotors started spinning the instant Natsu's helmswoman steered her vessel to the right. Soon the Wraith would leave its chasers behind, but first, it had to evade the cannonballs while it was still picking up speed, which shouldn't take too long—hopefully—with all the men down below deck feeding the engine with coal.

"Come on. Come on," Natsu muttered, now able to see the cannons of the two Turtles coming from the left. As the Wraith became faster, the failure of the coastguards' attempt to intercept it became evident. Still, it was in the range of their cannons. "Head east!" she instructed Mushi. "We need to keep those two behind us!"

"That might allow the Turtle behind us to catch up, boss," the helmswoman pointed out.

"Just do it!" Natsu howled, having no time to explain the point of this maneuver. While the Wraith was still in the range of the cannons of the two Turtles coming from the northeastern gulf, Natsu's priority was to give the coastguards a smaller target to aim at. Striking the stern of a ship should be *relatively* harder than hitting any part of its entire port. *Right after we get outside their range, we shall restore our course to the north before the first Turtle comes...*

Three consecutive thundering explosions interrupted her train of thought. The first cannonball was too far to threaten Natsu and her crew—a desperate shot from the single Turtle from the south. The second and the third were from the two Turtles of the northeastern gulf. One cannonball barely missed the rearmost part of the Wraith, which was still turning right. The second crashed into the Wraith's port, shaking the entire vessel like a leaf in the wind.

"*Breach!*" one of her crew cried, and from her spot, Natsu could hear the tumult of shouting that broke out downstairs. She could also hear the clamor of the massive rotors of the ship. Miraculously, the engine was still working, but it was only a matter of time before the water flooded the cargo hold and the engine room. If Natsu didn't order Mushi to turn back to the island of Yoshi at once, the Wraith would end up sinking in the Koyan Sea. But that implied surrendering herself and her crew to the coastguards on a silver platter.

The seabed or the executioner's blade; those were here options at the moment. *Think, Natsu. Think. You cannot die today. You are not allowed to. A five-year-old boy is waiting for you.*

Natsu scurried to the stairs, and on her way to the engine room to assess the damage, she realized that the cannonball had breached the hull at the cargo load, which was flooded already. "Stay upstairs, Natsu! We will handle this!" Pantu yelled at her, his men blocking the gap with anything they found nearby—most of these things were parts of crates they had smashed. "Just keep your eyes on the coastguards! Make sure they don't catch us!"

Natsu noticed that most of her oarsmen were now at the breached cargo load. "And you keep feeding the engine! Do not let the ship stop for any reason!" she demanded, then hurried upstairs to the stern. The pursuers were now too far to threaten her with their cannons. For the time being, the real threat was the sea itself.

To her surprise, the Wraith took a sharp turn to the left until it was facing the two Turtles sailing together. "What are you doing?" she blustered, sprinting toward Mushi.

"We won't make it to Hokydo or even Oyoto!" Mushi said nervously. "Yoshi is the nearest land to us!"

Didn't her foolish helmswoman take note of the two Turtle ships obstructing their way to the shore of Yoshi Island? "The coastguards will sink us with their cannons!" She gritted her teeth. "Turn back to the north!"

"Don't you see? We are sinking already, Natsu! If we are not going to Yoshi, then we must abandon the ship!"

Abandon the Wraith? The masterpiece her brilliant late husband Botan had built? "We can't do that! We're nothing without this ship you want us to…"

"Do you all see this?"

Sogeki-hei's question interrupted her from his spot in the crow's nest. Looking where he was pointing, Natsu doubted in the beginning that her eyes were playing tricks on her. "Is that…?"

"A whirlpool." Mushi's jaw dropped, unintentionally assuring Natsu that her eyes were fine. Because right now, she was not looking at a *normal* whirlpool.

It was the mother of all whirlpools.

Caught in a huge vortex in the sea that had been calm all day, the two Turtle ships coming from the gulf twirled as the maelstrom grew faster. They spun and spun, and in less than a minute, the two vessels vanished as the gigantic whirlpool sucked them into its core. Much to the astonishment of Natsu and everybody watching, the sea that had just swallowed two ships of the finest unit in the Koyan navy was calm now, as if that monstrous maelstrom had never existed a few seconds ago.

"A miracle!" the superstitious helmswoman exclaimed. "My prayers are answered!"

Natsu couldn't argue. "We need another miracle, then." She gazed at the remaining Turtle that had been chasing them from the southern coast. Obviously, the 'miraculous' maelstrom didn't intimidate its crew.

But suddenly, the Turtle sank. Yes, suddenly. *Instantly.* As if it headed with all its speed to the bottom of the deep blue sea. No whirlpools this time, though.

"Sogeki-hei?" Natsu called out, but instead of answering her, the sharpshooter strapped his crossbow to his back and climbed down the mast in a hurry. Why was he abandoning his post without her permission?

Sogeki-hei approached Natsu and whispered into her ear, "We need to get as far as possible away from here."

Now he was acting really strange. "Why should we?" She didn't whisper as he did. "The way to Yoshi is clear now."

Sogeki-hei signaled her to lower her voice. "The water between us and the island is cursed," he whispered again.

"Cursed?" exclaimed Mushi, who heard him somehow. Without hesitation, she steered the Wraith again toward the north.

"What is wrong with you both?" Natsu barked, her crew's erratic behavior enraging her.

"You didn't see the hands, but I did," Sogeki-hei snapped. "Monstrous hands, Natsu."

"What are you talking about?" Natsu asked impatiently.

"The hands that pulled that Turtle to the bottom of the sea!" Sogeki-hei glared at her. "For the sake of the Light, Natsu, we must *assume* they belong to the same creature that created the maelstrom!"

Natsu would belittle what she had just heard if it came from anybody else. But even with her undying faith in Sogeki-hei's senses, she still needed time to digest what he said.

"The light behind the mountain!" Mushi exclaimed, pointing to the island of Yoshi, where a shimmering fireball floated over the summit of a mountain by the sea. "It was a prophecy from the Light! I knew it was a miracle!"

"I don't mean to disappoint you," Natsu said, squinting at the distant figure lifting both arms up, as if holding the ominous fireball without touching it. "But this has nothing to do with your prayers and the miracles you believe in." She turned to Mushi. "Now take us to the island before we join the sunken Turtles."

8. AKIRA

All the *recruits* in the Sun Castle were allowed to venture outside its walls for one day. The reason was Lan's funeral, which would be held in the city at the Shrine of the Dead.

Akira had no problems with the late lad, but attending the funeral was just an excuse to spend as much time as possible away from this prison. He would quickly pay his condolences to Lan's parents and siblings, and after that, he would find the nearest tavern to drink what the lips of *the Soldiers of the Light* were prohibited from touching. A simple plan, it was. But it almost failed because of Kim.

"The pain is unbearable." Clutching her blanket with both hands, she explained to Akira why she wouldn't be able to attend Lan's funeral. "That's why I sent for you. I need someone around just in case, you know."

Standing by his cousin's bed, Akira glanced at the other empty ones in the dorm room. All the girls here must have left already lest they miss the funeral. What was he going to do now? He couldn't leave his cousin in this condition on her own.

Unless he found a volunteer. Yes, there must be, at least, one person who wouldn't go to Lan's funeral for any damned reason. The late lad was not that popular after all.

"What will the others say after they find out that I haven't attended the funeral?" Akira warily asked.

Kim arched an eyebrow. "You fear they might judge you? I thought you stopped caring about anything related to Sun Castle."

Akira heaved a deep sigh. "It doesn't matter how I feel about anything, Kim." He shrugged. "I just have to do what I'm supposed to do, right?"

His cousin clenched her jaw, certainly because of the colic. "The damned red mantle." She took in a deep breath, and then she went on, "You won't get over it, will you?"

Akira wasn't in the mood for this conversation for the time being. *Not now, not ever.*

"You know what's funny?" Kim smiled wryly. "None of us got what they wanted, did we? I guess that's how this world works."

Footsteps approached the dorm room, and it was Minjun Sen who entered. "You still here?" he chided Akira, his hands clasped behind his back as he slowly approached Kim's bed. "The last coach is about to leave."

Akira exchanged a silent look with his hurting cousin before he said to the slender, dark-haired tutor, "I'm staying, Minjun Sen. Someone must look after her."

Minjun's eyes betrayed his concern. Kim's complaint must have reminded him of the novice that had died in his hands yesterday. No one would be ready for another shock like this.

"What's wrong?" Minjun asked her.

Kim feigned a smile. "I guess it's last night's dinner."

"Nobody had problems with last night's dinner." Minjun laid his palm gently on Kim's forehead. "You are slightly feverish. Did you take any medicine?"

Kim shrugged. "I drank some anise to alleviate the colic."

"Anise?" Minjun Sen curled his nose in disdain, then turned to Akira. "You should hurry to that coach before it leaves. I will take care of her."

Akira wanted to thank Minjun Sen heartily for saving his day, but come to think of it, he realized how that might sound to his cousin. "I know you will, Minjun Sen." Akira bowed to the Red Cloak, then gave Kim an apologetic look. She seemed irked that he was abandoning her in such a condition, but that didn't stop him from striding to the door then across the hallway outside the dorm room.

Yes, Kim was right about him. He had stopped caring about anything related to Sun Castle.

* * *

The Shrine of the Dead, where the funeral was held, was more crowded than Akira had imagined. Family, friends, peers, tutors, even the Archmage himself; all of them had come today to bid Lan farewell before his soul started its journey to the spirits' realm, all of them donning white cloaks to remind themselves that when death came, all colors and ranks became obsolete.

So many familiar faces surrounded Akira in the yard outside the shrine, where the monks would soon perform the salvation rituals, but only a few bothered to greet him. His 'dear' uncle Kungwan Sen was not one of those few, though. *Maybe he is just busy*, Akira thought, his eyes fixed on the short, gray-haired lady talking to his uncle in a low voice away from the crowd. Why would Hanu Sen, the former Head of the Imperial Court, attend a mage's funeral?

There was a moment when Akira felt the weight of stares on him. Scanning the yard, he found a bunch of people pointing and nodding their chins toward him as they murmured. While Akira was wondering what that was about, a broad-shouldered man split off from the burbling group and approached him.

"They say you were by his side when he died," the broad-shouldered man said bitterly. From the concern on his face, whose similarity to Lan's couldn't be mistaken, Akira safely presumed he was talking to Wei Sen, the Commander of the Imperial Guard; a man you wouldn't see quite often. *Took him a son to lose to appear in a public gathering.*

"I'm sorry I couldn't save him." Akira pressed his lips together. Maybe he should say no more to the grieving father.

"It was fated." Wei Sen waved dismissively, then sighed. "Lan's mother and I will be grateful if you join the coffin carriers."

Because I was close to Lan during his last moments in this life, Akira reflected. It was an old tradition that belonged to the people of Hokydo. Did Lan's family have roots in that wretched island? Anyway, now wasn't the time to discuss their origins.

Akira thanked Wei Sen who ushered him to the door of the shrine and closed it behind him. Plainly, the man couldn't stand the sight of his son in the wooden box resting on the ground.

Akira's boots echoed in the vast, empty hall as he advanced toward the coffin. Nobody was in the shrine except the carriers and the monk, of course. Though Akira recognized none of the eight men in the hall, the monk called out to him, "Come here, Akira son of Chiaki."

Akira was taken off guard, he had to admit. "You know my mother?"

"She used to teach my daughter in the Foundation School." The monk motioned for Akira to come closer to the coffin. "Take your position. About time the people outside took a last look at their deceased boy."

Akira couldn't help staring at Lan, who was clad in a white cloak, his head shaved, the scent of cinnamon bark wafting from his bathed body. It wasn't Akira's first funeral, but he had never been this close to a 'processed' corpse. *So, this is what it will be like.*

"Akira?" the monk called, and at once Akira did as instructed and took his position on the left side at the back. Following the monk's lead, Akira and the seven other men lifted the coffin up together on their shoulders as they exited the shrine. The crowd outside made way for the monk and the carriers to advance across the yard toward the pyre at its end, which was a long walk with this hefty wooden box almost dislocating Akira's shoulder.

Akira and the carriers placed the coffin carefully on the pyre and stepped back, leaving the monk to intone his prayers right in front of it. After he was done, one of the shrine servants standing at the back scurried to him and handed him a torch. As the monk set the pyre on fire, a woman started sobbing, the people around her trying to comfort her. Akira hadn't seen that woman before, but he would be surprised if she was someone other than Lan's mother.

Pay your respects to the parents and leave as soon as possible; that was the plan. However, Akira found himself standing still, staring at the flames that ate through the coffin holding Lan's body inside. Even when people started to leave, he didn't abandon his spot, unable to dismiss from his mind this intrusive image of his corpse instead of Lan's. *It is my inevitable fate, isn't it?* he thought to himself. Back in the day—which was not a long time ago anyway—when he still had hope to don the red mantle, he used to claim he was ready to die in the War of the Last Day for his nation. Was it some boyish gibberish? Perhaps. Easy for you to brag you are a swimmer when you are in the heart of the desert.

A gentle hand on his shoulder startled him, and then he realized it was the monk who knew his mother's name. "Is your mind still troubled, son?"

Alright, this monk knew too much. "It seems that you and Mother still talk, Your Eminence," Akira said, not so politely though.

"You are as smart as she says." The monk grinned. "And yes, we still talk."

"Clearly, she has told you too much."

"Your mother is a good woman, Akira." The monk's smile faded. "And you give her all the reasons to worry about you."

Worry about him? The only thing she cared about was her name among her peers in the School. "I am fine," Akira said curtly. "Tell her this the next time she comes here."

Before Akira could walk away, the monk gripped his wrist tightly. "You will never find peace unless you understand, son." The monk's voice was firm yet too low to be heard by anybody else in the yard. "The Light has spared you for a reason."

Akira looked from the pyre to the monk. "You say I would have been in Lan's place if I took the red mantle?" he scoffed. "You say the Light did me a favor by denying me the thing I wished for the most?"

"I say you have been denied for a nobler mission."

Nonsense, Akira would say, but he would be damned forever if he did. "What mission could be nobler than fighting the Light's holy war?"

"Fighting the holy war is something, winning it is something else, son." The monk gestured toward the pyre. "You can be one of its heroes if you save the Light's soldiers from this fate."

Akira was relieved when the monk let go of him and went to Lan's parents. *Such a waste of time*, Akira thought as he strode out of the yard. He hadn't escaped from the Sun Castle to listen to the same hollow speech his mother had given him about *becoming one of the heroes of the War of the Last Day*. Without doubt, that monk did exert some decent effort to memorize and recite her words back to him.

Wait. What if it was the other way around? What if his mother was the one reciting the monk's words?

Akira was already getting away from the shrine when the thought struck him. *Who are you really, Your Eminence?* Akira wondered, heading toward the nearest tavern to entertain his restless mind a little bit. Had he just talked today to the very seer who had told his mother that the Last Day was sooner than they thought?

9. NATSU

The gulf of the northeastern coast of Yoshi was a natural harbor. After Natsu's crew docked the Wraith there to resume the repair works, her deputy wanted to accompany her when she disembarked. "No, Pantu. You must stay here to keep order on the ship," she demanded. "I want that breach sealed by the time I return."

"Very well. I will stay. But at least, take one of us with you," Pantu pleaded, glancing at the mountain atop which the mage was waiting.

"It is not necessary." Literally. All of Natsu's crew combined would never do her any good if that mage up there decided to hurt her. Had her deputy forgotten the horrific display that had cost the Koyan empire three of their mighty Turtle ships? "Just keep the men working and make sure they stay calm in my absence. Tell them there is no reason to panic here, do you understand? That mage I'm going to meet is not a threat. Actually, he is the only ally we have in these waters."

"If you insist." Finally, Pantu acquiesced. "Be careful in your ascent, then. Pick a path that is not too steep."

Natsu hadn't survived all she had survived so far to allow a mountain to defeat her. "Then, I need to go while the sun is still up in the sky."

Fortunately, finding a less steep side of the mountain didn't take much time, but the ascent itself was a little bit hairy because of the sharp rocks everywhere. One misstep might prove costly in this desolate place. "Blast! Why don't you just come down?" she muttered, hoping that mage might hear her and spare her the trouble of climbing a mountain after barely surviving being chased by three Turtle ships. *And after barely sleeping last night.*

The ascent was taking too long, but she didn't regret ignoring Pantu's advice. As she was not in need of 'actual' help from her crew, any company would just be a distraction while she was collecting her thoughts for the upcoming meeting with the intimidating mage. He had had the upper hand last time; something she shouldn't allow to happen again. *He rescued us because he wants something from us,* she thought. *Those bastards never do any favors without something in return.*

Natsu was nearing the summit when she found huge rocks blocking her way upward. Too smooth to climb, too huge to turn around. And she had gone too far to go down and restart her ascent somewhere else. After scanning the rocky barrier ahead of her, all Natsu found was a small foothold, but it would do for her to resume her climb. Gripping on the only handhold she saw, she strained her arms to pull herself up as she tried to lodge her boot into another foothold.

And that was when she slipped.

Natsu cried out the instant she lost her footing. Panicking, she moved her legs hysterically to find a foothold before her tired arms—the only things preventing her from falling down—would fail her. But her hysteric movements added more weight to the body hardly hanging on to the rock. And before she knew it, she was holding on to nothing but air.

Natsu's fall didn't last a whole second, and yet it was the most horrifying feeling she had ever experienced. She was still screaming even after she felt herself being pulled *upward*. When she raised her head, she saw the masked mage standing at the cliff, his arms stretched forward, his fingers moving as if he was beckoning Natsu over. Except that Natsu had no say in that.

The moment Natsu landed in front of the robed mage, she blustered, "What was all this horror for? You could have just met me at the foot of the bloody mountain!"

The mage wearing the crimson mask tilted his head. "I've just saved your life. Haven't the good people of Hokydo heard of the phrase 'thank you'?"

"Saved my life? You are the one who put my life in danger in the first place," Natsu snapped, still infuriated. "Tell me: Was it entertaining to watch me climb all this distance to reach you?"

The provocative mage shrugged. "You have come to me voluntarily. I didn't ask you to do so, did I?"

Now he was treating her as if she was a fool; another reason to be enraged. "The fireball floating above you; you created it to show me where you were."

The robed mage gestured toward the sea. "Because I saw that you needed to repair your glorified ship."

Mocking the Wraith irked Natsu, she had to admit. "What do you even know about my ship?"

"More than the tales you spread about it. That it is not faster than lightning as the seafolks believe."

With anybody outside her crew, Natsu would deny the existence of the Wraith. But that mage mentioned it for a reason. *He is here for it*, she thought, and the idea scared her. How could you stand between a mage and something he wanted?

"How did you know about the ambush?" she asked, and at once, a guess came to her mind. "It was you." She gaped at him. "You and your people set that ambush for us."

"My people?" Leaning forward toward Natsu, the masked mage clenched his fist. "Did you hear anything about them?"

Natsu didn't get what that menacing tone was for. Regardless of the consequences, she said, "That they are planning for the Third Crossing. It's not a secret now, I presume."

"It is not. And it's why I sent the Turtles after you. I wanted to see for myself if you could outrun them." The mage relaxed his hand. "Plainly, it needs some enhancements."

"You almost killed us just to test our ship?"

"My demon wouldn't have let them kill you. You saw for yourself, didn't you?"

His demon? "Those huge hands..."

"They belong to *Shnakar*, our servant in the Koyan Sea."

At this moment, Natsu realized she was wrong about the masked man standing two feet away from her. He was not just a mage; he was a *summoner*. The rarest and most dangerous kind of mages. "I thought demons only occupied the Boiling Eyes."

"We have left them untamed in the Boiling Eyes to limit the outsiders' naval access to our islands."

Damn him! He was casually talking about *untamed demons* as if they were pets of his own. What was this mage's problem? "You tell me we have been sailing over them across the Koyan Sea all this time?" Natsu exclaimed.

"They are confined here." The mage shrugged. "They can't harm anybody unless we decide so."

Still digesting what she had just learned, Natsu held her temples with both hands as she thought for a moment. "You control the demons. You control the Koyan navy. What would you need from simple people like us?"

"Something neither the navy nor the demons could help me with. But as I said before; your ship needs a little enhancement."

The fact that a summoner stated clearly that he needed her help instilled some confidence in her. "With all my due respect to your unparalleled powers, I doubt your eligibility to give me this advice. You don't understand how the Wraith works, to begin with."

The masked mage folded his arms across his chest. "You mean the ship that works on a steam engine? It's a brilliant idea, but we all know it wasn't your husband's."

How dare he? "What is this nonsense?" she snapped. "All know that Botan the Squid was the one who built this ship."

"Using the documents he had bought from the Goranians. Darov's *stolen* documents."

"Botan didn't steal anything," she said without thinking, but after pondering her statement, she realized how ambitious she sounded.

"Someone else did when the Rusakian chemist was in prison. That 'someone' sold the documents to the Byzonts, who in turn sold them to your late husband. He did a great job in building the engine, though."

The father of the Wraith; that was how Botan had cemented his name in the smuggling business. Being the Squid's successor as the commander of the mythical ship was a way to earn her rivals' respect, if not their fear. Realizing now that a major part of the *father's* legacy was based on a lie would be a shock to Natsu's crew.

"You know more about us than we do," she said bitterly.

"Your deputy's spies were not the only ones who were doing their job," the mage scoffed. "We have eyes as well."

Again, the mage won in the leverage game, but Natsu wouldn't admit her defeat. *He needs the Wraith*, she reminded herself. "What kind of enhancements are you talking about?"

"You rely on coal as a source of heat to produce the steam that will eventually move the rotors, right?" The mage was not waiting for her answer, obviously. "I can augment your engine by adding a faster way of heating."

Now he piqued Natsu's curiosity. "And what is that faster way?"

The mage spread his palm, then flexed his fingers without totally closing them. A small fireball appeared out of nowhere, floating a few inches above the mage's hand. "Our way."

10. AKIRA

Focus was as important as stamina for wielding jumuns; Akira had been taught that, but it wasn't the real reason why mages were prohibited from drinking. Poor Pink Cloaks, like Akira's humble self, would rarely need to make complex bonds—scrutinizing scrolls and preparing potions required a more basic level of focus. Those *inferior* mages should drink whenever they wanted, right?

Well, Akira might have changed his mind after tonight's little ride back to Sun Castle. All that occupied his head the instant he hopped off the stagecoach was one idea: to reduce this colossal, stony structure he was gazing at to ashes. *Plainly, they are right about banning wine*, he thought, waddling toward the locked gate of the castle. *A drunken mage is a dangerous being. Be they wearing red cloaks or pink ones.*

The guards posted atop the bulwark glared at Akira, their hands reaching for the crossbows strapped to their backs as he approached. *You can't be seen like this, Akira*, he told himself as he straightened his back—or at least, he tried to. "I was in the city." Akira put his fist on his mouth to suppress a belch. "I was attending the funeral. See?" He managed a smile, clutching his cloak. "I'm wearing the white."

The guards made way for their captain to come and look at the late visitor, which he did, looking him over dubiously, his hands on his waist. "Everybody has returned from the funeral hours ago."

"Yes, I left them for a short while, but when I came back, I didn't find anybody waiting for me." Akira shrugged. "Without my pink cloak, I had trouble finding an unoccupied coach headed here."

The captain didn't seem convinced as he smacked his lips. "It's not up to me to decide. Your tutor is Jihoon Sen, right?"

Akira nodded reluctantly. He was mostly sober, yet a voice in his head—the same voice that tempted him to burn the entire castle down—reminded him that he was a mage. With a single jumun, he could send all these clowns flying to the ground and break their spines. Fortunately, he came to his senses before committing a foolish act that would alarm an army of Red Cloaks to thwart the drunken mage. Not that they would need an army, to begin with; one Red Cloak was enough to defeat him single-handedly.

Fidgeting in front of the locked gate, Akira waited for the guards to summon his mentor Jihoon Sen. The minutes felt like hours, invoking the same insane voice to muddle his head with more reckless ideas. *What is taking you so long, big man?* he thought, clenching his fist. But when Akira took note of the guards aiming their crossbows at him, he raised his open palms to show them he was standing down now.

Akira sat down on the ground as the waiting continued. *Is Jihoon punishing me for my late return?* he wondered, taking deep breaths to calm himself down. Reminding himself that his punishment would be worse if he turned his back to the castle and went the other way, he brushed aside the idea.

The iron gate squealed as the guards opened it at last. Akira groaned as he rose to his feet and entered, but the mage waiting for him in the courtyard was not his beefy mentor. "You picked quite the night to show your lack of discipline," said Kyong Sen, his lips clenched in a firm line. "Soon, we shall know whether you are too lucky or totally the opposite." The tutor of potions and chemistry signaled Akira to follow him as he walked ahead toward the main building. Why were there too many guards posted at its door?

This doesn't feel right. "Where is Jihoon Sen?" Akira warily asked, walking behind the black-bearded tutor.

"He has a more serious issue to attend to," said Kyong Sen without looking at him as they both traversed the guarded vestibule. Usually, those soldiers with lamellar armors paid more attention to the walls and the gate. That issue Kyong was referring to was apparently *way* more serious than the tardiness of one worthless student.

"That *more serious issue* didn't harm Jihoon Sen, right?"

"We shall know after the investigations are over."

Investigations? What did this irksome tutor hide? "Is it too hard to tell me what has just happened here, Kyong Sen?"

"There was a fire in the chemistry study." Finally, Kyong deigned to give him a quick glance as they stopped in the thronged hallway. "Wait here until you hear your name."

Akira was alarmed when he realized that the waiting line ahead of him led to nothing but the office of the Archmage himself. "Am I a suspect?" Akira was totally sober when he dared to catch Kyong by the hand before the latter might leave him at the back of the line. The bearded tutor's reaction was a hard look that urged Akira to release the hand immediately and apologize.

Kyong Sen didn't walk away, though. "The investigation shall determine to what extent you have been involved with the primary suspect." He leaned forward toward Akira. "With your cousin, I mean."

* * *

Akira's stomach was in knots when his turn to enter Kungwan's vast office came. Sitting at the head of the table in the center of the room was none other than the Archmage himself, Jihoon and Tashihara next to each other on the side facing the door, all wearing grim faces.

The Archmage was not looking at Akira when Tashihara beckoned the *suspect* over, Jihoon folding his arms across his broad chest. "Sit," demanded the most fearsome lady Akira had ever encountered. Why was he so nervous despite his certainty of his innocence?

"Do you know why you are here, Akira?" Jihoon asked. Despite his attempts to sound impassive, you could sense a hint of empathy in his voice. *He* hopes *that I have nothing to do with this grave accident.*

"I was told there had been a fire today." Akira was not sure if he should reveal all he had heard from Kyong Sen.

"We have our reasons to believe it was your cousin Kim." Akira couldn't help stealing a glance at his uncle upon hearing Tashihara utter Kim's name, and to Akira's surprise, the Archmage didn't flinch. "Is it true she shared her intentions with you before the incident?"

The tension was enough to nullify the impact of anything Akira had drunk tonight. The devious lady was luring him into a trap, and he could see it. "With all due respect, Tashihara Sen; I find it hard to imagine that a sweet, disciplined girl like Kim would do something like that." He mustered all his courage to add, "You have been her mentor for a while; you should know that very well."

"We deal with the facts at hand, not our gut feelings," she countered. "And the facts at hand point to her."

"What facts, Tashihara Sen?"

"We are the ones who ask, and you are the one who answers," she said firmly. "Now tell me; of all her peers, can you name one person closer to Kim than you?"

Again, Akira saw the trap, and it was inescapable this time. A yes would just land him right into the middle of it. A no would be considered a lie. "Not that I know of."

Tashihara glowered at him. "Yes or no?"

May the demons take your soul. "No, I can't." He leaned both elbows on the table, looking Tashihara in the eye. "What does this prove anyway?"

"Akira," Jihoon called. "You had better calm down. Stick to answering our questions."

Akira didn't wish to argue with his mentor in front of Tashihara and the Archmage, but you shouldn't back someone into a corner and expect him not to defend himself. "Your 'questions' betray nothing but a prejudice against me and Kim, Jihoon Sen. How should I feel *calm* about that?"

The sounds in the room hushed down when Kungwan Sen heaved a deep sigh, both Tashihara and Jihoon staring at their superior in anticipation.

"If there was a prejudice, it would be in favor of the Archmage's daughter, not the other way around," Kungwan

Sen spoke at last, his voice flat, yet Akira sensed his concealed fury. "You think anyone with enough sanity in this place would be eager to prove her guilty?" He clenched his jaw when he went on, "You think I would do that to my own blood, young man?"

Akira wondered if he was included in his uncle's 'own blood,' but he didn't dare to ask. "Why do you assume that everybody in this castle is glad you are assuming the seat of the Head of the Imperial Court, Kungwan Sen?"

Tashihara was about to protest, but a firm gesture with Kungwan's palm silenced her. "Go on," he commanded, nodding his chin toward Akira.

Now not obliged to stick to Tashihara's leading questions, Akira should be more relieved. Surprisingly enough, it didn't eliminate the pressure; it just made it different. The space Kungwan had just allowed him was a chance Akira had to seize.

"I don't know about the facts you all have against Kim, but I believe there are more facts you should heed as well." Akira was addressing the three senior mages, but it was Kungwan Sen who got most of his attention. "Of all people who dined tonight at the same place, the daughter of the newly-appointed Head of the Imperial Court got sick because of the food, so that next day, the day of Lan's funeral, she would be the only student staying at the castle when the fire incident happened." Akira paused for effect before he continued cautiously, "Which also makes me wonder why you accuse Kim in particular. As far as I know, there were guards, maidservants…and *other* mages when the fire started."

Kungwan Sen gnashed his teeth. "Accusing a Red Cloak is a grave act, son."

"Your daughter is a Red Cloak too, Kungwan Sen."

The Archmage slammed his hands across the table. "Except that she was the first one seen coming out of the hall right after it was set on fire."

That took Akira off guard. Now he understood what facts Tashihara was talking about.

"Who saw her?" Akira asked his uncle.

Tashihara cleared her throat, and on Kungwan's behalf, she answered, "That's none of your—"

"Minjun Sen did," Kungwan cut her off.

Akira never liked the former prodigy of Sun Castle. "And you believe him while you doubt your own daughter?"

"Here, I'm the Archmage. My own daughter is there at home."

"Whom do you trust more, Kungwan Sen?"

Akira's uncle inhaled deeply. "Minjun Sen has always been devoted to our sacred cause. He has no reason to do something like that."

"Kim didn't have a reason either."

"Kim has always had her own beliefs about the Last Day, Akira, and you know that." Kungwan wagged a firm finger. "Don't you dare lie in my face and pretend she never told you."

The foolish girl! Has she shared her brilliant thoughts with her father? "I don't understand," Akira shook his head, astonished, "why are you so desperate to prove her guilty?"

"If she is the one who did it, then she deserves to be punished," Kungwan said firmly. "That's the code we live by."

Kungwan's ruthlessness was not something Akira was unfamiliar with, but in such a situation? With his own daughter? *The old man has lost his mind.*

"Akira." Jihoon was back after watching his master for a while. "Do you agree with Kim that the Last Day could be a threat to the entire human race?"

Again, more traps, and this time, it was Akira's *kind* mentor. "I never said she said that in the first place."

Tashihara leaned forward toward him. "You agree with that belief or not?"

For this question in particular, his mentor could vouch for him, but Akira was now aware he had no allies in this room. "Of course not. I have been striving to wear the red mantle so that I too can be part of the army fighting the Light's holy war one day." He gestured toward Jihoon Sen. "You may ask him, and he will tell you if I'm telling the truth."

Ignoring his last statement, Tashihara asked him, "What do you know about the Tree of Amagesdon?"

On a regular day, Akira would boast about his knowledge, but tonight? With these people? He would hurt Kim if he showed that he knew much more than he should. "What tree is this?"

Jihoon leered at Akira. "Hiding the truth is as useless as lying, young man. So, do us and yourself a favor; we are already having a long night."

How does he know if I'm hiding something? "And I can't wait to walk out of this room, Jihoon Sen. So please, tell me what you want to hear."

Jihoon fixated his gaze on him. "Something that you can say without affecting your pulse."

Hells and demons! Akira had heard about the *sensors*, but he never knew that his mentor was one of them. Continuing this charade of ignorance was absurd now.

"It's an ancient weapon that we are going to use in the Third Crossing." Akira shrugged as he went on, "That's all I know."

Tashihara cast him a studying look. "Didn't she tell you that it can destroy an entire city as big as Oyoto in a blink of an eye?"

"No, she didn't." *She wanted to, but she didn't have the chance.* All she had told him was something about the Light not being pleased with such 'atrocity.'

Akira noticed that slight nod Jihoon gave the Archmage. "I'm done with this session," said Kungwan firmly, waving dismissively at Akira. As neither Tashihara nor Jihoon protested—as if they could commit such a crime, to begin with—Akira pushed to his feet, bowed to the respectable mages, and took his leave.

"What do you think of this, Akira?" Kungwan Sen asked from behind Akira before the latter reached the door. "A weapon that reduces a whole city with all of its people to ashes. Do you think the Light would approve of burning innocent children, women, and elders with their blazed homeland?"

Akira's investigators were saving their most baneful trap for last. A trap by the Archmage himself. What they didn't know was that it was actually the easiest. "We don't question the Light's will," Akira answered confidently. "And if they are innocent as you say, Kungwan Sen, then we are just sending their souls to the Light's eternal paradise."

Kungwan raised his eyebrows before he exchanged a quick look with Jihoon, the mage with the sensors' abilities. "Of all the answers we heard today," Jihoon glanced at Akira, "this one was by far the most truthful."

Tashihara pressed her lips together, surely not thrilled by Jihoon's statement.

"You are free to go, son," Kungwan said, a hint of a smile on his face. "We are proud we have someone like you among us."

Akira could have never imagined himself saying that, but this interrogation could be the best thing that had ever happened to him since he joined Sun Castle.

11. NATSU

Following Pantu's advice, Natsu forbade Mushi from setting a straight course back to Hokydo. Instead, they turned around the island of Jopen and headed to their homeland from its eastern coast. The helmswoman had her concerns about taking a longer route with the Wraith in its current condition. "We are not sure how long that 'magical' seal will hold," she said, referring to the mage's trick that didn't just repair the breach; it made it *vanish*. As if the hull of the ship had always been intact.

"It will hold." Natsu didn't have a hint of doubt, still unable to forget the sight of the wooden parts sticking together and fusing with the gap in a smooth fashion. According to the mage, who had descended to the mountain foot to aid Natsu's crew yesterday, 'binding the particles of wood' was the explanation for his trick. As if he owed anybody an explanation in the first place. "And it's too late now anyway, Mushi. If you want to say something useful, then pray we won't encounter any more Turtles."

Natsu couldn't tell whether Mushi's prayers worked or it was just a coincidence, but fortunately, the Wraith made it safely to their secret cove, which you would never spot from the sea unless you were foolish enough to come close to the waterfall covering the entrance. After docking at the wharf, Mushi and the sailors stayed to replenish the ship's supply of coal, and also to guard the vessel if necessary. Pantu, Sogeki-hei, and Jirou followed Natsu through the cave from which they would emerge in the middle of the eastern hills, then traverse the abandoned area until reaching the main coastal road, and from there, they would move north toward the town. If they didn't encounter any more hurdles on their way, they should arrive by nightfall.

They were exiting the cave when Pantu walked alongside Natsu. "You think of anything other than sticking to our deal with the mage?" her deputy asked. He would always be worried about her recklessness, Natsu reckoned.

"Why would we break our deal with him? All he has done so far is help us."

"To deliver him the Wraith on a silver platter."

"You think he couldn't steal the Wraith from under our noses if he wanted?"

Pantu's mouth clenched in a firm line as he nodded. "You have a point." He fell silent for a moment, then said, "But there is something in the assignment he has given us that bothers me. Why all the secrecy about the cargo he wants us to transport to Gorania? If we are working for the Koyan Empire, then we shouldn't be hiding from the coastguards."

"We never cared who paid us as long as they *paid*."

"He hasn't shown us a damned coin yet, not even of copper."

Natsu heaved a sigh. "Don't you realize that he doesn't even need to lie to us? He could have just threatened us with his 'domesticated' sea monster." *Shnakar* was its name. If only that mage agreed to unleash his hellish pet upon Qianfan's boats…

Natsu's retinue reached an abandoned warehouse near the main road, where they had hidden the carriage that had brought them to this place. As they approached the front door, Sogeki-hei drew his crossbow and mounted a bolt into it, and at once Jirou drew his falchion. Natsu and Pantu halted and looked around, but nothing alive was there except their shadows. "What is it?" she asked nervously.

As the sharpshooter aimed at the door, Natsu shot Jirou an inquisitive look. "I don't know," the brawny man whispered, shrugging. "I just saw Sogeki-hei draw his weapon."

"Someone is inside the warehouse," the sharpshooter said in a low voice without looking at Natsu or Jirou, his crossbow pointed at the door as he warily approached.

"Our coachman, perhaps?" Natsu asked.

"Someone else is with him." Sogeki-hei nodded his chin toward the ground, where he must have spotted the tracks of the outsider.

"Someone? You mean we are only facing one man?" Jirou arched an eyebrow, and then he rushed toward the door and barged into the warehouse despite Sogeki-hei's disapproval.

Jirou's noisy entrance startled the two men inside for an instant before they all realized they were on the same side. Standing next to Natsu's coachman was Manshik, the boss of one of the small gangs that had pledged to join her in her feud against Qianfan. What brought him here? How had he found her, to begin with?

"I have been praying to the Light you will come back safely," the stocky boss said, his hands clasped in front of him. "I knew you wouldn't fall that easy."

Manshik's words didn't bode well. "What are you doing here, Manshik?"

"Qianfan and his men have been everywhere since you left. He amassed them and went to all the gangs in Hokydo, telling them that your days were numbered if not even over, and now they must only answer to the man in charge. To *him*. Otherwise, the answer would be blood."

So, Natsu's clash with Qianfan had just begun. "And blood is what he will get," she bristled. "Gather your men at the southern road while I summon the rest."

Manshik swallowed. "You don't get it. Qianfan wasn't just threatening. He killed all who resisted on the spot, leaving the rest no option but to join him."

No, no, no! She couldn't lose now. Not after all the measures she had taken. "Blast!" she blustered, walking away from Manshik, her mind still unable to process the situation. *I took too much time preparing! I should have acted at once,* she thought, biting her lower lip until it almost bled. "What about you, Manshik?" She glanced over her shoulder at him. "Why did Qianfan let you live if you were still loyal to me?"

"I ordered my men to flee from the town the moment I heard about Qianfan's moves. It was obvious he was targeting all those who joined you, so I knew our turn would come."

Running away was better than betraying her. "How did this happen? We had as many men as he had," she rambled, not addressing anybody in particular.

"Our people were scattered, Natsu," Manshik explained. "On the other hand, he gathered all his men and moved as one unit to each gang in turn, one after the other. The few who didn't join him perished by his order."

"He is even stronger now," Natsu muttered, unable to find a way out of this predicament.

"You should all flee from Hokydo," Manshik provided. "Most probably, my men and I will do the same. On this island, we can never be safe from Qianfan."

"He is right," Pantu seconded Manshik. "Qianfan's next target will be us. He will sweep the island until he finds his only rival."

With the news this stout fellow had just brought, Natsu was far from being anybody's rival. Her feud with Qianfan was something she should forget about for the time being. "Riku and Mother." She balled her hands into fists as she went on, "I can't leave them in that bloody town on their own."

"They are safer the farther they stay away from you," Pantu remarked.

"Nonsense," Natsu insisted. "If Qianfan doesn't find me, he will use them to get to me."

"So, you make his job of finding you easier?" Pantu swept an arm toward Manshik. "This man is still alive, not because he managed to flee from Qianfan. It was Qianfan who wanted him to flee. He left you someone to warn you, so that you would feel the urge to hurry to the very place he would be waiting for you at."

What Pantu said made Natsu even more determined to return as soon as possible to the town. "Listen. I don't care if I die while trying to save my family. If you want to run away, then go. I'm not forcing anyone to go to the town with me."

"I'll go where you go, boss," said Jirou without any hesitation. Maybe he was not the cleverest member of her crew, but definitely, he was one of the most loyal. Like Sogeki-hei, who just shrugged, as if his stance should be too clear to ask him about.

"Alright." Pantu exhaled. Clearly, he realized that nothing would change his boss's mind. "Sogeki-hei," he turned to the sharpshooter, his hands on his waist, "go ahead of us to scout the road. If you don't come back before sunset, we shall leave."

Sogeki-hei nodded, and while he was untying one of the two horses that were supposed to drag the carriage, Manshik harrumphed as he took one step closer to Natsu. "I'm afraid I won't be able to join you, Natsu."

Natsu patted his shoulder, allowing herself a smile. "You did better than most, Manshik. Don't let the bastard find you."

Mounting his horse, Sogeki-hei offered to drop Manshik on the main road, and the stout man accepted. After they both left, Jirou asked both Natsu and Pantu, "You want me to stand outside as a lookout?"

Jirou would rather bring unnecessary attention to their hideout than be useful as a lookout. "We will watch from inside." Natsu gazed through the nearest window at the apparently deserted area outside the warehouse. "Before sunset, we shall leave as Pantu suggests."

* * *

Natsu was relieved when Sogeki-hei returned before sunset. The news he bore didn't bode well though. "Qianfan's men are lurking all over the southern territory. We can't take the main road."

Sogeki-hei's announcement loomed large in the minds of everybody in the warehouse, it was plain. Going to the town was a suicide mission; Natsu was fully aware of this fact, and surely, she was the only one who didn't care. "We will draw too much attention if the four of us go together," she said to her men. "Qianfan's men won't expect me to enter the town on my own."

"That's out of the question," Pantu said firmly.

"We need to put our emotions aside and think rationally," she countered. "It's the only way for us all to survive."

"There is nothing rational in going to the town now, Natsu." Her deputy sneered. "But as long as you decide to go back there, we can't leave you."

"She is right, Pantu. We can't enter the city together if we want to make this work," Sogeki-hei interjected. "That's why I will do it alone."

Natsu hadn't seen this coming. "No one is going to risk himself for me. It's my family that's trapped there; I must be the one to rescue them."

"You were just talking about *thinking rationally*, weren't you?" Sogeki-hei smiled crookedly. "If you put your emotions aside indeed, you will realize that I'm the best one for such a mission. None of you can sneak in and out of town better than me."

Natsu found herself at a loss for words right now. Truth be told, her sharpshooter was the only one in this room who said something sensible. Instead of arguing with him, she asked, "Do you have a plan in mind?"

"Qianfan won't expect any of us to enter the town from its northern borders," Sogeki-hei began. "Also, he won't expect you to run away from the island while your child and your mother are still there." He glanced at both Pantu and Jirou as he added, "We will do everything he doesn't expect."

"That will never happen," Natsu snapped. "I will never leave my boy behind!"

Pantu shook his head, his arms folded across his chest, making Natsu not sure whether he disapproved of her reaction to Sogeki-hei's idea or to the idea itself.

"You will not leave anybody," Sogeki-hei explained. "Because I will bring them to you in the middle of the sea, where you will be waiting for me aboard the Wraith."

Pantu's eyebrows rose in astonishment. "You will sneak Natsu's family out through the sea?"

"Through the northern coast."

"It could be easier for you to cross the mountains there on your own. But with an old woman and a child in your company?" Pantu smacked his lips, shaking his head again. "I don't know, but it will take too much time, if it works at all."

Sogeki-hei grinned. "That's why Qianfan won't expect us to come in or out from that side of Hokydo."

Pantu didn't seem convinced as he shot Natsu an inquisitive glance. He was waiting for her to weigh in, it was clear.

"Your plan sounds a little bit reckless," Natsu said to her sharpshooter. "But I guess it is our best alternative so far." She peered at Pantu. "You have a better idea?"

Pantu puffed nervously. "It's the best idea I have heard so far, and that's what worries me."

"Every voyage we made was always a risk," Sogeki-hei pointed out, smiling at Pantu. "Why do you expect this one to be any different?"

"This one *is* different." Pantu didn't seem in the mood for Sogeki-hei's humor. "This time we are chased by everybody on land and in the sea."

"Only for a while, Pantu," Natsu promised, and she did mean every word of it. But right now, her priority was putting Riku and her mother somewhere safe. She would hide them in the forbidden lands of Gorania, if that was what it took. Because after that, with the arrival of Bilguun's Skandivian mercenaries, it wouldn't be a chase anymore.

It would be a bloodbath.

12. AKIRA

The only building in Koya that rivaled the sheer size of the Imperial Palace was Sun Castle. But even in such a vast building, where all of its people woke up, had their meals, attended their sessions, and slept at the same time, it was unlikely not to run across your cousin for three whole days.

Unless she didn't want to.

Right after breakfast this morning, Akira decided to look for her in her dorm room. The girls standing by the door gave him a judging look when he strode toward them, and that was when he realized that he should slow down a little bit. "I don't mean to barge in like this…" He cleared his throat, asking himself what on Earth he was saying right now.

"You are looking for Kim, aren't you?" One of the girls was decent enough to relieve him from his embarrassment. When he nodded, she continued, "She has just packed and left."

"What?"

The girl's lips curled into a mocking smile. "You didn't know she was leaving today? Or you didn't know she was leaving in the first place?"

The 'decent' girl was not as decent as Akira had presumed, it turned out. "When did she leave?" he asked, unable to conceal the anger in his tone.

"A few minutes ago." She shrugged. "You might still…"

Akira didn't wait for the girl to finish and sprinted away from her and her friends, ignoring their irksome laughter. Nothing preoccupied his mind as he rushed down the stairs except his unhinged cousin. He could understand her inclination for seclusion after the recent incident she was accused of, but avoiding him of all people? To the extent of leaving Sun Castle without even telling him? Well, Akira wouldn't settle down until he got some answers.

The first thing he heard upon reaching the courtyard was the sound of clopping hooves. "WAIT!" he yelled, running after the carriage passing through the open gate of the castle. The carriage didn't stop, though, forcing Akira to chase it outside the walls. To his surprise, the guards showed some understanding by not standing in his way.

Akira caught up with the carriage as it halted not too far away from the gate of the castle. Mad with fury, he resisted the urge to punish the coachman with a fireball for this uncalled morning sprint. After a second thought, he reminded himself that the poor man was just obeying the orders of his passenger.

The daughter of Kungwan Sen, the Archmage of Sun Castle and Head of the Imperial Court.

While Akira was about to shout at Kim, his cousin jumped off the carriage, scowling. "What are you doing, you idiot?"

Kim's move took him off guard for a second. He was the one who should be chiding her, not the opposite. "What is your problem?" he snapped.

Kim gripped Akira's hand and walked him away from the carriage until they were out of earshot. "I'm doing my best to keep you out of this, but you insist on framing yourself with your own hands!"

"Frame myself? I'm not accused of anything."

"I was told bits of your *impressive* performance during the investigation. Still, not everybody believes you are totally innocent." Kim glanced over her shoulder at the coachman to make sure he was not following them. "That you might not have helped me burn the chemistry study, but somehow you were involved. That's why I have been staying away from you, you fool!"

The casual way she mentioned burning the chemistry study worried him. "Wait a second. You…did it for real?"

Kim furrowed her brow. "You mean setting that damned hall on fire? I wish I did," she scoffed. "Unfortunately, someone else beat me to it."

His cousin had lost her mind indeed. "This is not you, Kim. You are the one who loathes destruction."

"After seeing what I saw in that hall, I wouldn't mind causing some little destruction to prevent a greater one." She attempted a sardonic smile. "Fortunately, someone else wasn't glad about that place either and took action."

His cousin might not be lying about not setting the chemistry study on fire, but something was not right about her. Something that made him feel she was not telling him all that she knew.

She is the one who is not totally innocent.

"Kim, please, tell me: What happened exactly that night? What made them accuse you?"

Kim heaved a sigh before she walked Akira a little farther from the carriage and its coachman. "I wasn't planning to burn the entire room; it was only the Tree of Amagesdon that I came for. I wanted to destroy every document—or chemical if necessary—related to it."

"So, your sickness during that day…?"

"I was pretending, yes. Sneaking into the study was easier when there were fewer people in the castle."

"Minjun was there to look after you." Akira couldn't utter the name without showing his aversion. "How did you get past him?"

"It wasn't that hard." Kim shrugged. "After he made sure I was 'stable,' he left to attend to his business. That was when I made my move and sneaked into the study. It took me quite some time to search the whole place, and all I found was a bunch of scrolls *mentioning* the Tree of Amagesdon, nothing about the components and the formula. So, I kept scanning for a while until I heard the footsteps of someone entering the study very cautiously, as if he wasn't supposed to be in that place." She smiled wryly. "Like me."

"You didn't see him, did you?"

"No, but I saw the fire he set." The satisfaction in Kim's tone when she said that was a little bit awkward for Akira. "The whole act didn't take more than a few seconds. Footsteps then fire."

"You were inside the study when it was set on fire?" Akira exclaimed.

She shrugged. "It wasn't too hard for me to make my way out of it."

Of course, Akira forgot; she was a Red Cloak after all. With a simple jumun, she could figure this out. "You could have saved the study as well, but you didn't," he rebuked her.

"Why would I?" She curled her lip in disdain. "Actually, I wouldn't have forgiven myself if I had."

His cousin was beyond saving. "You didn't say that in the investigation, did you?"

"It was unnecessary," she scoffed. "Seeing me emerge from the burning hall was enough to condemn me."

"Were there witnesses?" Akira had a guess already.

"Minjun himself."

Of course. "How convenient!"

Kim tilted her head. "You can't be inferring that he is the one who did it. Whether you like him or not, Minjun is one of the highly regarded mages in Sun Castle for a reason. His dedication to the Light's holy quest is unquestionable."

She might change her mind if she learned about Akira's conversation with Minjun the night Lan had died. But anyway, Akira didn't believe it was about the Third Crossing, to begin with. "What if that fire incident was not meant to be an act of sabotage to hinder the preparations of the War of the Last Day?"

Kim didn't seem convinced. "What else would it be done for?"

"Making the Archmage look bad by framing his daughter." Actually, both the fire incident and Lan's death were enough to serve such a purpose.

Kim wrinkled her fair forehead, and for a few seconds, she seemed to be ruminating on Akira's question. "I'm not saying this because he is my father, but I can't think of anybody who has problems with him. All mages of Sun Castle are loyal to their Archmage."

Akira stared at her. "A man who has no enemies is a man who does nothing." A sudden idea crossed his mind, so he asked, "And who said anything about the dedicated mages of Sun Castle?" He leaned forward toward Kim. "What if the whole matter was from someone *outside* the castle?" A familiar feminine figure came to Akira's mind. "Someone whose objective is to show the Emperor that the Archmage is losing control over the castle after he has become Head of the Imperial Court."

"Hanu!" Kim's eyes widened. "Hells and demons! You might be right." She scratched her chin reflectively. "But you know what? She wouldn't be able to execute her scheme without allies inside Sun Castle."

His cousin's assumption made sense. "I saw her at Lan's funeral. Is she friends with any of his parents?"

"She is Wei's cousin," she said, then shook her head. "But I never heard about any disputes between the man and Father."

"Perhaps there weren't any previous ones. But that wouldn't matter for the time being if he blamed your father for the death of his son."

"This is insane." Kim bit her lower lip as she kept shaking her head. "Hanu is a devious woman. If she is behind this, then Father is in great danger." She stared at Akira for a moment before she added, "You might be as well."

Really? That was a little surprising. "Because I'm his nephew?"

"Because you could be part of his plans. That would make you a hurdle to Hanu one way or another."

Akira couldn't help chuckling. "Me? Part of Kungwan Sen's plans?"

"I know nothing." She gritted her teeth. "But the night I was searching the chemistry study, I found one of your documents there. That essay you wrote about how to produce extremely powerful stamina-boosting potions using only local herbs."

Akira had to admit he was flattered to hear that. "My essay was about several kinds of potions, not just stamina-boosting ones."

"I'm not surprised that Father is only interested in the latter." Kim dug into her pocket, then took out a small purple flower and showed it to him. "Does this give you any clue? This is the only whole flower I found in the study. The rest were a few petals scattered all over the floor."

Akira scrutinized the flower he gently took from her hand. "That's a cherry blossom. What was it doing there?"

Kim cast him a studying look. "Doesn't it have anything to do with your potions?"

No, but the flower, which was about to wilt, evoked an idea in Akira's mind. "I thought you were disgruntled about my beliefs as well as your father's plans," he teased her.

Kim didn't look amused when she said, "That's where you and I differ, Akira." She leaned forward toward him. "For me, it's family that comes first, not faith."

Akira nodded pointedly toward the carriage behind her. "Is that why you are leaving your family?"

"It's Father's decision, not mine. He wants me to leave before he announces my expulsion from Sun Castle."

Akira couldn't get it. "If you are not guilty of an act of sabotage, then you must stay. But if you are…"

"Death will be my sanction, then." Kim smiled nervously. "But that's not what I'm expelled for. I'm punished for manipulation—my pretense of sickness, you know—and sneaking into the study and thus violating the rules of the lofty Sun Castle."

Given Kim's current situation, Akira couldn't consider this bad news. "What about burning the study? Who is taking the blame?"

"Until this moment? Nobody." Kim shrugged. "The investigations are not over yet."

They wouldn't be over before Kim went as far as possible from this place, Akira reckoned. *Well played, Uncle.* The heartless Archmage cared about his daughter after all.

"You are not returning home, I suppose?"

Kim grinned. "You are smart enough to understand that I must not tell you. It's better this way." She paused, and silence reigned over them for a moment. Both of them knew it was time to bid each other farewell, but neither of them wanted to be the first one to say goodbye.

"I know you're not fond of the old man that much," Kim broke the silence, averting her eyes, "but would you watch over him for me, please?"

Fortunately, I don't loathe him as much as Mother does. He nodded without saying a word. She did the same, pressing her lips together as she walked back to her carriage.

And that was their farewell. *At least, I got a flower.* He contemplated the cherry blossom in his hand, then buried it in his pocket before he headed back to the *lofty* Sun Castle. A storm of irrelevant questions invaded his mind as he stalked past the guards posted at the gate. He needed somebody to exchange his thoughts with, but that somebody was getting away from here as fast as possible. Yes, they had their differences, but she was always blunt about them, and that was why she was the only person he felt comfortable with. Even with his mother, he had to weigh every word before it slipped out of his mouth; a stress Kim never put on him.

Akira hurried toward the main building, where the first session of the day was about to start. Later, he should pay a visit to the plants' section in the library. Because if he remembered right, cherry blossoms only grew on the southern hills of the island of Hokydo. Why would anyone bother bringing flowers of no use from there?

13. NATSU

Natsu jumped off the boat as she and Pantu reached the dark, abandoned beach. If they didn't stop for rest, they would make it to the northern side of the town before midnight.

"Hopefully, we run into them," Pantu muttered as they walked through the defile between the mountains of the northern coast. "Maybe he was waiting for nightfall to make his move."

Natsu hoped her deputy was right about Sogeki-hei, who had taken longer than expected to return with her son and her mother. Though Pantu had begged her to stay on board the Wraith while he went on his own to look for Sogeki-hei and her family, Natsu had insisted on joining him. Actually, Pantu was the one joining her. *It was my task from the beginning. I shouldn't have let anybody else undertake it on my behalf.*

"We should slow down a bit lest we get tired out," Pantu offered. As Natsu ignored his piece of advice, he added, "Slower is faster sometimes."

"Pantu, please." Natsu wanted to avoid arguing with her deputy right now. With her anxiety getting worse by the minute, she might not be able to control whatever words were coming out of her mouth.

Thankfully, Pantu didn't share more of his wisdom with her until they reached the end of the defile, which was not too far away from the quiet edge of the town. "Where are we going?" she asked her deputy after noticing he was not taking the shortest path to her house.

"You and I need to get cloaks before we wander around the town," he justified. "Qianfan's men could be watching now."

It was dark already, but Natsu wouldn't protest against Pantu's precautionary measure, as long as it didn't imply wasting too much time. "Daiyu's house then?" The drunken widow Natsu mentioned was not just a tailor; she was one of Pantu's informants. "Most probably, she is not home yet."

"Let's hope she abandons the tavern earlier tonight," he said, his eyes betraying his doubt. Everybody in town knew that Daiyu was always the last to leave the tavern. Most of the time, it was the tavern keeper who threw her out because he needed to shut the place and go to sleep.

The widow was sitting on the doorstep of her cottage when Natsu and Pantu found her. Still not done with the bottle of ale in her hand, she didn't notice her late visitors until they stood right in front of her. "Hells and demons." Daiyu gawked at them, her eyes wide. "I'm not hallucinating, am I?"

"The filth you drink is never that strong." Pantu helped the old widow up and walked her into the cottage, Natsu following them, closing the door behind her.

"What are you doing here, you two? Shouldn't you be hiding somewhere?" Daiyu asked them, the bottle still in her hand. "Wait a minute. You are not going to hide here, are you?"

Without taking Daiyu's permission, Pantu rummaged through the pile of outfits cramming the table in the center of the small reception hall. "Don't worry, young lady. We will borrow two cloaks and leave."

Even that lonely widow who lived at the edge of the town was aware of the current situation with Qianfan. Curious to hear what that drunken lady knew, Natsu asked her, "Why do you think we should be hiding?"

Daiyu slammed the bottle on the table. "You don't know? Qianfan's men have been sweeping the entire town to find you." She winced, shaking her head. "Too much blood and fire in the past few days." Grimacing, she stook a gulp of ale, then said, "You haven't heard about your family and your house, have you?"

Mentioning Natsu's family alarmed her. *Please, no.* "What happened to them?" Natsu gripped the widow's wrist. "Is my son alright? Speak!"

Pantu hurried to Natsu to pull her off Daiyu. "Easy on her, Natsu. She is a friend."

"Get away from me!" Natsu shoved him, then held Daiyu's shoulders and shook her. "Speak quickly, woman! What do you know?"

Daiyu got rid of Natsu's grasp. "They didn't find his body. So, there is a chance he is still alive."

His body? "What on Earth are you talking about?"

"They found the corpses of your mother and the man who was trying to sneak her out of the town. Whoever stabbed them to death left their bodies on the street, in the heart of the marketplace, so that the merchants would find them when they went to their shops next morning."

* * *

Sitting on her own in Daiyu's cottage, Natsu needed an hour to grasp what the drunken, wrinkled woman had told her.

Her mother was killed. Sogeki-hei, whom Natsu had sent to get her family out of this damned town, was killed. Her son Riku hadn't been seen since then. And her house was reduced to ashes. Too much for her troubled mind and broken heart to deal with.

Natsu hadn't been there when the bastards had done it, and yet she couldn't dismiss the intrusive imagery of her mother's torn abdomen. Couldn't dismiss her mother's screams of fear, her shrieks of agony. *Those lowly sons of whores! They didn't bat an eye when they killed an old woman! With everything precious in this world, I swear I will make them face my wrath before they face the wrath of the Light in hell!*

And where had they taken her son? Had the rascals dared to lay their filthy hands on him? Every time she tried to imagine how terrified her poor little boy would be right now it tore her heart apart. *I must find him tonight*, Natsu thought as she lurched to her feet and strode to the door. *He can't stay all that long with those monsters.*

Pantu, who had been waiting outside with Daiyu, hurried toward Natsu upon seeing her exit the cottage. "Where to, Natsu?"

"I have a son to bring back," Natsu rasped as she went on her way.

"Natsu, wait!" Pantu scurried after her and caught her wrist. "Did you forget what I told you?"

"Let go of me!" Natsu wriggled to break free from his grip, but he held her tight with both hands. "My boy must not stay one more hour with those bastards. Do you understand?"

"It's you who must understand!" To Natsu's surprise, Pantu yelled at her. "This is exactly what he wants you to do! To act mindlessly until you get yourself killed! Is that what you want to do? Is that how you want to save Riku?"

For a second, Natsu's wrecked mind tried to consider Pantu's words. Another second later, she found herself bursting into tears, Pantu allowing her to bury her face in his shoulder. For a second, it felt wrong to show how vulnerable she was in front of her deputy. But above being a boss, she was a daughter who grieved for her murdered mother. A mother who was scared for her lost son. A mere person who felt too helpless to protect her loved ones.

Yes, she was vulnerable. She had the right to show that.

Natsu pulled herself away from Pantu and muttered, "I just want him back."

"We will find a way to bring him back," Pantu promised softly. "But we need to be calm and reasonable to do that."

Calm and reasonable. Two words that had become too absurd for her to use.

"You can resume this conversation inside," Daiyu urged them, scanning the dark, desolate area around her cottage. "We can never know who might be watching us right now."

Natsu didn't argue, and silently headed back into the cottage, Pantu and the widow following her. When Daiyu offered her one of her bottles, Natsu waved at her dismissively as she picked the nearest chair. "My mind is shattered already. I need whatever remained of my sanity to think of my next move."

Pantu nodded approvingly as he stood facing Natsu, his arms folded across his chest, his back against the wall. "That's a good start." He turned to Daiyu. "Are you sure Qianfan didn't leave a message for Natsu to state his demands?"

Daiyu shook her head, then said, "Doesn't that mean it's possible he doesn't have the boy?"

"He is only five," Pantu pointed out. "It's unlikely he wasn't with his grandmother and Sogeki-hei when Qianfan's men found them." He paused thoughtfully. "He wants to throw Natsu off balance. He wants her to rush into town to look for her son blindly, with her guard down, so that he could easily strike her dead."

"Alright." Natsu clenched her jaw. "Now I'm not going *blindly*; what is the plan?"

Pantu heaved a sigh. "I must talk to my eyes here to find out Riku's whereabouts. Someone must have seen something."

"And after we find out?"

Pantu peered at her for a moment. "Natsu, it must be me only. You and the rest of the crew will flee to Oyoto while I handle—"

"That's not going to happen, and you know that."

"Natsu, please." Pantu looked her in the eye. "I need you to trust me with this mission."

"I have always trusted you with missions, Pantu. But this is my son we are talking about. My everything!"

"If you want to stay on Hokydo, then I must remind you that Qianfan's men are not leaving a stone unturned," said Daiyu. "If they find you, what remains for your little boy?"

We need to be calm and reasonable. It was hard to do that just one hour after hearing today's shocking news. "You are right, good woman. I had better stay away and let my men handle this matter." She rose to her feet, gesturing toward Pantu. "Just give this man a cloak, and then he will leave and let you be."

Pantu seemed confused as Natsu went to the door and exited. After a minute of waiting, Pantu joined her outside the cottage wearing his new cloak. They stood facing each other for a moment before Pantu broke the silence. "You really meant what you just said? You will let your men handle the matter while you flee to Oyoto?"

"I didn't say I'd go to Oyoto." Natsu lowered her voice. "I will take the Wraith back to our cavern, and from there I will head to the southern hills."

"The southern hills?" Pantu furrowed his brow. "Why?"

Natsu poked his chest with her finger. "Because you are going to hurry to that common friend between you and the mage. Tell him that I need an extremely urgent meeting at our usual place."

14. AKIRA

Seven. That was the number of cherry blossom petals Akira had picked up from the floor all the way from the burned chemistry study to the place he hated the most in Sun Castle; the Portal Yard.

The last week was a dull, peaceful one in the castle—well, if compared to the week before, which had witnessed the death of a student, the chemistry hall incident, and the following investigations—but it wasn't that peaceful to Akira. Not because studying portals was hard; it was just traumatic. *And I thought I could stay away from them forever.*

In a moment of temporary weakness, Akira thought of divulging everything to Jihoon, hoping he would persuade his mentor to guide him through the passage across the dreadful void that connected all portals together. Luckily, the faint voice of wisdom in his head saved him from committing such a foolish act. *Since when have you started doubting yourself, Akira? Memorizing the locations of portals shouldn't be any different from memorizing any formula you have learned before.*

Today was the day, Akira decided. The senior mages would be preoccupied until noon with that 'important' meeting Kungwan had called for; an opportunity that Akira shouldn't miss. None of those senior mages would feel his absence for hours. *Hesitate today, and you shall regret it forever.*

Akira was expecting Kyong to keep his apprentices busy during the meeting with Kungwan Sen, and the potions' tutor didn't disappoint. Right before leaving the hopeless Pink Cloaks in his workshop, Kyong demanded loads of potions to be prepared before sunset. Some of the young mages mumbled in frustration, but none of them dared to protest straightforwardly, and the reason was his warning at the end of his session: "Those who don't finish their assignments today will be denied their next city visit."

Akira was possibly the only one who wouldn't bother. Thanks to the day of Lan's burial, he wasn't yearning for another taste of ale. And honestly, he wasn't that enthusiastic about seeing his mother any time soon. If it were not for your loved ones or a few sips of ale, why would anybody be eager for a city visit?

Akira waited until he couldn't hear any footsteps in the corridor outside Kyong's workshop. *The meeting must have started*, he deduced, and that was when he mustered his courage and went to the door to exit. As he strode across the corridors, he kept revising the map of portals in his head. *No accidents today*, Akira reminded himself, trying to prevent the memory of his last attempt to cross the void from overwhelming his mind. But it seemed that the more he tried, the more he remembered from that disastrous day. His panic when he had almost lost his balance. His perplexity when he had suddenly been unable to identify the right portal. His shame when Jihoon had interfered to get him out of the void before the closure of all portals. Most probably, the decision of not raising Akira to the rank of Red Cloak had been decided on that day, regardless of his results in the last trial which had been held one year later. Not that he questioned Jihoon's fairness, mind you. Had it not been for his mentor, Akira would have been lost in the void until the end of times.

Enough of the memories, and focus, he told himself as he reached the vacant yard. The only thing he needed to remember now was all the instructions regarding portal crossing. *First, the antiemetic.* He dug into his pocket, took out the flacon of red ginseng decoction, and drank half of it. After he waited for a minute, he closed his eyes, gathering his focus to bind his anerjy with Earth's pulling force. The crack startled him, although it indicated that he had unlocked the portal here.

Akira could feel his accelerating pulse as he stared at the shimmering oval that grew in front of him. *The hardest part is yet to come,* he thought, taking a few slow breaths to relieve his stress. *You wanted to become a Red Cloak and fight in the War of the Last Day, right? What kind of a Red Cloak would fear the void? Maybe they were right about not choosing you, son of Seijos!*

Now his fury overcoming his anxiety, Akira drew one long breath, then walked through the shining portal. Instantly, he was in the place he feared the most.

The void. That dark, silent emptiness that connected all the portals in the world together.

Don't look down, he reminded himself, lest he fall into the bottomless space for eternity. "It doesn't matter if you can't see it. Just trust your feet," he recalled Jihoon's instructions about dealing with the invisible 'ground' he was actually feeling right now. "Keep your eyes on the portal you are going to cross next."

Akira, still overwhelmed by his presence in the ominous void, almost forgot about the other portal he would have to open to go to the other side. "The more you concentrate, the fewer portals you open in the void," was another piece of advice from Akira's mentor. "But it shouldn't be a hurdle anyway if you memorize all the portal sites."

One more time, he gathered his focus to open the portal that would take him to the only portal site with cherry blossoms around it; the southern hills of the island of Hokydo.

Luminous ovals started to appear in the void ahead of him until he counted eighteen, which was not something unusual for a novice. "Even a seasoned Red Cloak would unlock four or five portals in the void." In this dreadful passage, there couldn't be a better companion than his mentor's warm voice in his head. "Now walk to your portal, neither too slowly nor too fast."

Taking a deep breath of air—or whatever filled this void, which was a totally different part of the world—Akira squinted at the portals on the left. Three of them would take him to Hokydo, only one of them to the desired destination. *Pick one before the anerjy of the portals fades,* he urged himself as he walked onward.

Suddenly aware that he was not looking down, Akira could feel his heart racing again. "Please not now," he muttered, resisting the urge to slap himself. Until today, he had never been closer to completing a passage through the void.

Akira wasn't sure if his eyes were playing tricks on him, but he thought that the portals were slowly fading away. "You can't channel your anerjy inside the void if the portals are closed," Jihoon's voice echoed in his head as he picked one of the three portals of Hokydo. Getting out of here was his priority now. Later, he might worry about the right destination. Any 'destination' other than the void would do for now.

The portals were shrinking indeed. Without thinking twice, Akira strode toward the portal in the middle. The instant his foot hit some solid ground, he found himself stumbling. Panicking, he gasped, but one second later, he noticed the blue sky.

He did flee from the void. Now he could worry about where on Earth—literally speaking—he had gone.

He was near the edge of a hilltop. *A wooded hilltop,* he thought, the sight of the cherry blossom trees around him making him chuckle. "I did it," he said excitedly, congratulating himself for picking the right portal, for reaching the right destination. After his excitement faded, he realized that there was a question he should find an answer to.

What would a mage do here in this abandoned place?

Except that it is not this abandoned.

"I see you," Akira called to the lady watching him from behind the trees. He wouldn't be surprised if she ran away, but this one didn't. On the contrary, she emerged from her hideout, her eyes scanning him as she straightened her back. She was older than Akira, that was for certain, but how much older? When it came to estimating ladies' ages, he was no expert, but he surmised that she couldn't be older than thirty-five.

"You are not the one I was expecting," she gruffly said, an expression of disappointment plastered on her round face.

Don't let anything dishearten you. Akira drew a deep breath. "Whom were you expecting?"

"I never saw his face," she warily said. "But he surely sounded older than you."

Seems I've come across something. Akira did his best to hide his eagerness. He had better handle this lady carefully to extract from her whatever she knew about that 'something.' "Being younger doesn't mean I can't offer whatever he offered you."

The lady smirked. "And I was thinking he might have sent you in his stead."

Akira shouldn't ruin this. "How do you know he didn't?"

The lady scowled, her lip curled in disdain. "Listen, boy. I haven't traveled all that distance for some stupid game." She wagged a firm finger. "Now open that portal you came from and take me to your superior."

This was not going well. But if playing nice didn't work, then he should try something else. "Who do you think you are?" Disapproval was surely obvious in his tone, but it was an actual question. The journey to the top of this hill must have soiled her outfit, but the dust wouldn't fool him. Only a wealthy lady would wear this silk tunic and trousers. "Do you have any idea what I can do to you in a blink of an eye?"

"I do, and I don't care," she peered at him, approaching without any hint of being intimidated, "as long as you are not going to help me bring my son back!"

Alright. Akira could still make this work. He just had to ask the right questions. "Why would *he* bring your son back to you?"

The lady in silk arched an eyebrow. "You are not even his subaltern." She paused thoughtfully, and then she continued, "Actually, you are digging to find something you can condemn him for."

Clever. "Did he do something that could condemn him?"

She shrugged. "Who am I to judge?"

"I surely can if you tell me."

"Why should I?" She stepped forward and stopped right in front of him, fixing him with her gaze. "Because I must *fear* you?"

Intimidating her wouldn't work. No creature is as fierce as a mother who fights for her child. "Because I can help you."

"You help me, then I will tell you everything I know."

Helping her would probably imply violating numerous rules that would get Akira expelled from Sun Castle, if not arrested or even worse. *Not if she leads me to the culprit who burned the study and framed an innocent girl to hurt her father.* Kim would be able to return, and surely, the Archmage of this castle wouldn't forget such a favor. "We have an agreement, then."

15. NATSU

Natsu almost dropped her cup of tea when the door of the safe house was opened. Upon realizing it was nobody other than her loyal deputy Pantu, she sighed in relief. In terms of composure, she was not doing an impressive job, which would be enough to kill her today.

"They are coming," Pantu announced.

And so it begins, Natsu thought, filling her lungs with air one more time. "If you are sure of what your eyes have told you, then you must leave me here, Pantu."

Pantu furrowed his brow. "We are in this together, Natsu."

"No, we are not." Natsu had been mulling over this desperate situation for a whole day. "If Qianfan is after the Wraith, then it's only me whom he needs alive."

Pantu was at a loss for words, his eyes wide, as if her conclusion had shocked him.

Natsu put the full cup on the table next to her, then approached her dumbfounded deputy, trying to cast him her best smile in the last few days. "It's alright. You have already done enough, my friend." She held his hand, then gave him what was probably her last order to him. "You must leave now."

Gnashing his teeth, he quickly looked through the window before he turned to her. "You won't be alone in this, Natsu," he promised. "My eyes and I will be watching."

Natsu patted Pantu's arm, signaling him to hurry. Giving her an apologetic look, he bowed and took his leave.

Now alone in the safe house—which wouldn't be safe much longer in the next few minutes—Natsu sat at the table facing the door and took a sip from her tea, which was still warm. The thudding footsteps approaching her door were so many that she wondered how Pantu could evade all those men surrounding the house.

Two men rammed the door with a log. "She is here!" one of them yelled. Their noisy entrance didn't deter her from drinking her tea, though.

"Drop your weapons and raise your hands!" The second man scanned the hall, pointing his sword at her as he slowly stepped forward. She was cornered, ridiculously outnumbered, and yet those bastards found some reason to worry about her. Even in her darkest moment, it was satisfying to see how those armed men still feared her. Less than a year in the shadow business, and she had built quite a reputation for herself.

"I'm not sure how you regard a cup of tea, but I'm unarmed." Natsu took one last sip, put the empty cup on the table, rose to her feet, and walked toward Qianfan's men. "Let's go, boys. Your boss must have been waiting for this moment for long."

THE THIRD CROSSING

* * *

Four more men were waiting for their two fellows outside the safe house. But as they tied Natsu's hands behind her back and walked her a few buildings away, she realized that Qianfan had sent a small army to ring the perimeter of the whole area. So far she counted four carts loaded with murderers armed with swords, falchions, and crossbows; a force that a commander would deploy to capture a gang, not an unarmed woman. *Quite a disappointment for those men,* she thought, but she couldn't deny that the sight of the convoy escorting her was flattering.

From the road they were taking, Natsu guessed they were heading to Qianfan's 'humble' house at the center of the town. *Why would the most powerful man in Hokydo need to hide?* she reflected, sighing as she gazed at the slums of this dreadful town. The miserable folks of Hokydo were just watching the train of carts traversing their streets. Some of them were surely aware that the lady surrounded by all those outlaws was in trouble, but none of those maggots would dare to help her. They were Hokydoans, and that meant they already had their own share of trouble to deal with on a daily basis. Nobody was eager for more.

As expected, the procession halted at the walls of Qianfan's house, and that was when Natsu realized the weight of the grave mistake she had made. *I should have done a better job in protecting them,* she thought sorrowfully, contemplating the guards posted at the gate and the crossbowmen atop the walls. She should have turned her house into a fort, like the one she was beholding right now. She should have assigned a decent force to guard her family wherever they went. A few things she had *forgotten* to do, just because she wanted her mother and her son to live the delusion she was living. That there was nothing to worry about in living her husband's life. That she was just a *merchant*; a lie that had initially been intended to silence her bickering mother. With the passing of time, Natsu herself had started to believe her own lie until she had become oblivious to the dangers accompanying her profession. Oblivious to the fact that she was a *smuggler*; that she was one of the dangerous names in her business. And usually dangerous smugglers had dangerous rivals.

Without any sort of resistance, Natsu let Qianfan's underlings walk her through the small garden to the door of the two-story house. The minion holding her arm tightened his grip when they stepped in, and she was not surprised. The instant she saw Qianfan's face, she felt the blood boiling in her veins. She was not ready for this moment, for this 'reunion' with the rascal who had murdered her mother and abducted her son. But surviving long enough for this meeting was not something she would bet on.

Qianfan motioned for his men to bring Natsu to the table he was sitting at. A round table that had no plates, bottles, or any utensils on it. *It's just a barrier for protection*, she reckoned. *As if being tied up, unarmed, and outnumbered is not enough for him to feel safe in his own fort.*

The black-bearded man grinned gloatingly at her as she sat across from him. He turned to his minions and asked, "Did you face any unexpected hurdles?"

One of Qianfan's men shook his head. "She was alone in the house that old woman told us about."

Daiyu. Natsu's face must have betrayed her shock; she could tell from Qianfan's odious smile that even grew wider. "Your last ally has sold you for a small pouch of silver," he said.

"She couldn't be cheaper than the bastard who killed my mother and took my child."

"You are starting to disappoint me, Natsu." Qianfan didn't seem offended, though. "I thought you could do better than throwing around some insults."

Natsu was eager to do much more than insulting him indeed. But not before she got what she was here for. "Where is my boy, Qianfan? I must see him."

"*Must?*" Resting his hairy chin on his right hand, he smiled in amusement. "You are too demanding for someone cornered."

"Let's not fool each other." Natsu looked him in the eye. "You could have killed me, but you didn't because I have something you want."

Qianfan met her gaze, still keeping his wry smile. "You do, but that's not the only reason why I'm keeping you alive." He leaned forward toward her. "You see, you are an interesting woman, Natsu. You are not the kind one would meet very often in this country. You deserve to understand why I did what I did to your people before I eventually kill you."

His nonchalance while making such an announcement took her off her guard. After drawing in a deep breath, she said, "If killing me guarantees my son's safety, then so be it. I will do whatever it takes."

Qianfan leaned back in his seat, curling his lip as he shook his head. "Look at you. We both could have become the kings of Hokydo, but your greed got the better of you. *Crushed* you. And now, you are *nothing*."

Look who is talking about greed, like a whore preaching virtue.

Should she remind him that he was the one who had started the bloodshed by claiming what didn't belong to him? *Are you fooling yourself now? It's totally not worth it.* "You won," she admitted. "Hokydo is all yours now. Is it too much for a crushed woman to spend the remaining years of her miserable life with her son?" She couldn't help glaring at him as she continued, "Her only family, after *you* killed her mother?"

"No, it is not." Qianfan shrugged carelessly. "But I don't like to leave loose ends, Natsu. Sparing you after our first meeting was a mistake that I will not repeat." He gave her a studying look. "Now tell me which is a better option for you: killing both you and your son, or killing only you?"

"It doesn't have to be this way." Natsu was not begging him, was she?

"Yes, it *does*." He slammed his palm across the table, then he pointed an accusing finger at her. "You are a murderer too, Natsu. You take lives to get what you seek. Even your people; you don't mind sacrificing their lives to save yours. You are ruthless, and that's how you get things done. That's how you rose quickly in this business! But you never understood the notion of rivalry. Botan and I were rivals, but we were never enemies. We set rules, respected them, and that's how we both grew wealthier. But *you*?" He clenched his jaw. "You always want to play alone. You loathe the rules of this business, and that makes you untrustworthy. Makes you *dangerous*. And I only know one way to deal with dangerous people."

"Was my mother one of those dangerous people?" Natsu snarled.

"Oh, please! Don't you dare pretend that you cared for her, or even for your son! Any woman in your place would lose her mind over her dead mother and roam this damned town to find her lost boy. But you, Natsu? You are too practical, too sane, too *heartless* to do that! When I let your informants know that I'm after the Wraith, I thought you would reach out to me at once to trade for your son's life. But plainly, you needed some time to decide which was more precious to you; your only child, or your fabled ship."

The likes of him would never understand it was the other way around. She had lurked, but not because of her sanity. She had lurked *in spite of* losing it. She had wanted to roam every corner in Hokydo, to scream her son's name, hoping someone would answer her and tell her where he was, but she had had to fight that urge. She had reined back her fear, her *rage*, because she had clung to the faint hope of reuniting with her son. "I needed some time indeed," she said absently. "But not to decide which is more precious."

Qianfan tilted his head, squinting at her.

"I knew I had one chance to catch you," Natsu added, leaning forward toward him. "I wanted to make sure it would count."

"Catch me?" Qianfan chuckled. "Well, I think there might be a *slight* deviation in your ambitious plan."

"On the contrary. It's working perfectly so far."

Natsu's curt announcement did carve an impact on Qianfan's face. "Daiyu," he said, his eyes wide. "Was it you?"

"You can't say she lied to you. I was exactly where she told your men I was, right?"

Qianfan lurched to his feet. "Tell them outside to keep their eyes open," he commanded the minion who walked her into the house. The *king* of Hokydo didn't seem as confident as he had been a few minutes ago. "And send three patrols to—"

A thunderous explosion outside the house interrupted Qianfan's orders, the shatters and the door swinging open, the floor beneath Natsu's feet shaking. While everybody inside and outside the house was still in shock, she took the liberty of leaving her seat to have a better view of the smoke and fire rising above the ruins of what remained of the walls of Qianfan's fort.

And from behind the smoke, came the roars. Roars of warriors who didn't belong to this island. No, not just the island of Hokydo; from the whole Empire of Koya.

"This is impossible." Qianfan gaped at the brawny, muscular warriors tearing his men apart with their axes and war hammers. "They were too far to be here this soon, I was told."

The Skandivians were too far from this part of the world indeed. But thanks to Natsu's new ally who had the ability to open portals, she had assembled thirty warriors from the far northwestern lands of Skandivia in nearly five hours. Though they didn't outnumber the guards here, it was plain that against the battle-hardened Skandivians, Qianfan's minions wouldn't stand a chance.

"It's over," she said firmly to Qianfan, who was still watching the Skandivians slay his men in the garden one after another. "Now tell me where my son is, and I shall make your death swifter than you deserve."

"You still lose." Qianfan drew a dagger from his belt, and before he might lunge at Natsu, she kicked her chair toward him. The wooden thing hit her raging rival, but it didn't hinder him for long. "After you die, your mercenaries will need someone to pay them."

Natsu, whose hands were still tied, stepped back to dodge Qianfan's stab. But she lost her balance when she bumped into the table. Growling, Qianfan lunged at her, but she rolled on the ground, barely evading another strike. Lying on her back, she kicked him below the belly when he lunged again. The hit stunned him, giving her a moment to rise to her feet, but with her hands bound together behind her back, she didn't have a fighting chance. "You whore!" Qianfan grunted as he slashed at her. To protect her chest, Natsu instinctively turned, screaming as the blade cut her arm instead. The next stab was a low one. But just an instant before it might touch her skin, Qianfan was sent flying in the air until he hit the wall with his back.

"You are late!" she bellowed at Akira, who stood by the doorstep, his hands stretched out.

"If you haven't noticed, there is a fight ensuing outside that I had to get past." Akira strode toward her, then nodded his chin toward her fallen rival. "What do you want me to do with him?"

After bringing reinforcements from Skandivia and destroying the walls with his magical tricks, Natsu couldn't ask him for more. "You have done enough," she said, her eyes fixed on Qianfan. Still lying on the floor, the bearded bastard groaned, his dagger fallen not far away from him. "Untie me, and I will take care of the rest."

Akira seemed a little bit confused for a moment before he stalked past Natsu, collected Qianfan's dagger from the ground, and returned to her.

"Seriously?" She couldn't help chuckling as the *mage* used a normal blade to cut the rope binding her hands together. No magical tricks this time.

"For your hands' safety." After he was done with the rope, Akira handed her the dagger. "He is all yours."

One of Qianfan's men returned from the garden, obviously to aid his master, but Akira stopped him with another telekinetic slap that slammed the armed minion against the wall. "I'm watching your back," Akira assured Natsu.

Gripping Qianfan's dagger, Natsu approached her foe who seemed unable to rise to his feet. The slam against the wall could have broken his spine—not that she cared—and now, all he could do was groan, move his head, and surely, breathe.

"This can end swiftly or ugly." Natsu sat on top of Qianfan, laying the flat of the blade on his cheek. "Where is my boy?"

Qianfan's answer was nothing but a groan.

"You've become mute now?" Natsu gritted her teeth before she planted the dagger into Qianfan's right hand, his cry of agony giving her a slight feeling of satisfaction. "SPEAK!"

Qianfan mumbled incoherently, as if he was trying to overcome the pain to say something. To give him some help, Natsu snatched the dagger from his hand, Qianfan howling but not for long this time.

"You…you'll…kill me…after… after I…tell you."

Natsu's patience was running thin. Though she didn't loathe anybody or anything like that bearded creature beneath her, she would never be keen about killing him more than she would care about her son's return. "I might change my mind if you tell me *now*."

Qianfan opened his mouth, but instead of uttering the answer she was eager to hear, a thin smile tugged at his lips for a second. "You lie."

Mad with fury, Natsu grunted as she drove the blade through Qianfan's good hand. While he was howling again, she barked, "WHERE IS HE?"

After a minute of gasping, Qianfan finally said, "I will…take you…there."

A desperate attempt from him to escape from the corner she had backed him into. Did he think she would fall for that? "You are not going anywhere."

Grimacing, Qianfan seemed to be mustering all the strength he could. "You want…your son…or not?"

"Listen carefully, you whoreson dog! Because this is how it's going to work. You say where my son is, I hold you in my custody while my men and I bring my son back. If I don't find him there, I'll return to dismember you."

Qianfan should know better she wasn't not bluffing. "What if…you find him?" He glowered at her.

She wanted him dead. She wanted her son back. *Priorities, Natsu!* "You don't deserve to live," she spat. "But I will spare you if my son comes back to me safe and sound."

Qianfan looked at her doubtfully, and after a moment of hesitation, he said, "The cellar."

Was there a cellar? *Here,* in this very house? That was news to Natsu. "How many guards?"

"No guards." Qianfan winced, glancing at the dagger in her hand. "Just locked."

Lying now would bring him more bleeding, more agony; he must have learned that already. "Go find that cellar," she said to Akira as she rose to her feet. "I can take care of myself." The fight outside was almost over anyway.

"You're sure you—"

"Just go at once," she urged the young mage. Couldn't he understand how impatient she was right now?

While Akira was looking for that cellar, Natsu kept looking from Qianfan to the door and back. Her Skandivian mercenaries were winning the fight in the garden, and her rival was still on the floor. He appeared to be surrendering to the fact that he was defeated, but that wouldn't make her let down her guard. Not until Akira returned with her son safe and sound.

"A mage." Qianfan grimaced, putting one bleeding hand over the other. "How did you persuade him?"

Natsu pointed the dagger at him. "What kind of an answer do you expect from me?"

"Nothing. I'm just impressed. You can't tempt these people with coin because they don't need it." He took a deep breath, clearly struggling with his pain, and then he tiredly continued, "That's why I can't help wondering," he flinched, "what you might possibly have that he needs so badly?" He switched his eyes from his hand to her. "You understand he will be punished for what he did here, right?"

Natsu peered at him. "You dare to make threats now?"

"I'm not making any," he said hurriedly. "I'm talking about the folks from Sun Castle."

Curious to hear more, she asked, "What about them?"

"They have strict rules about wielding sorcery outside the walls of their fortress." Qianfan was checking the impact of his words on her face, she was aware. "I hear they don't take unauthorized use of sorcery lightly. Especially when used for violent purposes."

What was the game her cornered foe was playing? "What if this was *authorized*?"

Surprisingly, Qianfan was able to manage a crooked smile that irked her. "You want me to believe that the boy you are shouting your commands to is sent by Sun Castle?"

Footsteps were coming from inside the house. Footsteps of more than one person, some of them light.

"Riku!" Natsu's heart quivered the instant she saw her son holding Akira's hand. The young mage let go of him as Natsu sprinted and squeezed her son against her chest. Ignoring everything around her, she was unable to hold her tears when she buried her face in his black soft hair. It didn't matter that Qianfan or Akira were watching. It didn't matter how she seemed to them right now. With Riku in her arms, nothing else mattered.

With Riku in her arms, she was whole again.

Natsu held her son's face with both hands. "Sweetheart, did they hurt you? Tell me, and Mama shall punish them."

"They hurt *Obaasan*, Mama," Riku whimpered, his innocent eyes betraying his horror. Had those bastards made a five-year-old child witness the murder of his own grandmother?

"They won't hurt us anymore, sweetheart." Natsu kissed his head softly and turned to Akira. "Hold him for me, please."

The young mage took Riku's hand, staring at her quizzically. Ignoring him, she strode toward Qianfan, who was struggling to lean his broken back against the wall. "What are you going to do?" her foe asked in alarm, his eyes fixed on the dagger she was gripping. "You gave me your word!"

"I gave my son my word too!" With all hatred and fury in the world, she howled as she stabbed him hysterically, blood gushing out of his abdomen and his chest, splattering all over her face and tunic. She stabbed and stabbed until her arm stiffened. The bastard stopped gurgling, his motionless body thudding on the floor.

Natsu beckoned her terrified son over. "There is nothing to fear now, sweetheart. Just come closer to your mother," she said softly. When her hesitant child approached her, she pointed her red blade at Qianfan's corpse. "You see, Riku? This is what Mama does to whoever *thinks* of hurting you. No evil people shall ever dare to come close to you again. Do you understand me?"

Blood was still dripping from her blade when her astounded son nodded silently. Truth be told, she wasn't sure which scared her child more; Qianfan's body that lay sprawled in a pond of blood, or his mother who had slain a man in a moment of rage.

The fight in the garden was over. When the Skandivians started to trickle into the hall, Natsu said in their Goranian tongue, "Whatever you find in this house is all yours."

The mercenaries voiced their approval. While they were collecting their trophies, Akira came to Natsu. "Your turn to deliver," he said, his hands on his waist.

Her son was back. Her foe was dead. The young mage had delivered his end of the agreement in full. "I'm in your debt forever." She sighed, collecting her thoughts after this nerve-wracking encounter. "This is everything the masked mage has told me."

16. AKIRA

Opening a portal could be exhausting for the uninitiated. How about opening thirty on a single day?

I could be doing it all wrong. There must be an easier way to teleport all those Skandivians than escorting them one by one through the void, Akira thought, barely standing at the portal site, where he was about to start one last passage through the void to go back to Sun Castle. Was there a possibility that nobody there had noticed his absence for an entire day?

Missing sessions, be they studying or sparring, never went without consequences. And in the case of someone like Akira—someone who was a suspect in the chemistry study incident—the sanction could be exaggerated.

But right now, that sanction was the least of Akira's concerns. It shouldn't be a concern, to begin with. With the information he had gathered from the Hokydoan smuggler, he should be thinking of his *reward*.

What reward, you petty fool? If all that Natsu said was true, then the Third Crossing, and consequently, our entire holy cause, could be in grave danger.

Akira would kill to get some sleep, but first, he had to get out of the island of Hokydo. Draining the red balya decoction he carried with him enabled him to muster his focus and bind what remained of his anerjy with Earth's pulling force. The shimmering portal opened with its usual cracking noise, and hurriedly, Akira stepped into it. Just a few days ago, he would have never believed what he was capable of now. What could be a better exercise than teleporting thirty people in a couple of hours? *I still have a lot to learn, though*, he reflected, gazing at the dozen portals on the other end of the void. Perhaps he should find a veteran Red Cloak to teach him how to avoid opening irrelevant portals.

When all this mess was over.

Akira crossed the luminous oval that took him back to the Portal Yard at Sun Castle. Quiet and abandoned, just like he had left it yesterday.

Or that was what he thought until he heard a firm voice from behind him commanding, "Don't move."

Akira froze in his place, and cautiously, he glanced over his shoulder. He couldn't recognize that mustached Red Cloak, but he was sure he hadn't seen him before. And since it was unlikely for Akira to come across a new mentor after spending four years here, he could safely presume that the thirtyish Red Cloak behind him was a battlemage. Usually, the likes of him were as powerful as the mentors, yet far less smart, and thus more dangerous.

"I'm Kungwan Sen's nephew, and I must see him now," said Akira, doing his best to sound confident.

"It's your lucky day, then," the battlemage coldly said. "He demands to see you too."

Akira wasn't exactly expecting a warm reception upon his return. But to be taken straightforwardly to the Archmage himself? "May I ask why he does?"

"You may ask him yourself," the battlemage curtly replied. "Now move."

* * *

The fact that his uncle, *the Archmage*, had been waiting for him was a little bit unsettling, although the old man was surely the right person to inform of the suspicious news from Hokydo. Jihoon was a logical option too; he was the tutor Akira would trust the most. The only doubt Akira had was how Jihoon would react, though. Either he would do nothing, or worse, he would divulge the secret to the wrong people. *I didn't shake hands with a smuggler from Hokydo to end up expelled from Sun Castle.*

The battlemage escorted Akira to Kungwan's office. Without saying a word, the Red Cloak knocked on the door, opened it, then motioned for Akira to enter. "Shouldn't we get his permission first?" Akira asked hesitantly, the battlemage casting him a hard look. "Fine. But I will tell him it was you who made me barge into his office." When the battlemage puffed impatiently, Akira felt that his caution could be a bit exaggerated.

The moment Akira set foot in the office, he sensed the tension in the room. Sitting behind his desk, Kungwan Sen let his quill fall on the document he was writing, his glowering eyes fixed on Akira as the latter advanced warily. *There is nothing to fear, Akira,* he reminded himself. *Just tell him all you know, and your unauthorized absence will be nothing.*

"What were you thinking?" Kungwan blustered, before Akira could figure out where to start.

"Uncle Kungwan, I can explain—"

"You know, *this* is the problem," Kungwan cut him off, an accusing finger pointed at him. "You and Kim do not understand that I'm *not* your family in this castle. We are all soldiers here, and I mean by 'we' every single person in Sun Castle. That has been the norm for decades. But when you or my silly daughter commit something foolish, they remember that you two and I are related."

Kungwan's fury was over something beyond Akira's mistake, his *nephew's* mistake. "Who are *they*, Kungwan Sen?"

His uncle heaved a deep sigh, his eyes dropping down to the parchment on his desk. After a moment of uneasy silence, he turned to Akira. "I didn't choose to be the Head of the Imperial Court, and I never wanted to, but it happened nevertheless. And that did gall a bunch of Blue Cloaks." He nodded his chin toward Akira. "You've become old enough to understand; I saw that already during your investigation."

Akira was flattered that the Archmage was sharing this with him. "Is Hanu causing problems for you in the court?"

Kungwan smiled nervously. "In the beginning, she tried to convince the Emperor that I would be more of an Archmage than a Court Head."

Tried? "I take it that she didn't succeed."

"Not yet." Kungwan shot him a blaming look. "But thanks to the recent unfortunate events—Lan's death and the fire incident—I seem to be losing control over my own turf. And now *you*? I can't even control my own family. How am I supposed to lead this nation in one of the most critical moments of its history?"

"Trust me, *Uncle*." Akira knew it was a risk to utter the word, let alone stress it, but he took his chances anyway. "You will thank me if you just listen—"

"*Thank you*?" Kungwan retorted. "For what? Your absenteeism? Or stealing our material?"

Akira had *borrowed* some chemicals and herbs to gear himself up for Natsu's quest. Had Kyong Sen identified the missing items this fast? "Please, give me a chance to explain. The matter is much graver than a few missing vials—"

"It is not!" Kungwan put in, slamming his palm across the desk. "You think I'm oblivious to your desperation to prove your worth? I knew, even before their announcement, that the trials results would frustrate you more than the rest of your peers. But I never expected you to take it that far. To involve my silly daughter in your foolishness." He wagged a firm finger at Akira. "You are the one who should have been expelled, not her!"

Hells and demons! The course this conversation was taking didn't bode well at all. "There is a huge misunderstanding here."

"You might fool my daughter, but not me, boy!" Kungwan gnashed his teeth. "We know about the experimental potion you have produced without our approval."

Experimental potion? Was that how they referred to the potion he had prepared on his own to boost his stamina ten times more than red balya does? "I created the formula of that potion."

"That formula belongs now to Sun Castle, and hence to the Empire. It shall be used to serve a holy mission, not some absurd boyish ventures."

When would the stubborn old man listen? "I didn't make any absurd boyish ventures," Akira said, with an edge to his voice.

"Really? Then why did you prepare an extremely powerful stamina-boosting potion before teleporting outside Sun Castle? Did you go to the outskirts or even to Hokydo Island so that you could assault some outlaws at their dens? Isn't it all about achieving a personal victory that might heal your hurt pride?"

His uncle's interpretation of the whole matter was all wrong. *Is that so? Why do you feel as if punched in the face, then?* "This is not about me." Akira cleared his throat, his voice not convincing himself even. "This is about—"

A knock on the door interrupted him, Jihoon Sen entering without receiving the Archmage's permission. While Akira was wondering what was wrong with the people of this place, the beefy mentor announced, "Hanu is here."

"What?" Kungwan snapped. "How could she come here without informing us beforehand?"

"Should we tell her to wait until you are ready for her?"

"No, don't do that." Kungwan pushed to his feet, the legs of his chair scraping against the floor. Pointing a firm finger at Akira, he demanded, "Stay here. Nobody shall see or talk to you until I'm done with you."

Kungwan closed the door behind him as he followed Jihoon outside the office. *He didn't say a word to me*, Akira thought, a little bit irked that his mentor had ignored his presence completely. *Is he mad at me too?*

It could be Hanu's surprising visit, though, Akira reflected, recalling Kungwan's reaction upon hearing the news. *Her uncalled visit did hit a nerve in him, more than my 'crime' did.* Not that Akira was surprised—not after his uncle had bluntly complained about her to him. He just couldn't imagine the extent to which the enmity between the former Head of the Imperial Court and the current one had reached.

Pacing around the vast office, Akira couldn't help mulling over his uncle's last command to him. He could have just asked Akira to wait for his return so that they could resume their urgent conversation as soon as possible. But no, that was not a priority, Akira believed. First it was that battlemage who had been assigned to watch over the Portal Yard to bring Akira upon his return to Kungwan Sen. And then, there was this clear statement: *Nobody shall see or talk to you.*

Was the Archmage so ashamed of his irresponsible nephew he wanted to hide him for the time being? Or forever?

You are the one who should have been expelled, not her! Maybe that was what this closed meeting was all about.

Akira was trapped here. That grand Kungwan-Hanu encounter would not end any time soon. At least a couple of hours later, Akira guessed. And surely, leaving Kungwan's office was not an option. It would be another crime to add to Akira's record, if the battlemage posted outside allowed him in the first place. He was still out there, wasn't he?

Bored, and also curious, Akira found his feet taking him closer to the desk, *the Archmage's* desk. *This is wrong, Akira*, he told himself, but what could possibly be the harm of skimming an unfinished document?

A letter to the Emperor?

Alright. Akira was unable to resist his curiosity now. Instead of having a quick look from the opposite side, he moved around the desk and stood right in front of his uncle's seat.

From the Light's humble servant Kungwan Okimoto to the Light's shadow on Earth His Radiance the Emperor of Koya,

I beg your forgiveness for my delay in answering your call. All I ask is two more weeks to settle all the pending matters in Sun Castle. After that, I will be honored to serve Your Radiance by your side as long as it takes.

I almost decided on my successor. But first, I must make sure...

Obviously, that was the point when Kungwan had dropped his quill upon Akira's arrival. But there was no need to read more to understand what this letter was about. His uncle was going to cede his position as the Archmage and move to the Imperial Palace to be fully dedicated to his role as the Head of the court. Were Akira and Kim to blame for this? Should anybody be blamed, to begin with? Maybe that should have been the right arrangement from the beginning. Juggling both responsibilities in full was not a simple task, even for the great Kungwan Sen.

Akira's curiosity was getting the better of him; he was aware of that, his eyes fixed on the few parchments stacked next to Kungwan's incomplete letter. *No harm done,* he told himself, picking up one particular parchment with extreme care. A letter with a broken seal.

The Emperor's Seal.

Without thinking of the consequences, Akira allowed himself to scan the short letter. It was not that interesting, though. Just an invitation. No, *an order* to the Archmage to present himself to His Radiance at the Imperial Palace, urgently. The brief letter mentioned nothing about any 'pending matters' or Kungwan's resignation, though. But plainly, these topics were discussed elsewhere.

Growing more comfortable in his uncle's office, Akira checked more documents on the desk, but he didn't find anything intriguing. Just a couple of official papers that had Kungwan's seal on it: an approved coin dispense form, a signed supplies request from Kyong Sen, a proposal of a new training schedule for the newly-joining battlemages…

Akira stopped browsing. *If I'm caught checking those useless documents, I'll be punished to no avail,* he thought, turning to the magnificent library behind Kungwan's desk. Sorcery, history, chemistry, herbs, the human body, world geography, philosophy, even poetry; there was not a single topic these books didn't cover. Had his uncle read all of them to become an Archmage?

Any books of these would do to kill the time, but Akira was not in the mood of reading. He would find similar books in the castle library if he wanted. But a rare chance to wander the Archmage's office? No way would he miss that.

Akira kept his ears open to any sound coming from outside the office as he ambled toward the closed door of an antechamber. *Bad idea, Akira.* If Kungwan was keen that nobody else read those documents, he would have put them in the drawers for instance. But this room? It was closed for a reason. And Akira should respect…

WHAT. IS. THIS?

Akira hoped that his eyes were playing tricks on him, but he became certain they were not when he picked up that thing from the ground.

A petal of a cherry blossom flower.

No, no, no. It can't be true. My uncle? The Archmage? He is the one who is supposed to lead us in the…How could he…?

Akira needed a moment to pull himself together. That purple petal didn't necessarily imply that Kungwan was the mysterious masked mage who had struck a deal with Natsu the smuggler. It could mean that the mysterious mage had recently come to the Archmage's office. *Very recently*, Akira thought, contemplating the clean floor of the office, recalling a particular part of Natsu's account in their last encounter. "He was supposed to meet me on that hilltop, but you showed up first. I guess my message didn't reach him that fast."

The masked mage had been here, in this very office, today, right after his return from a fruitless journey to the abandoned hilltop. Natsu's absence must have frustrated him.

That should limit the list of suspects. But first, he had to inquire about those who had met the Archmage here…

What if…? Akira was unable to dismiss this shocking possibility from his head. Only one thing could silence this inner voice of doubt.

The door of the antechamber was not locked, which was surprising and somehow also relieving. *If he has something to hide, he will surely lock the door,* he thought, stepping warily into the dark, windowless room. Despite his exhaustion, Akira managed a small fireball and kept it floating between his hands until he found a torch attached to the wall. A single torch was enough to illuminate the antechamber, which was much smaller than the office. Unlike what Akira had assumed, this wasn't designed for the Archmage's private meetings.

This was simply the Archmage's bedroom.

In the center of the chamber was a square dining table, where his meals were brought to him every day, Akira could imagine. And next to the bed was a wardrobe and a hanger on which nothing was hung. *Seems he was in a hurry today*, he thought as he spotted a cloak, which was thrown on the bed carelessly. He even stumbled on a boot when he approached his uncle's bed. *Too clumsy for the wisest mage of Sun Castle.*

Hoping he was wrong, Akira turned the boot upside down to scrutinize its sole. As he didn't find any purple petals stuck to the boot, he heaved a deep sigh of relief. It didn't prove his uncle's innocence, though. But at least, there wasn't anything that would definitely incriminate…

"Hells and demons!" Akira muttered, pulling the cloak that hid a big part of a *mask*. He grabbed the thing and held it next to the torch to have a clearer view.

Crimson. Like the one Natsu saw on the mage's face.

* * *

Running away had never been a tempting idea like it was now.

After extinguishing the torch of the antechamber and closing its door, Akira dragged his feet to one of the chairs opposite his uncle's desk. Head down, he leaned his elbows on his thighs as he sat. Lost. Terrified. Furious.

"With the help of two of his mages, he wants me to transport more than a hundred crates to Shezar; a coastal city at the southeastern corner of Gorania." Akira was recalling what Natsu had recounted to him about her masked hirer. "If I succeed, he will pay me fifty thousand golden dragons."

Everything about Natsu's account was bizarre, starting with the destination. Why Shezar? Why not a much closer port like Dibal? Or even Yetsuda? And fifty thousand *golden* dragons? Akira didn't have the least clue about the treasury of Sun Castle, but he doubted it could be much bigger than this insane sum.

And that had led him to one logical question. "If he is a Red Cloak—as you say—why would he pay for something he could do without charge? The whole Turtle Fleet is under our disposal. For the sake of our holy mission, the Emperor would never…" The look of contempt on her face had made him feel like a fool. "Hells and demons! He is not transporting our gear. He is *stealing* them!"

"Forgive me if I didn't care." Natsu had shrugged. "With this fortune, my family won't have to work for the next two generations."

"You can't accept that job, Natsu."

Natsu would never be glad to do as Akira had asked. "Say I don't *want* to accept it. How could I ever say no to a man who could summon a sea demon? He doesn't need to pay me, to begin with. He could simply command me, and I will have no choice but to obey."

That mage didn't need to pay her indeed. He was just draining the resources of Sun Castle. That massive act of sabotage dwarfed the infamous fire incident.

"You must not fear him, Natsu. Once I return to Sun Castle, I shall tell the Archmage. He will know what to do."

"You really think the Archmage would believe you, young man?" Natsu had asked skeptically.

"I don't mean to brag," Akira had scoffed. "But the man I'm talking about is my uncle."

Except that his uncle was not exactly whom he thought he was, it turned out.

Akira had to flee; that he knew. Where he should hide was not something he could easily figure out. He was not just escaping from Sun Castle. He was escaping from his uncle; the man he never loved, but always respected for everything he represented. The holy mission his mother had been preparing for. The ultimate aspiration Akira had been pursuing. Simply, Akira's entire life.

And it was all based on a lie.

Akira could wield a jumun and stun whoever was guarding the door outside. But even if he pulled that off and made it to the Portal Yard, he would tempt every mage in Koya to chase him for the rest of his life. A miserable life, that would be. More miserable than his current one.

You could do better than this, Akira. If he managed to compose himself until his uncle's return, resumed their meaningless conversation, and concluded it on good terms, Akira would easily walk out the door of this damned office and head back to the Portal Yard without provoking anybody to follow him.

When the door of the office was opened, Akira realized that he didn't prepare himself for that 'meaningless' conversation. *Hopefully, he forgets,* Akira thought, staring at his uncle who entered the room. Without saying a word to the nephew he had detained in his office for an hour, Kungwan returned to his seat behind the desk, a scowl on his face. *His meeting with Hanu didn't go well, I surmise.*

Or maybe his uncle was still wondering why his smuggler hadn't come to the meeting she had requested.

Kungwan exhaled, then said, "I know what you might be thinking, but I was helping you by holding you here."

Despite all Akira had seen just a few minutes ago, he was still unable to digest the fact that this man, of all the men in the world, was a traitor to his nation. A traitor to the Light. Did Akira misinterpret the clues he had gathered? *Clues? He sought a smuggler because he wanted to avoid the coastguards. He chose a destination that nobody would expect. If he had the Emperor's approval, he wouldn't keep that matter a secret.*

"Akira?"

Who else knows about this? "You said you were helping me." Akira feigned a brief smile. "I just wonder how."

Kungwan clasped his fingers together, leaning his elbows on the desk. "I was preventing you from saying anything that could be used against you. Hanu has eyes and ears here."

Does Kim know what *you really are?* "In Sun Castle?"

"You said it yourself once, remember? We shouldn't presume that everybody here is glad to see me occupying the seat of the Head of the Imperial Court. I guess some will find it really convenient to ally themselves to the lady who shares their feelings toward me."

Akira didn't like that implicit menace in the Archmage's tone. "You are not going to lock me up for good, are you, *Uncle?*"

"I won't, unless you deserve it." Kungwan peered at him. "Now tell me: What did you do on your little adventure?"

Akira pretended that he was hesitant about telling him. "Alright, I admit it." He exhaled, head down. "I was seeking a personal victory I needed. I wanted to prove my worth; that I'm not less than any of the Red Cloaks you recently picked."

Akira paused intentionally, prompting Kungwan to ask, "And did you eventually find what you were seeking?"

Akira sighed. "I just spent a night on the road." He managed a nervous smile. "I was lucky enough to come across four bandits to beat."

A hint of a wry smile tugged up one side of Kungwan's mouth. "Was beating four bandits worth stealing from Sun Castle?"

"Well. I saved a man and his wife, to say the least." Akira had just invented this story. But did his lying skills impress his uncle?

"Is becoming a guardmage what you want?"

Akira shrugged. "What if that makes me less useless?"

"You are not useless here," Kungwan snapped. "Never underestimate a role you play in a great cause."

For a second, Akira almost believed the act his uncle was putting forth. Seriously, this old man didn't fail to impress him. In a different way this time.

"I'm not going to expel you, Akira," Kungwan went on. "But I'm quite certain you understand that I can't allow you to go unpunished."

17. NATSU

The sun was mild, but the humidity was unbearable today. For the third time since she rode that carriage with Pantu this morning, Natsu dampened a scarf with water to wipe her face with it. "Couldn't we just postpone that meeting until nightfall?" she complained. "Or dusk at least?"

"Just a precautionary measure. My eyes are scouting the meeting venue for any possible ambushes, so I want to make their job easier." Pantu tilted his head, adding, "Besides, a little sunlight won't harm."

Contemplating the Skandivians escorting her carriage on foot, she said, "They won't dare to ambush me; not after they heard about what I had done to Qianfan. All gangs do fear the Murderous Widow now."

"Sometimes fear makes men act stupidly."

"Let them act stupidly, then." Truth be told, Natsu was itching to find an excuse to punish all those cravens who had once surrendered themselves to her rival.

The Fishermen's Village was on the horizon when Jirou, their coachman on this ride, steered the carriage off the southern road and headed east toward the mountains, the western coast behind them now. In half an hour, they should reach their destination.

"I've been thinking how we should answer the masked mage if he contacts us again," Pantu began.

Natsu hoped the masked mage would just forget about her after she had failed to meet him as agreed. "Most probably, he is seeking an alternative partner for his operation." *His huge operation,* she thought bitterly. Nobody in the history of smuggling had earned, or would earn, that titanic amount of gold in their whole life. "If he hasn't found one already."

"What if he is looking for us to *punish* us?"

"Punish us for what?" Natsu swallowed, a picture of *Shnakar's* gigantic hands crossing her mind. "I wasn't able to meet him because of personal matters, and that's it."

Pantu raised his eyebrows in astonishment. "So, you don't mind undertaking his big job? What about your new ally who brought your son back to you? You gave him your word."

"I did." Akira, that young mage from Sun Castle, would surely be disappointed if he learned that she was helping the masked mage again. But what options would she have if that powerful mage found her again? "But it's on him if that happens. He told me he was connected to important people in Sun Castle; he would take care of that masked mage."

Pantu pressed his lips together, giving her words a thought. "I don't think our young friend will approve of this justification."

"You saw what one mage could do, Pantu. Imagine a war between two armies of mages." Voicing the thought out loud was enough to scare her. "That's something greater than our capabilities. Better we stay away and don't take sides while they lay waste to each other lest they crush us in the middle."

Natsu's convoy halted when they reached the meeting venue Pantu himself had picked. Like he had described it to her before; a barren plain with no buildings or hilltops nearby. *No hidden shooting spots for archers.* If anyone set an ambush here, it would be spotted from miles away. Natsu had nothing to hide, though. On the contrary, she wanted her counterparts to be well aware of the Skandivian band guarding her. That should let their imagination run wild about the rest of her army that had not come.

Natsu led the way as she clambered down from the carriage, her eyes scanning the small crowd waiting for her. *Who are these clowns?* she wondered, both disapprovingly and quizzically. According to Pantu, she was supposed to be meeting with a bunch of 'bosses,' but all the men she recognized so far were a bunch of *nobodies*. Most of the faces here were unfamiliar in the first place. *Did Pantu bring me to meet with some lowly pickpockets?*

She heaved a sigh when she found Diachi, the man who had called for this gathering. He was the oldest 'boss' here. Though it was no secret that he was nothing more than a small-time smuggler, the gray-haired man commanded everybody's respect. *Most of them, to say the least,* she thought, curling her lip in disdain when her eyes and Diachi's met. Respected or not, that wrinkled coward had shaken hands with the bastard who had murdered her mother and kidnapped her son. The proper way to greet Diachi and the likes of his was to spit in their faces. Maybe she would have the chance to do this soon enough.

An eerie silence fell over the place for a moment as Natsu stood facing those jokes of bosses, her hands on her waist, the fearsome Skandivian warriors behind her and Pantu by some distance. Of the bosses attending this meeting, she had brought the largest single retinue. Only if those bosses joined forces would they outnumber her.

And yet, they all seemed wary.

Diachi was the first boss who found the courage to approach her. "Natsu Sen." He bowed to her. "I'm grateful for your coming here."

Some respect at last. Natsu gave him an acknowledging nod, still wearing her stern face. "Now I'm here; may I ask: Why am I summoned to this place?" She glanced at the other bosses behind him. "Why are they?"

Diachi managed a smile. "To write a new page. Enough blood has been spilled already."

Natsu couldn't help snarling, "You should have considered that when my mother's blood was spilled."

"I lost dear ones in that bloodshed too, you know?" growled a stout man as he advanced to stand on Diachi's right. "All of these men did." He gestured toward the remaining bosses behind him, then pointed accusingly at Natsu. "Because of you."

More bosses voiced their approval as they stepped forward to join the conversation. *Those pigs! They helped Qianfan destroy my family, and yet they have the audacity to blame me for rescuing my son!* "I'm not the one who started that war, to begin with."

"You started the war with your greed," stated a boss with a thin mustache.

"Call it as you like," Natsu retorted. "If you consider making a stand for your right greed, I will consider abandoning me an act of cowardice and betrayal."

The insult aggravated the bosses, that was for sure, and she didn't care. "Quiet!" Diachi bellowed at the protesting men, then turned to Natsu. "I want to make this work, Natsu Sen, but you are not helping."

"I didn't ask for your 'peace' anyway," she said nonchalantly.

"Natsu." Pantu's jaws clenched when he gripped her wrist. "Diachi Sen is trying to do something good with his initiative." Her deputy's voice was intentionally loud enough for the old boss to hear, it was plain. "Let him speak first."

Natsu had thought she would be able to have a conversation with those traitors, but it seemed that she had overestimated her patience. Just the sight of their horrendous faces was enough to make the blood in her veins boil, provoking her to draw her dagger and plunge it into the chest of the nearest bastard to her. Had it not been for the glorious name of peace, under which this meeting was held, she would have given her Skandivian warriors another bloody task to accomplish.

Pantu took Natsu aside and whispered into her ear, "We need this peace, Natsu. It's good for the business."

For sure, it was. But what about her peace of mind? Didn't it matter as well? "Anything for the good of the business, right?" She feigned a smile. "I'm listening."

Diachi seemed more relieved now. "Good, Natsu Sen." He glanced at the other bosses flanking him. "Because I believe that we all need to move on and think of the future. A better future, where we can all get richer. Does anything else matter to any of you?"

Some of Diachi's clowns chuckled, others didn't show any reaction, while a few peered at Natsu who wasn't amused at all.

"Very well," Diachi went on. "Qianfan's fall has left a lot to split between us all. Let everybody here walk away with a fair share that shall satisfy each and every one of us."

The clowns cheered for the old man who had gathered them. Actually, Natsu wouldn't be surprised if all of this was nothing more than some staged farce.

Diachi lifted a hand to silence his folks. *He is enjoying it*, Natsu thought, taking note of the faint smile that had fleeted across his face for no more than a second.

"Before we split anything, we all must swear an oath." Diachi glanced at Natsu as he added, "That none of us shall ever dishonor the peace we all have agreed upon here, on these abandoned lands." He looked at his clowns. "Do all of you swear on that?"

Unable to hear any more of this nonsense, Natsu whispered into Pantu's ear, "I will be waiting in the carriage to hear the conclusion from you."

Natsu was about to leave him behind when Pantu caught her by the elbow. "Wait," he demanded, his voice low. "You can't walk away now. It will be disrespectful to all of these men, especially to Diachi."

"This meeting is disrespectful to me," she said firmly, pushing his hand away. "You shouldn't be attending it either."

No sooner had Natsu left her deputy behind her than Diachi called out, "Natsu Sen, where are you going?" As she didn't reply, she heard his hurried footsteps after her. "Did something upset you?"

"Are you serious?" she snapped as she turned to him. "Half of these men used to work for me, the other for Qianfan. What was on your mind when you thought that I would be glad to deal with them as equals?"

"I promise I had no ill intentions," Diachi explained. "I was just buying their peace, nothing more."

"You think I *need* to buy their peace?"

"I think it's better for all of us to conduct our businesses without having to watch our backs."

Natsu glared at the gray-haired smuggler who had obviously forgotten his place. "Is that a sort of threat, Diachi *Sen*?"

"Many of the men behind me think *you* are the threat, Natsu Sen," Diachi said grimly. "What I'm trying to do here is prove them wrong. But I can't do this alone without your help."

Natsu couldn't help chuckling in contempt. "By 'my help' you mean: accepting your terms."

"Fair terms."

And the nonsense continues. "I'm sure they are to you and your friends."

"Just think of it, Natsu Sen." Somehow Diachi sounded pleading yet commanding. "A few days ago, you had nothing but enemies. Now I'm giving you a chance to resume your business without worrying about your safety or your child's."

The bastard dared to threaten her blatantly this time.

"You are wrong, Diachi Sen," came Pantu's voice, before Natsu might bluster at the old bastard. When the latter turned to her deputy, Pantu went on, "Until this current moment, the entire Mankol coast still belongs to us."

Diachi stammered, rubbed the nape of his neck, then said, "Let me make sure I understand this right. You want to take over the whole business with the Mankol merchants?"

"The Mankol business has always been ours; that was the deal with Qianfan," Pantu stated, looking Diachi in the eye.

"As an act of generosity from our side, we will let you divide his business among you all."

Diachi smiled nervously. "Pantu Sen, you are a reasonable man."

"I guess my boss disagrees." Pantu nodded his chin toward Natsu, a crooked smile on his face. "Because I'm offering you much more than you could dream of."

Satisfied by her deputy's quick-witted interference, Natsu remained silent as she observed the grim look on Diachi's face. *What were you thinking of us when you summoned us here, old man? A bunch of gullible fools?*

"Very well," Diachi muttered, nodding. "Maybe I should have mentioned this earlier." He paused, looking from Pantu to Natsu, his hands clasped behind his back. "While you were assaulting Qianfan's warehouses to lay waste to his men, I took over his ships. And I must tell you, not all of them were empty." He leaned forward to Pantu. "You see? I don't need to *dream* of what you offer."

The old bastard was in a better position than Natsu and Pantu had estimated. "So, all you said about everyone getting their *fair share* was just some farce?" Natsu glared at Diachi.

"They are no sailors, so they have nothing to do with Qianfan's small fleet." The old man gestured toward the nobodies he had gathered today. "I was talking about his many unclaimed warehouses."

Qianfan's warehouses were not that many. Unless…

"What you call 'unclaimed warehouses' doesn't include the ones Qianfan took from me last week," Natsu said gruffly.

"You need men to run those abandoned warehouses."

Natsu smirked, glancing at the Skandivians behind her. "You see that I lack them?"

"I see you have warriors who do not understand our business."

"For now. Until I'm done teaching them, they will make sure nobody will dare to come close to my warehouses."

Diachi scowled. "Is that it? I call for peace, and in return, you threaten me?"

Natsu kept her calm as she said, "I'm just stating the facts that should help us all realize the peace you have called for."

Diachi opened his mouth as if to say something, but Pantu was faster than him when he suggested, "Don't rush into a decision now, good man. Take all the time you need to think about it."

Daichi swept an arm toward the crowd behind him. "I gave these men my word. They are expecting a future of more coin to each and every one of them."

Hells and demons! The demented rascal does believe he is a real boss now. "Then it's your fault that you have promised them what you don't own." Natsu gritted her teeth.

Pantu harrumphed. "There is still enough coin in the arrangement we are proposing, Diachi Sen. And more importantly, there will be *peace*. I'm quite sure you can convince them that peace with us is not a cheap item."

"A peace with the Murderous Widow." Diachi nodded. "I guess they will appreciate it."

Pantu exchanged a quick look with Natsu before he asked Daichi, "So, we have an agreement?"

"No doubt, we will." Diachi gave him a toothy grin. "Let's meet in three days after I'm done convincing everybody."

"They are here already, so let's finish this today," Pantu said. "Go talk to them now, and we shall wait."

"I need to talk to everybody, I said." Diachi kept his irksome smile. "Those are barely half of the bosses I could invite."

Bosses. And now he is the boss of bosses, Natsu thought, suppressing a mocking laugh. "Understood," she said. "Three days, it is."

Diachi took his leave, Natsu's eyes following him on his way back to his clowns. "Find Manshik now," she ordered Pantu. "Tell him to take his men away from this place before we attack."

Pantu's eyes widened. "Attack? Wait, Natsu, we just—"

"Were you even listening?" she put in, snarling. "The old clown has amassed a crowd to intimidate me. Now he is going to amass more men to fight us."

Pantu still looked astounded. "All he was talking about was peace."

Peace with the Murderous Widow. "Diachi will turn into another Qianfan, but only if we let him."

"This was a call for *peace*." Pantu gnashed his teeth. "If we attack anybody today, we will be everybody's enemy forever."

"We are everybody's enemy already," Natsu countered. "If we don't strike first, we will just be giving them a chance to take us off guard."

"You can't just kill everybody, Natsu. This can't be the way to conduct business."

After all she had been through, Pantu still couldn't understand. This was not about conducting business. This was about protecting the little boy she had promised to always be safe. "I don't need to kill everybody. Killing those will keep the rest who didn't come in line."

Pantu puffed, shaking his head, his hands on his waist. "I'm sorry, Natsu, but this is absolute madness. I can't allow you to hurt us all, including yourself."

Diachi was already among his people while she and her deputy were still arguing. "You are wasting my time, Pantu." She turned to her burly subaltern, who was standing with the captain of the Skandivian band. "Jirou!" She whistled, beckoning him over. As her brawny man hurried to her, she added, "I have an urgent task for you."

"No, Natsu!" Pantu protested. "Stop it!"

Ignoring her disgruntled deputy, Natsu ordered Jirou to find Manshik, the only 'boss' who had stood by her, when everybody else had abandoned her. As he always did, Jirou didn't argue with her, and at once, he hurried to the crowd to get the job done.

"Natsu!" Pantu called out as she headed back to her Skandivian band. "I can't be part of your crew if you give that order!"

That made her halt right in front of the mercenaries' leader. *It's just a hollow threat, isn't it?* she wondered, staring at the ground, unable to imagine the notion of losing her trustworthy deputy. Yes, they had their differences sometimes, especially when it came to matters that required assertive measures, but she couldn't deny that he had always been there for her since Botan's death. She wouldn't forget that he was the one who had introduced her to the world her late husband had been keeping her away from.

"Something wrong?" the towering Skandivian asked in Goranian, rousing her with his gruff voice.

He wouldn't dare to abandon me. Not now. Not after all we have endured together.

"My deputy doesn't believe you can defeat these..." Pointing to Diachi's crowd, Natsu groped for the word 'clowns' in Goranian, but she couldn't recall it. "These *men*."

The Skandivian leader made a few steps forward, his eyes scanning his foes like a hawk eyeing its prey. Waiting for him to weigh the odds, Natsu stood next to him with sealed lips.

"We won harder battles than this one," the Skandivian said nonchalantly, then peered at Natsu. "But my men will demand more coin for it."

Natsu had already let them keep all they had looted from Qianfan's quarters and warehouses to themselves. But as Bilguun had warned her once, those Skandivians never had enough. "Don't ever worry about silver with me."

The burly Skandivian grinned. "Then consider your enemy dead," he said, before he signaled his muscular fellows to advance.

"Wait for my mark," Natsu demanded, her eyes seeking Jirou and Manshik's gang who were yet to walk away from the party that was about to be slaughtered. After she finally spotted Jirou leading Manshik and his men away as agreed, she ordered the Skandivians to attack.

The instant the mercenaries advanced toward Diachi's folks, Pantu walked the other way toward the main road. "Where do you think you are going?" she harshly called to her deputy.

"Anywhere far from here," Pantu answered, and not so warmly, without stopping or even looking at her. "Far from you."

18. AKIRA

A one-month ban from entering Sun Castle. From wielding jumuns. From donning the pink cloak. That was Akira's punishment.

Going to his mother's house was not an option. She would never understand why her dear son was not allowed to wander the streets of Oyoto wearing the prestigious attire of mages, the devoted soldiers of the Light in His holy war. She would never understand why the guards at the gate of Sun Castle would not let her son enter their sacred headquarters.

She would never understand that the War of the Last Day was a lie.

Akira took a carriage to the city, where he would hop off at the door of the first tavern he would come across. However, the sight of the Shrine of the Dead perched on a nearby hill tempted him to make a slight change in his plans for today. That cup of ale he was yearning for could wait a couple of hours.

To Akira's astonishment, the bald monk—the one Akira had briefly chattered with on Lan's funeral—was standing at the entrance of the shrine when Akira clambered down from the carriage. A loud harrumph from the coachman brought to Akira's attention that he should do something he had never done before: pay in coin for a service he had received. Who could imagine that one day he would miss the very pink cloak he had always despised?

"Believe me, I'm a mage," Akira told the coachman, feeling his empty pockets. "You saw me come out from Sun Castle."

"Believe me, I need to eat," the coachman countered.

Akira should have thought this through before deciding not to go back to his mother's house. While he was wondering how to get out of this ridiculous situation, the monk sauntered in his loose robe toward the coachman and put the fare in the hand of the furious man. The coachman nodded respectfully to the monk, and then he rode away with his carriage.

"You have my gratitude, Your Eminence," Akira said to the monk, rubbing the back of his head in embarrassment. "Wait, did you know I was coming? Or was it a coincidence you were just standing here?"

"Coincidences do not exist, son," the bald monk said impassively, his hands clasped behind his back. "It is always fate."

"Can you see fate, then?" *Because I believe you are more than you pretend, old man.*

The question didn't move the monk, not in the slightest. "I only see what I am allowed to see."

I knew it. He is a seer. Akira had a thousand questions to ask such a man. Why was his mind too clouded to pick one of them to start with? Was it the monk's unnerving stare? He didn't need it to actually 'see' through Akira, did he?

"You look lost," the monk stated matter-of-factly, not a hint of empathy in his voice.

"Is that why you are mad at me?"

"You should be more concerned about the Light's fury, not mine."

Not the mood he was expecting for this conversation at all. "What have I done to anger the Light?" *He is not referring to my ignoble quest in Hokydo, is he?*

"Sometimes it is about what you are hesitant to do." There was a tone of rebuke in the monk's voice. "When the right course of action is plain to you, but you insist on giving too much weight to irrelevant considerations that hold you back."

Why the riddles? Akira wondered, but he didn't dare to ask the stern seer monk to speak less vaguely.

Considerations that held Akira back? Only one crossed his mind at the moment. "Isn't protecting my family a sacred mission?"

"Is it more sacred than protecting the Emperor? The Light's shadow that protects his chosen faction on this Earth?"

"I've always been faithful, the Light knows," Akira said defensively.

"Save your hollow words for the tutors you have fooled, boy." The monk gave him a dismissive wave. "The Light only judges us by our deeds."

Only now did Akira realize that he had balled his hands into fists, and all to blame was this intimidating monk. *What am I being scolded for?* Not that Akira had done something wrong. If he was to ask, the question should be: What exactly?

"In my defense," Akira shrugged, "my deeds were for all the good reasons."

"You were meaning to save your dearest, not the Light's holy war." The monk frowned. "Your selfish reasons deter you from doing what is necessary because you fear you might hurt a mortal person."

Kim. That mortal person the monk was talking about was Akira's dear cousin. Akira might have all the reasons to loathe her father, but surely, she cared, even a little bit, about her old man.

"How do I know if I'm saving the Light's holy war for real?" Akira found some courage to add, "What if I just hurt *my dearest?*"

"We are all tools to realize the Light's will. We don't think too much about consequences. We just do the right thing."

Easy for the monk staying in his shrine to say. "It is not that simple, Your Eminence. I'm just one person against a man who has an army under his disposal." *An army of mages, mind you.* "A man who answers only to the Emperor!"

"Then don't face him as one person," the monk said, with an air of authority. "Find an ally who answers only to the Emperor too."

Kungwan was the Head of the Imperial Court *and* the Archmage. Literally, all of the Emperor's subjects. Which allies was this monk talking about?

Wait. He said 'ally,' not 'allies.' It was only one person. One person who would dare to defy the second most powerful man in Koya.

One person who used to be the second most powerful *woman* in Koya. Akira's uncle did fear her for a reason.

"When you told Mother that I would be the hero of the War of the Last Day," Akira began. "Is this the moment you were talking about?"

The monk looked disappointed when he shook his head. "Still thinking selfishly." He leaned forward. "This is not about you being *the* hero. There will be heroes, and it doesn't matter who they are. What matters is their deeds. *Your* deeds, boy."

The monk dug into his pocket, then handed Akira a few silver dragons. "For your next trip," the monk said.

Before Akira might pose more questions, an empty carriage showed up on the road they had been standing by since Akira's arrival. The monk waved at the coachman to stop, patting Akira on the back when the carriage halted in front of him, as if urging him to leave immediately.

The instant Akira was about to hop on the carriage, he turned to the seer monk. "I can't help wondering; if you are aware of everything I know, why are you keeping quiet about it? Why haven't you taken action yet? After all, you are a monk; your word would be trusted. More than that of the young mage who was recently expelled and prohibited from wielding jumuns."

For the first time in this dry encounter, the monk granted Akira a thin smile. "Because it's not supposed to be me." He pointed a finger at him. "That task must be yours."

* * *

For the second time today, Akira missed his pink cloak.

Thanks to the handful of dragons the monk had granted him, Akira was able to pay for another trip. But he needed more than that to go past the guards of the Imperial Palace.

The guards posted at the gate were a mix of battlemages and *Seijos*. Proving he was a real mage from Sun Castle shouldn't be a hard task, especially to mages like him. Explaining how he had lost his cloak was not something he would love to explain; it would just rouse the battlemages' suspicions. And the battlemages here deal with their doubts seriously.

A Seijo guard donning the lamellar armor came out from the fortified gate of the Imperial Palace. "She will hear you. Drop every single weapon you carry."

The only weapon Akira carried was a knife he sometimes used to peel oranges. After handing it to the guard, the latter shot him a suspicious look. "I carry nothing else." Akira lifted his arms.

The guard exchanged a concerned look with the captain of the battlemages. "Hands behind your back," the captain commanded, and Akira did as he was asked. One second later, he felt the cold texture of steel around his wrists. No, this was not steel. This was something totally different. *Tunjesten?* he wondered, a strange feeling of 'disconnection' washing over him. He wasn't sure what that feeling was; he hadn't experienced it before. But the first thing that crossed his mind was that unique element that blocked all kinds of anerjy binding. *How did they mold it, though?* he wanted to ask, but a guard killed his curiosity by covering Akira's head with a woolen mask that only had two breathing pores. Wasn't cuffing him with tunjesten enough?

Handcuffed and blind, Akira let the guards march him into the palace that he had never set foot in before. Feeling the cobblestone beneath his boots, listening to the chorus of rustling leaves shaken by the evening breeze, he imagined himself walking a path through a vast garden that stretched for a mile or even more. A few minutes later, he was ascending a staircase inside a building that didn't allow the breeze to kiss his cheeks anymore, then he was led across several hallways that he didn't bother counting.

When the guards removed the mask, Akira found himself in the center of a room, a ring of Purple Cloaks and Seijo guards surrounding him. Sitting in front of him was an old lady donning a light blue cloak. The former Head of the Imperial Court.

Hanu Sen. The lady, and probably the person, Kungwan feared the most.

Squinting at Akira, she started, "You look familiar."

"I saw you at Lan's funeral." Fortunately, Akira was sober enough to remember that moment quickly. Thanks to Akira's stop by the shrine, he had missed the dose of ale he had promised himself.

"Lan's father is a dear cousin of mine. One of Koya's finest mages, but he was more of a fighter than a tutor." She stared at Akira for a moment. "You told my men you were from Sun Castle. What are you exactly? A messenger from Kungwan Sen?"

All the way to the Imperial Palace, Akira had been mulling over how to start his conversation with Hanu. Thankfully, she was making his job easier. "I'm here to talk about Kungwan Sen." He glanced at the Purple Cloaks surrounding him. "Without his consent, though."

He had Hanu's attention now; he could tell from her wide eyes. "Leave us," she commanded the Purple Cloaks and the Seijo guards.

"Hanu Sen?" The guards' captain didn't seem to be approving of her order.

"I will be fine." Hanu gave all her men a dismissive wave. When she was alone with Akira, she said to him, "Remind me of your name."

He had told the guards, but no problem. "Akira."

"And you are really a mage from Sun Castle as you claim?"

The doubt in her voice irked him. "I *am* a mage, Hanu Sen."

"If so, what brings you here without your attire?" Hanu's eyes were fixed on his face. "Or was it *taken* from you?"

"Taken, Hanu Sen," Akira decided not to lie about this part, "By order of Kungwan Sen."

"I'm sure he has his reasons," she prompted, her eyes betraying her anticipation.

"I'm not here for the cloak, Hanu Sen. Eventually, I will be getting it back in a month," Akira clarified. "I'm here to save the War of the Last Day."

Hanu tilted her head. "The War of the Last Day is inevitable," she said warily.

"Does that mean we shouldn't stop those who are trying to foil it?"

Hanu looked really upset. "Who might dare to think of such an atrocity?"

"I know it's hard to believe, but it's Kungwan Sen himself." Akira sighed. "I know he has agreed with a smuggler from Hokydo to transport a huge cargo of supplies from Sun Castle to Gorania. To the Murasen coast, to be specific."

The senior member of the Imperial Court seemed unable to digest the news; a reaction Akira had expected. "This means nothing. It could be an arrangement to start the Third Crossing."

Was she listening well? "An arrangement with a *smuggler*? What happened to our Turtle Navy?"

Hanu was taking her time to ponder what she heard. Yes, Kungwan was her rival, but nobody would imagine that, of

175

all people, the Archmage might betray the very cause he was supposed to be fighting for.

"Kungwan must have his reasons," she muttered. "He must have planned this with the Emperor."

"I wish that was true." Akira felt hesitant about revealing that now. *Better she hears it from me.* "He is family anyway."

Hanu's eyebrows rose as she cast him a long look. "You are that nephew of his." She lifted a finger to her chin. "But why?"

Akira heaved a deep sigh, thinking of Kim to help himself look sincere. "Believe me. What I'm doing is not easy on—"

"Why would he do that to himself?" she interrupted, with an edge to her voice, as she pushed to her feet. "He has dedicated his entire life to this mission. Why would he ruin it now after decades of hard work?"

Truth be told, Akira was impressed by Hanu's fairness. Despite their enmity, she still acknowledged Kungwan's worth.

"People change, Hanu Sen. Even archmages do." Akira himself wondered if it was Kim who had convinced her father with her ideas.

"So, the chemistry study," Hanu was obviously voicing her thoughts, "setting it on fire was his doing."

"To destroy the formulae documents of our weapons, yes."

Hanu nodded. "I remember now. He was never enthusiastic about the Tree of Amagesdon."

The Tree of Amagesdon was not the only weapon that Kungwan wanted to destroy. But now was not the time to brag. Actually, he was curious to hear more about his uncle. "What did he think of it?"

Pacing back and forth in the room, she didn't seem to be listening. "It doesn't make sense, still." She wiped her face with her hand, shaking her head in disapproval. "If he was planning to do that, why would he draw so much attention to Sun Castle with all the recent incidents there?"

Her question made sense. The letter Akira had found on his uncle's desk inspired him with an answer. "He needed time to finish his preparations for his sabotaging operation. These incidents were the perfect excuse to stay in Sun Castle *and* away from the Imperial Palace."

"An excuse?" Hanu winced. "A boy your age died, just to be an excuse!"

The idea sounded horrendous to Akira too. His uncle might be a traitor, but not a murderer. Actually, that was the reason why he betrayed his own people. To spare the lives of unworthy Goranians.

"I don't know." Akira shrugged. "Maybe Lan's death was just a coincidence."

"Maybe," she muttered, staring at Akira. "But your coming here is not. The question is: How do I know that you are not lying to me?"

Akira had no proof except what he had seen and heard. *The cunning old man never wrote to his smuggler. Always meeting her in person.* "Ask yourself first: Why would I do that to my uncle?"

"You don't seem to be that fond of him."

Akira couldn't deny that. "He is family, Hanu Sen. And yet, I'm here to fulfill my duty."

Hanu huffed in frustration. "Who else is involved with him?"

"I have no idea. That's why I've come to you, Hanu Sen. I don't know who I can trust in Sun Castle."

"Hells and demons!" Hanu gritted her teeth. "I can't inform the Emperor of anything until I confirm your story."

The cuffs started to irritate his wrists. "Then you *must* do this fast, Hanu Sen. My uncle was planning to make his move next week. I might have delayed him by making him lose his smuggler, but I'm sure he can find someone else soon."

"You made him *lose* his smuggler?" Hanu leered at him, her narrow eyes betraying her doubts. "What did you do to her?"

"No, not what you think." Akira should heed his words with Hanu; she was a member of the court after all. Anything could be used against him. "I just prevented her from meeting him."

Hanu's eyes were still fixed on him. "You might not be lying, but you are not telling me everything either."

How would Hanu Sen react when she heard that he had taken part in the inglorious war of smugglers on the island of Hokydo? Would she be understanding enough to let him get away with his 'crimes' unpunished? Would she spare him for the sake of the greater good?

"I need to know that I have your protection, Hanu Sen," Akira said gently, the cuffs rattling as he shook his hands. "I need to feel that I'm an ally, not a suspect."

"An ally, you say?" The way Hanu grimaced made him realize that he might have gone a little bit too far with his request. *Too late to take it back now.* "Guards!"

Akira swallowed when half a dozen men stormed the room, three of them drawing their swords already. The other three clenched their fingers, ready to hit him with jumuns. "Wait! Wait! WAIT! I did nothing wrong! I just—"

"Uncuff him," Hanu demanded, a gloating smile spreading over her face. "Let's make my *guest* feel more comfortable."

19. NATSU

The tavern by the sea was bustling with activity tonight, which was the case every night a ship was departing or arriving at the docks. Not long ago, Natsu would pray to the Light to make the next boat belong to her, but now she would not need to. With Qianfan's removal from the scene, the entire coast of Hokydo was hers to claim. All boats around the island were part of Natsu's fleet. Any piece of gold and silver exchanged through any transaction here would eventually end in her pockets.

The pockets of the Murderous Widow.

Natsu put her chopsticks on the empty plate when Manshik, her new right-hand man, entered the tavern. He might not be as clever as Pantu, but his loyalty was not something she would ever question—not after his heroic stand with her against Qianfan. Loyalty was all that mattered these days.

Natsu grabbed a cup of ale to wash down her dinner, glancing at her new deputy, who stood away from her table, as if respecting her moment of solitude. She beckoned him over, and at once he dragged forth a chair to join her.

"What is the frown for? Any trouble with the coastguards?" Natsu asked the stocky man she had temporarily delegated to handle all business matters on her behalf. Overseeing the works of her new quarters was more laborious than she had expected, but for the time being, it had a priority over everything else.

"It's the new recruits, Natsu." He clenched his jaw. "I'm far behind the number you demanded."

After plundering more than enough from Qianfan's coffers, the Skandivian mercenaries had had no desire to stay any longer in Hokydo. Natsu had to rebuild her own army now. "Do you imply that fifty men is an exaggerated number?"

"It's not about the number you set." Manshik seemed hesitant to continue.

Natsu put her half-full cup on the table. "What is it about, then?"

"It's our reputation, Natsu." He swallowed before he added, "It's not helping."

"*My* reputation, you mean," Natsu scoffed.

"Forgive my candor, Natsu, but what you did with Diachi and his folks was not the best way to attract new followers."

"I wasn't trying to tempt the men to join me. I was deterring them from even thinking of hurting me."

"They fear you; that's for sure." Manshik gnashed his teeth. "But they also fear the enemies you always create. No one can fight everybody and win."

"Did they believe so when Qianfan fought them all? Or was it alright because he was *not* a woman?"

Manshik heaved a sigh. "The men are afraid, Natsu. Afraid that with you, there will be more blood than coin."

"Cravens," Natsu spat. "If they are too faint-hearted for the sight of blood, then they had better plow fields and milk cows."

Manshik smiled nervously. "Maybe you should have prevented the Skandivians from leaving." After a moment of uneasy silence, he asked, "How are the building works going?"

Natsu had a strange feeling about this question. Manshik was not the chatty type. "Good," Natsu said curtly, hoping her vague answer would prompt Manshik to reveal whatever was crossing his mind right now.

"Good." Manshik nodded, his eyes hollow. "Hopefully, your new fortress is ready soon."

Alright. This is becoming too irksome to tolerate. "Does my new fortress bother you, Manshik?"

Her stout right-hand man exhaled. "It doesn't. The shortage of coin does, though."

After acquiring Qianfan's business, coin should be the least of her problems. But building a fort with stone walls and watch towers was eating through her coffers like fire through dry grass. "It's temporary, Manshik. Once the building works are over, we shall never have such a conversation again."

"My men are growing uneasy by the day. Business is flourishing, they know that, and yet, they get scraps." Manshik leaned his elbows on the table. "I need to tell them when this tight situation will end. With the struggle I'm having with new recruits, I do hope to keep my current crew."

Natsu didn't wish to lose more men either. A fortress without soldiers manning it would be as useful as an empty scabbard.

Jirou, whom she had posted at the door of the tavern, hurried inside and strode toward her, his hand on the hilt of the new sword strapped to his belt. "Someone says he must meet you urgently."

Natsu eyed Jirou's blank facial expression. "Someone?" She couldn't help chuckling. "He didn't tell you who is?"

"I asked him about his name, but he insisted that it wouldn't matter." Jirou shrugged his broad shoulders. "He mentioned something about a meeting you missed with his master, though."

His master? Was that an errand boy of some boss she had promised to…?

The missing meeting, Natsu. Wake up! "Hells and demons," she muttered. "Let him in," she urged Jirou, and then she turned to the scowling Manshik. "We shall resume our conversation later." *Hopefully, not.*

Her new deputy nodded in understanding as he pushed to his feet. While he was walking out of the tavern, Jirou ushered the mysterious visitor to Natsu's table. A stout, clean-shaven man donning a grey cloak. *Pantu's contact*, she thought. *Did Pantu send him, or did he come directly to me?*

Natsu gestured for her visitor to sit and for Jirou to leave. Not sure how to start this awkward conversation with the masked mage's contact, she said, "I must say I didn't expect you to come to me." That was not a lie. It was his master whom she was expecting. "How is your master?"

"Furious and astonished," the cloaked man said flatly. "You were the one who requested that meeting with my master, and yet you didn't come."

Because Akira found me first. "Against my intention. My mother and my son were kidnapped, so I had to stay to rescue them." She looked the cloaked man in the eye. "I have no doubt your master would understand."

"My master doesn't like his time to be wasted." The cloaked man gnashed his teeth. "You still want the fifty thousand dragons or not?"

Natsu found herself swallowing. Yes, she had given Akira her word, but the sound of this insanely huge sum was mind-boggling. Especially, with the turbulence she was facing with her crew. The timing of this man's visit was surely a work of the Light Himself.

The cloaked man tilted his head. "Natsu Sen?"

Only one-fifth of this sum would cover *all* the expenses of her new fort. What was she even thinking of?

Was it her word to Akira?

You shouldn't have promised him anything, Natsu. You had already kept your side of the bargain when you revealed the plans of the masked mage to him. Your promise was just a moment of elation when your son was given back to you.

"When?" she asked.

A smile spread across the cloaked man's face. "Two days."

"What?" Natsu exclaimed, a few diners nearby looking at her. When she glowered at them, they pretended they were busy with their meals and drinks.

The cloaked man smiled crookedly. "Is it too hard for you to pull off?"

The way he undermined her was not amusing. "You sure *you* can pull it off? You need one day at least to return to Sun…" The way his smile grew wide made her pause. *He can't return faster than that. Unless…* "You are a mage yourself, aren't you?"

183

The cloaked man stared at her, the same crooked smile still plastered on his face. "Two days."

"I need a down payment."

The cloaked man's smile faded; something Natsu wouldn't complain of. "Your agreement with my master didn't include any down payments."

"My agreement with your master didn't include those two days either."

He stared at her thoughtfully, then said, "Your full payment is part of the cargo you are going to transport." He leaned forward. "You will be paid in full even before you complete your mission. How does that sit with you?"

It wasn't ideal, but the arrangement wasn't that bad either. *The reward is worth the trouble, though.* "Tell your master I will be there in two days."

"My master will be pleased to hear this." The cloaked man rose to his feet. "There can be no mistakes this time. Many lives are at stake, yours included."

Natsu folded her arms across her chest, peering at the man donning the grey cloak. "If you know me well, then you *must* understand that threats do not work well with me."

"It's *you* who does not understand." He gritted his teeth. "Your meaningless pride won't do us any good if you fail. This operation is huger than you think, and so is its reward." The right side of his mouth quirked upward. "I wonder if you will ever need to work again."

The cloaked man gave Natsu a slight bow before he ambled toward the door of the tavern, leaving her in a storm of thoughts about the idea he had just suggested.

The idea of retiring.

20. AKIRA

Without the tunjesten cuffs, Akira was officially not a prisoner—not in the eyes of the imperial guards, to say the least—but that didn't mean he was free to wander around the palace either. To put it more accurately, Akira was *free* to wander around the vast hall he was confined in.

Save for the guards, Hanu Sen was the only person Akira had talked to since he was dragged into the palace. By order of the *former* Head of the Imperial Court, lunch then dinner had been served to 'Akira Sen' in this very hall. Yes, Hanu had been removed from her high post, but it was clear that her recent loss hadn't taken a toll on her. The proud, old lady was still in charge.

Lifting a golden goblet of wine to his lips, Akira contemplated the empty seats on both sides of the long table he was dining at. A maidservant approached with agile yet quiet steps. She glanced at the platters he hadn't touched in a while, gesturing for him with both hands, as if making sure he was done with his dinner. Akira nodded with a grateful smile, giving her his permission to collect the half-empty platters. He did enjoy this brief feeling of authority over one person in this magnificent hall—without exaggeration, this huge hall alone, with its sumptuous furniture, was more worth than his mother's house in the city. *How does it feel to be the lord of a palace that has a few more halls like this one? How does it feel to be the lord of an entire nation?* Just imagining the idea was enough to make him feel drunk. No, it wasn't the wine. The delusion of power was enough to put him into this state of light trance.

The door of the hall was opened, Hanu Sen entering alongside a familiar broad-shouldered man donning a purple cloak. Wei Sen, the mage who had tragically lost his teenage son Lan.

Akira pushed his seat back as he rose to his feet, the wooden legs of his chair scraping against the parquet floor. "Hanu Sen. Wei Sen." He bowed to his two seniors. They nodded in acknowledgment, the old lady signaling him to be seated.

"Hanu Sen told me everything you recounted," Wei began, after he and his gray-haired cousin sat opposite Akira. "But I must ask you, *again*: Do you understand the gravity of throwing such an accusation at your uncle?"

Akira was getting bored of being doubted again and again. "I would have never come here if I wasn't certain of what I saw and heard."

"We need more than your certainty to inform the Emperor," Wei said firmly. "We need evidence."

Akira huffed in frustration. "You may find the evidence you want in my uncle's office."

"You think I can just send somebody to search the Archmage's office?" Wei shook his head, stealing a glance at Hanu. "It's not that simple, not without a solid reason."

"It will be even worse if we find nothing there," Hanu pointed out, her arms crossed as she leaned back in her seat, staring thoughtfully at the chandelier hanging above their table. "Kungwan will tell the Emperor at once, and we will all be in trouble."

"And we will get the biggest share of the blame," Wei added, then turned to Akira. "Forgive me, son, but it's the adults who pay for the mistakes of the younger reckless ones."

Reckless? Akira couldn't help digging his nails into the arms of his seat. "I don't think the Emperor will be pleased when he learns that you were alerted before Kungwan made his move."

"Children these days," Wei muttered, glaring at Akira. "Are you threatening us, boy?"

Hanu gripped her cousin's wrist, casting Akira a warning look. "I'm sure it's just a tongue slip, Wei Sen."

Only now did Akira realize how his last statement sounded like. He needed to clear the air fast. "I just wanted to say that foiling Kungwan's plan should be a priority now. While we take the time we need to gather evidence, we must make sure he doesn't take anything or anybody away from Sun Castle."

"Not bad as a strategy," Wei said, apparently not so convinced though. "You have a clear plan how to do this?"

Yes, Akira did. And all credit went to Hanu's *warm* reception to him when he had come to the palace. "Depends on how much tunjesten we can gather in one or two days."

Hanu narrowed her eyes. "How do you plan to utilize such precious material?"

The idea was still brewing in his head, but Akira had a good feeling about it. "Stopping Kungwan from taking the supplies out of Koya shouldn't be a problem as long as we keep their pickup point under watch. The problem is with Kungwan and his anonymous followers. They can simply teleport themselves to whatever destination they desire without us knowing about their escape in the first place."

"You suggest we watch the portal sites as well?" Hanu wondered.

"Opening a portal takes less than a minute," Wei provided. "We will need to watch *and* defend the portal sites."

Akira nodded his agreement with Wei Sen. "The thing is that we don't know how many mages we should assign to each portal site. And more importantly; *whom* we should assign? Until this moment, we have no idea who has joined Kungwan in his treacherous act and who has not."

From the way Wei looked at him, Akira could tell that the senior mage was not belittling him any longer. Hanu was still wearing that expressionless face, but surely, she wouldn't summon the mourning father urgently to the Imperial Palace if she didn't have a slight belief in Akira's account.

"That's why we need to rely on things, not people," Akira continued, allowing himself a smile. "Things that would render a mage unable to channel his anerjy."

"What?" Wei shrugged. "Tunjesten handcuffs?"

"Tunjesten fields," Akira corrected. "Spreading small particles of tunjesten around each portal site should do."

Hanu looked from Akira to Wei. "Is that possible?"

"In theory, it could be." Wei shrugged. "But we never tried a trick like this before."

"Shouldn't be a problem." About time Akira showed off his academic knowledge. "If you provide me with tunjesten now, we can just try it out in the portal site of this palace."

While Hanu was still keeping her face expressionless, Wei held his chin thoughtfully for a moment. "Even if your trick works, it won't be enough to foil Kungwan's plan. He and his unknown followers will head to the nearest portal site outside Sun Castle, and that's it."

Akira hadn't thought that through. The whole idea had arisen in his mind just a few minutes ago. "Then, we use the same trick with the nearest portal site as well."

"To what end?" Wei asked disapprovingly. "We don't have enough tunjesten to block every portal site in Koya."

"Maybe we don't have to," Hanu said, eyes on the table, "if we confine them to Sun Castle."

Wei shook his head, wincing. "We don't know if we have the numbers to do that. We don't know who we are facing, and how many there are, to begin with."

Hanu turned to him, fixing him with her gaze for a couple of seconds, then said, "Not every matter is settled by force. A piece of parchment adorned with the Emperor's seal can do miracles."

Was she serious? What happened to the need for *evidence* before informing His Radiance? "So, you will tell the Emperor?" Akira asked her.

Hanu rolled her eyes, as if she was listening to some naïve child. For a moment, Akira thought she would ignore him. But after she heaved a sigh, she explained, "The investigation of the fire incident is still ongoing, and the Emperor himself is following it up. It won't be hard to persuade him that an imperial order of confinement shall accelerate the progress of the investigations."

Wei's eyebrows rose as he nodded. Truth be told, the Purple Cloak was not the only impressed person in this room.

"What if they defy the order?" Akira wondered.

"No one would dare," Hanu said confidently.

Wei seemed to be considering the possibility Akira had just raised. "Even if few do, we will be able to handle them."

"Exactly," Hanu seconded her cousin. "The rest will find themselves choosing between staying trapped in the castle or fleeing via the sea, with their cargo. Even if Kungwan outnumbers us with his minions, it won't matter." She paused for effect, glancing at Akira, then she added, "Their numbers will mean nothing against one fast cannonball sending their ship to the bottom of the sea."

Though they were talking about traitors, Wei didn't seem comfortable with the notion of killing dozens of fellow Red Cloaks. As for Akira, he felt nothing. Jihoon, his dear mentor, might be one of those sunken mages, and yet, all Akira felt was *nothing*. Actually, all he was assessing right now was the efficacy of Hanu's plan. The only thing that galled him about it was the loss of that huge amount of supplies. *A costly victory, that will be. But better we lose those supplies than let the Goranians use them against us.*

While Akira was about to acknowledge the lady's brilliance, Wei said, "With Kungwan on board that ship, they might have a chance to survive that cannonball, I'm afraid."

The Purple Cloak's statement seemed to irk Hanu. "Overestimating this one man won't help, my dear cousin," Hanu coldly said to Wei.

"This one man was one of the youngest mages who had ever donned the red mantle in the last two centuries. The only mage I watched make nine simultaneous bonds. Nine,

Hanu! You would understand if you were a mage yourself."
He turned to Akira. "You sure do."

Akira nodded, finding no reason to disagree with the
senior mage, who must have witnessed the Archmage in
action long ago in their youth. "Then we must keep him
away from the ship," Akira provided, having no idea how to
make this happen. *Perhaps another order stamped by the imperial
seal, summoning the Archmage for an urgent meeting here?* he
thought, stealing a glance at the former Head of the Imperial
Court, but then, he remembered the unfinished letter on his
uncle's desk. *He is ignoring a call from the Emperor himself. Why
would he respond to an order from a lesser person?*

"Taking him away from the ship shouldn't be an issue,"
said Hanu. "The question is: How long can we keep him?
Without any solid proof, we won't be able to hold him
outside forever. He will eventually return."

Her confidence in her ability to lure his uncle outside Sun
Castle piqued his curiosity. "May I ask: How do you plan to
keep him away from his escape vessel?"

"His daughter," Hanu said nonchalantly. "He will hurry
to her if he learns that she is in danger."

Akira felt the heat inside his head upon hearing Hanu
coupling his cousin Kim with danger. "Is she?" he asked,
aware of his obvious eagerness.

"She is just a bait, *for now.*" Hanu peered at him judgingly.
"Do you have a problem with that?"

Opposing Hanu wouldn't be a wise idea now. And yet, he
was unable to stand helplessly, allowing Kim to get hurt.
"You won't punish her for her father's sins, will you?"

Wei glowered at him. "Is that an order, young man?"

"She is not important." Hanu gave both of them a
dismissive gesture to close the topic. "It's her father we want
to capture."

"We will need an army of mages to force him to surrender," Wei pointed out. "An army of imperial guards."

Hanu curled her lip. "Which will require an explanation to His Radiance why we are arresting his Archmage."

Capturing Kungwan was no longer Akira's main concern. Right now, it was Kim's safety that had become his priority. *The old lady would never care about my cousin more than I do,* he reflected, realizing that there was only one way to rest assured that Kim wouldn't be some sort of collateral damage in whatever Hanu was planning to do.

"You won't need to explain to anyone," Akira said to Hanu. "It will be me who deals with Kungwan."

Hanu remained resolved as usual, but Wei couldn't hide the contempt in his smile. "*You?*"

Akira grinned, not taking any offense at Wei's disdaining tone. No one would believe a young mage, let alone a young *Pink* Cloak, who claimed he could handle the unparalleled Archmage of Koya on his own. No one would believe that the aforementioned young mage could even do this in his dreams.

"Yes, *me.*" Akira held Wei's gaze. "I have a plan."

21. KUNGWAN

Kungwan was almost done writing his last letter when knocks sounded on his door. After jotting down the last line, he put it in an envelope, sealed it, and slipped it into the drawer of his desk, alongside the two dozen envelopes with the same message he had been writing for an hour. He knew how hard it was to make a decision like abandoning your homeland, which was more of abandoning your *faith*. Not everybody would follow him to Gorania now. Some would without hesitation because they believed in their Archmage. Others would need more time to ponder the facts and decide. For those, he had written these letters.

"Come in," Kungwan shouted, and at once, Jihoon pushed the door open and scurried to the desk Kungwan was sitting behind.

"Imperial guards, Kungwan Sen," Jihoon began, his eyes betraying his worry. "They stormed Sun Castle without informing us. We heard them say they were headed to the Portal Yard."

The imperial guards' sole job was to protect the Emperor. Seeing them outside the Imperial Palace was a rare event. What game was being played? A few days ago, the Emperor had sent his snake to investigate the recent incidents, and today, his dogs? *This is Hanu's doing.*

"Summon every Red Cloak in the castle to the Portal Yard." Kungwan pushed to his feet and stalked past Jihoon toward the door.

"We are not fighting the imperial guards, are we?" Jihoon asked, catching up with Kungwan at the corridor outside the office.

Kungwan hoped they wouldn't have to do that. Not on the eve of their escape. "Just be ready."

Jihoon went the other way to see to his master's orders. Kungwan himself, rushing through the hallways and down the stairs, urged every mage he ran into to join him. When he reached the Portal Yard, he was leading a squad of seven Red Cloaks against two dozen imperial guards under the command of his old friend Wei.

"What is happening, Wei Sen?" Kungwan asked firmly, eyeing the imperial guards who were hammering silver plates on the floor.

"Kungwan Sen." Wei inclined his head toward the Archmage, and then he gestured for his old friend toward the corridor behind him. "Why don't we talk elsewhere?"

"I'm not going anywhere before you order them to stop," Kungwan pointed at Wei's men. "Or I shall stop them myself."

"Kungwan Sen," Wei called out flatly. "All of these men look up to you. You won't make them watch their role model disobey the Emperor's orders."

Nonsense! Wei might fool anybody with this farce, but not Kungwan. Leaning forward, he whispered into Wei's ear, "You mean Hanu's orders?"

"She is acting on the Emperor's delegation to oversee the investigations," Wei justified, his voice low. "You do not question His Radiance's choice, do you?"

Kungwan heaved a sigh, staring at Wei's open hand. His friend's offer of resuming this conversation somewhere else was still standing.

Without saying a word, Kungwan walked Wei to the nearest unoccupied room, which happened to be a small chemistry lab. After slamming the door closed, Kungwan snapped, "This is becoming unacceptable, Wei. Your men can't just storm the castle without even notifying me!"

"You seem to forget how things are run here, Kungwan." Wei's voice was suddenly harsh, unlike the reserved tone he had used a few minutes ago in the Portal Yard. "Those *men* belong to the Imperial Guard. They answer to no one but His Radiance."

What Wei stated was the law, but Kungwan was talking about the *norm*. Out of respect, he expected a different kind of treatment. A treatment befitting his status as the most eminent mage in the Koyan Empire.

Kungwan wiped his face with one hand and took a deep breath. "What is your business here, Wei Sen?"

"I carry orders to fulfill." From his pocket, Wei produced two rolled parchments. He handed Kungwan one of them and continued, "This is a ban on teleportation until the end of the investigation."

He can't be serious. A ban on teleportation? Now? "What is the point, may I ask?"

A wry smile slipped from Wei's face. "That's something Hanu Sen might answer. I am here to execute the order."

More nonsense from his old *friend*. Only a fool might believe that Wei was not aligned with his malicious cousin. *What is she up to? Does she know anything about our escape?* Even if that was the case, Hanu's ridiculous order would delay his move, but it wouldn't foil it. Dozens of portals existed outside Sun Castle, still.

"I shall report all of this to the Emperor." Kungwan wagged one firm finger at Wei. "I shall let him know how his subordinates have misused their authority. And I'm quite certain he won't be glad when he hears that his soldiers and their commander have been disrespected in his name."

Wei curled his nose. "You are exaggerating, Kungwan Sen. These are just routine measures in such a situation."

Measures? The word echoed in Kungwan's mind as he glanced at the other parchment Wei was still holding. "What's in this?" the Archmage asked warily.

The Commander of the Imperial Guard cast Kungwan a crooked smile as he handed him the second parchment. "Just another routine measure."

Growing impatient, Kungwan broke the seal, spread the parchment, and skimmed through it. "A confinement order?" He almost tore the parchment apart in a moment of fury, but he knew better that he shouldn't do that to a document that had the Emperor's seal. At least, not in front of the Commander of the Imperial Guard.

"Once we arrest those who set fire to the chemistry room in the castle, all these measures will become invalid."

Kungwan glared at Wei. "Tell Hanu that whatever happens within the walls of Sun Castle is my business alone. After I'm done with my own investigations, I shall return to the Imperial Palace." He wagged a firm finger, hoping Wei would buy his act. "I shall make sure you and your cousin receive the sanction you deserve for this insolence."

Wei heaved a sigh. "If anybody else said what you said, I'd arrest them at once, but as a matter of respect to your glorious past, I'll pretend I've heard nothing. My piece of advice to you now is to keep your head together and try to right the wrongs you have done." He leaned forward toward Kungwan. "Your daughter and your nephew will be a good start."

Kungwan tried to sound calm when he asked, "What about them?"

"They have to be part of *your* investigation, Kungwan Sen," Wei said curtly. "May I ask why they are not here in Sun Castle as we speak?"

"They are punished."

"While the investigation is still ongoing?"

Inwardly, Kungwan cursed those reckless teenagers for putting him in such a situation. "I told you: Whatever happens in this castle is my business alone."

"Not anymore, Kungwan Sen. Not after you allowed vandals to sabotage *your* castle." Wei gnashed his teeth. "Not after you killed my son with your extreme training methods!"

Kungwan wasn't too surprised that Wei still blamed him for Lan's death. Still, it was a cheap move by Hanu to use her cousin's loss against a rival of hers. "I should have known it from the beginning." He nodded, smirking. "This is not about the damned investigation. It's just you and your cousin seeking personal revenge." He pointed an accusing finger at Wei. "I thought you were better than that, *my friend*."

"You accuse us of taking matters personally?" Wei sneered. "Perhaps you shouldn't have hidden your daughter before you say that."

"I didn't hide her anywhere," Kungwan lied. "Who knows where she went after her expulsion? She is an adult after all."

Wei nodded silently, a strange smile on his face. "Maybe you don't know for real. Maybe it's her dear cousin who does."

Hells and demons! Kungwan had made it clear to his daughter that nobody should know where she had gone, even Akira. *Especially Akira.* Entrusting her erratic, fanatic cousin with such a secret would be a foolish act.

For some reason, Wei's smile widened. After a moment of awkward silence, he opened the door of the lab, and before exiting, he looked over his shoulder at Kungwan. "I promise you; we will find her. And you both shall get the sanction you deserve."

Kungwan inhaled deeply, mustering all the composure he needed lest he crush the man who had just threatened him and his daughter. *Let him go, Kungwan,* he told himself, watching the rascal return to his men at the Portal Yard. *His words are just hollow. Hollow words mean nothing.*

To give himself a chance to calm down, Kungwan slowly walked back to the Portal Yard, the small crowd of Sun Castle mages making way for him to come through. "Everybody! Back to your duties!" he demanded, and at once, his mages swarmed out of the corridor leading to the Portal Yard. The only mage who lingered was Jihoon, who stared quizzically at Kungwan as the latter approached him.

"You ordered me to summon our mages," Jihoon reminded him, his voice low.

"And now I realize I don't need them."

Jihoon looked at him doubtfully, as if asking, '*Are you sure?*' Then he turned to Wei's soldiers, shaking his head in disapproval as he muttered, "They are almost done fusing the tunjesten with the ground. Now we must burn the entire floor before we can open this portal again."

"I shall fix this misunderstanding with the Emperor himself when the time is right," Kungwan said, making sure Wei and his men had heard him. "Until then, we shall prove how compliant we are." He patted Jihoon on the shoulder, stealing a glance at the clowns executing the orders of Hanu Sen.

If only they know how absurd this is.

* * *

Fortunately, today's encounter with the imperial guards ended peacefully.

After Wei's soldiers were done *tunjestening* the Portal Yard and left the castle, Kungwan summoned Jihoon and Tashihara to his office. The instant his two subordinates sat across his desk, Tashihara asked impatiently, "What is this all about, Kungwan Sen? Do they *know*?"

Those who *knew* were not supposed to be that many. "I'm not sure." Kungwan leaned his elbows on the desk, his hands clasped together, mulling over all he had heard and seen today. "Perhaps Hanu suspects something." It was just an assumption, but come to think of it, it made sense. "If she knew something for sure, she would definitely arrest us without hesitation."

"But the ban on teleportation. And the confinement order," Jihoon said, an inquisitive look on his face. "What is the point of these measures?"

Kungwan had no idea, but surely, Hanu wouldn't come up with these decisions unless she believed they would hurt him somehow. "It doesn't matter. These measures change nothing in our arrangements. Tomorrow night, you two will be on board the Wraith with our supplies. Natsu will need your help to boost the power of her engine during the entire voyage."

Jihoon didn't seem satisfied. "I don't know, Kungwan Sen. Don't you think we should postpone our move for a while? With that order of confinement, I'll be surprised if the imperial guards are not watching our castle right now."

"They will be watching our walls; that's for sure," Kungwan said confidently. "But a steep sea cliff? I don't think so."

Both Jihoon and Tashihara looked at each other. Their fear was understandable, even without Hanu's worrying actions today. *We are not just abandoning our homeland. We are abandoning all the beliefs we have been raised to embrace.*

"Before you load the Wraith with our supplies," Kungwan went on, "tell Kyong about the letters. He must make sure that every section in Sun Castle has at least one copy of my letter."

Tashihara looked down, a nervous smile on her face, and then she prompted, "You are expecting a lot from that letter, Kungwan Sen."

"It's our only way to bring more men on our side," Kungwan said. Without exaggeration, delivering those letters was as crucial as smuggling the supplies across the Koyan Sea. That was why Kyong would be staying a few days after the escape of Kungwan and his two senior subordinates. "They must know that we are not doing this because we wish to fight them in the future alongside the Goranians; it's the total opposite. All of this is about stopping a war that will doom us all."

Jihoon nodded, his lips pressed together. "And when they eventually decide to fight us nonetheless?"

Kungwan doubted that his actions in the coming few days would pass without consequences. Fighting his people seemed to be inevitable. The best he could aim for was delaying that fight. "Then, let's pray to the Light that we won't be on our own when the time for that fight comes."

"What about you, Kungwan Sen?" Tashihara asked. "If you're not coming with us, then you will definitely break one of Hanu's orders, if not both."

Hanu could burn with her orders. Kungwan had a daughter to rescue. Arresting her would complicate his situation. "You are not wondering how I'm going to sneak outside Sun Castle, are you?" He couldn't help smiling when he asked her.

"To me, it's obvious that Hanu is luring you outside the walls of Sun Castle to prove you have broken the order of confinement."

His daughter was a bait to catch him, he knew. But what choice did he have? If Akira did know where she was staying, then Hanu would eventually find her. "Two days later, I will be called a traitor. You think I'd care if I break an order or two?"

* * *

Knowing that he might be spending his last few hours in Koya, Kungwan gathered all the potions he might need and put them in the pockets of his dark-blue cloak. He doubted he would need any of his stamina-boosting potions—no mage in Koya would dare to start a fight with the Archmage—but it was better to be safe than sorry.

Despite the order of confinement, Kungwan demanded that his carriage be readied for a three-day trip as soon as possible. Shortly after, he headed to the courtyard, where he found his gray-haired coachman standing by the door of the carriage. "Are you aware of the recent order of confinement?" Kungwan felt obliged to alert the man who had been working for him for two decades.

The coachman grinned, as if telling him that he knew, but he didn't care. "Where do you wish to go, Kungwan Sen?"

"I shall tell you on the road."

Bowing, the coachman held the door of the carriage open as Kungwan hopped on. Through the open window, the Archmage craned his neck and took a quick look at the walls and the gate, and it was plain that the guards posted there were growing uneasy as the carriage started moving, the hooves of the horses clopping on the cobblestone.

When the nervous guards stopped the carriage at the locked gate, Kungwan yelled, "Don't be stupid, boys! Are you really going to stand in my way?"

One of the guards was bold enough to say, "We mean no disrespect, Kungwan Sen. We are just complying with the Emperor's orders."

"These are the orders of a Court Member; a subordinate of mine." Kungwan leaned his elbow on the edge of the window, showing the color of the Court Head's attire. "The Emperor shall hear of this insolence when I go to him." He pointed a commanding finger at the gate. "Now open the damned gate, or I shall open it myself."

The guards still had enough common sense to realize how futile their stand against the Archmage was. To Kungwan's relief, they unlocked the gate, letting the carriage venture outside the walls of Sun Castle. From there, he could head to the Imperial Palace.

Or to Kim's hideout.

Having no doubt that Wei's men would be following him on the road, Kungwan took a sip of the becoba potion to boost his focus. Even if the imperial guards were hiding in the woods on the left side of the road, he would be able to sense their anerjy. For half an hour of traveling down the road, he sensed nothing, though. *Can't be. Wei won't be relying only on my men to execute Hanu's orders. Unless I have been overestimating my foes' cunning.*

"Stop here," Kungwan ordered the coachman, and the latter didn't hesitate.

"You feel well, Kungwan Sen?"

"I'm fine. Now listen. I want you to tour the Koyan coast for three days. You hear me; *three days*. No less. After that, you will head to my house. If anybody asks you, tell them that you were doing as your master commanded."

The coachman looked over his shoulder. "I take it I won't see you for a while, Kungwan Sen."

If the plan works? No, you won't, Kungwan wanted to tell him. "Before you resume your trip, there is an act we need to play, just in case someone is watching us."

"I'm not sure I'm good at acting, Kungwan Sen."

"I'm sure you are."

Kungwan did his best to simplify the coachman's role. After five minutes of explaining, the coachman assured Kungwan that he could do it.

The coachman hopped off the carriage, pretending as if he was checking on the legs of one of his horses. Kungwan opened the door of the carriage to see what was going on, and then he clambered down to join the coachman. "He will survive the trip," Kungwan said after a moment of fake inspection on the horse's leg. "Let's go. We cannot afford any delays."

Hoping that whoever was watching believed this stupid play, Kungwan returned to the carriage, and before the coachman could close the door behind him, he mustered all his focus to surround himself with a lightshield and jumped quickly from the carriage. Bearing in mind that the transparent shield deflected both light and air, the invisible Archmage sprinted away from the road until he reached the woods. With one quick glance over his shoulder, Kungwan made sure that his coachman was on his way to start his tour by the Koyan Sea, dragging Wei's guards—if they had been stalking the carriage since it left Sun Castle—away from Kungwan himself.

The air inside the invisibility shield was running low as Kungwan ventured through the woods, away from the main road. After ten minutes of walking, Kungwan broke the shield and gasped for air, his eyes scanning his surroundings. He wouldn't need the lightshield here anyway; the ancient towering cedar trees would curtain his moves.

The cottage he had sent Kim to was an hour's walk away from here. He should reach it and take his daughter to the nearest portal before nightfall. And tonight, Tashihara and Jihoon would start their voyage across the Koyan Sea. After three days of sailing on board the fast Wraith, Jihoon and Tashihara would be far enough from the Turtle Ships. Hopefully, by that time, Kungwan's letter would bring him more followers. He would need an army, not to face his own folks in battle, but to prevent that from happening.

The cottage was visible when Kungwan sensed a sudden flow of anerjy nearby. He stopped and looked around, the external flow of anerjy growing stronger. Someone approaching, but where was he? The tree trunks were not helping at all.

And then, he appeared. Literally, out of nowhere. Kungwan was not the only one who had wielded a lightshield today, it was clear.

"Surprised to see me, Uncle?"

22. AKIRA

One hour earlier,

The dose of the potion Akira had administered to fulfill Natsu's quest was enough to open a portal and cross the void thirty times in less than five hours. But to stand face to face against the Archmage of the Koyan Empire, the great Kungwan Sen; well, Akira might need more than the stamina-boosting potion he had developed himself.

His options were not that many, though. All he could do was improve his own experimental potion. A little more red balya to boost his stamina, an extra pinch of becoba to enhance his focus, and triple the dose of dandelion to accelerate his body's ability to get rid of the traces of the red mercury that might have precipitated during the initial preparation of the potion. The result of all these alterations filled the vial resting in his palm.

Which was not the only vial he brought for this task.

Having no doubt that his uncle would rush to his daughter to protect her from Wei's men, Akira waited outside the walls of Sun Castle on horseback, away from the main road by some distance. The moment he caught a glimpse of the gates slowly opening, he drained a vial of the 'enhanced' version of his experimental potion, and in a minute, a sweet feeling of power washed over him. The power he needed to wield all the jumuns the likes of him— the so-called Pink Cloaks—could never do.

So, this is how it feels to become a Red Cloak. Did they ever become addicted to this feeling? Or did they just get used to it over the course of time?

Akira summoned a *flat* lightshield that didn't enclose him, yet it was large enough to cover both him and the horse he was mounting. As long as he kept this shield between him and the road Kungwan was taking, Akira wouldn't need the traditional lightshield that was even impermeable to air. Surely, both he and the horse wouldn't be able to hold their breath the whole trip.

For an hour, Akira followed his uncle's carriage until it halted in the middle of nowhere. The coachman jumped down to inspect one of the horses, and shortly, Kungwan joined him for a brief time before he returned to the carriage. In a couple of minutes, the coachman reassumed his position and spurred the horses onward…*without* Kungwan Sen. Thanks to Akira's enhanced focus, he sensed his uncle's anerjy as the latter wielded a traditional lightshield—the one that surrounded a mage completely— and headed into the thick woods occupying the left side of the road.

Akira trailed his uncle, but he didn't come close enough lest the horse give away his position. After dismounting and quickly tying his horse to a tree, Akira summoned a full lightshield and resumed the chase. *How long could you hold your breath, Uncle?* Akira wondered, feeling at ease so far as his lungs consumed the air trapped in the shield at a pace slower than normal. To give the old man some credit, Kungwan held the lightshield longer than Akira would imagine. *I'm decades younger than him, and I drank an enhancing potion. He can't do better than me. Not today.*

Akira could see a cottage in the heart of the woods when Kungwan broke his shield to breathe. That was where Kim was hiding, Akira surmised. If he was to stop the Archmage, he should do it here, far enough from the cottage to avoid involving his cousin. This was between him and his *dear* uncle.

Breaking his shield as well, Akira approached Kungwan from his left side, the old man furrowing his brow. "Surprised to see me, Uncle?" he teased the Archmage.

"What are you doing here?"

Both his uncle's tone and the question itself were a little disappointing. Wasn't Kungwan curious to know how his *average* nephew had managed to pull that off?

"I'm here to stop you, old man," Akira said, his fingers clenched, ready to wield a jumun.

"Stop me from doing what?" Kungwan asked flatly.

"I know what you are up to, Uncle. Believe me, it's over."

"It's you who must believe me, Akira; you know nothing."

His uncle would always belittle him. Maybe Akira should prove him wrong. "I know about the Wraith, Uncle." Akira shook his head, casting his uncle a crooked smile. "I'm afraid you will have to miss your voyage."

Now he had his uncle's attention. The Archmage sharply drew in a deep breath as he clenched his fingers. "Who else knows?"

Akira couldn't conceal his gloating smile. "Everybody in the Imperial Court, I believe."

The scowl on Kungwan's face did satisfy Akira. "The Light knows I have done my best to keep you out of this."

Akira looked derisively at the Archmage. "Because you didn't want me to reveal your betrayal."

"Because I didn't want you to get hurt."

"Nonsense!" Akira snapped. "You never cared about me. You have always been ashamed of the son of your Seijo sister!"

Kungwan muttered curses under his breath. "Listen, boy." His voice was low yet menacing. "I have no time to resolve your delusions. Go back to your mother and stay away from Sun Castle as long as possible. It won't be a safe place for you for a while."

"Your time of giving commands has just ended, Kungwan Sen." Akira bound his massive anerjy with the air around him and directed a telekinetic slap at his uncle. The Archmage deflected it with a simple wave of his hand, as if shooing some buzzing flies.

"Don't make me hurt you, boy," Kungwan spat.

"Just try." Akira channeled more anerjy this time to heat the air, a fireball growing between his palms in a few seconds. He threw it at Kungwan, but again, his uncle deflected it. Without giving the old man a moment to catch his breath, Akira sent more fireballs at a rapid pace, but none of them landed where he wanted. The Archmage kept blocking them effortlessly, and suddenly, he returned a fireball to Akira. Taken off guard, Akira lost his balance as he deflected the fireball at the last second.

"Stay on the ground and don't be stupid!" Kungwan growled. "How do you think this fight will end?"

I might be stronger, but as a fighter, he is more seasoned, Akira thought, the realization scaring him for a second. This was not a mere sparring session where both the winner and the loser would bow to each other after the fight. Here, the winner would be the one who emerged from the woods alive.

And only one would.

The moment Akira pushed to his feet, Kungwan stunned him with a telekinetic slap that sent him flying. Luckily, the hit against the grassy terrain didn't break any of Akira's bones, but the right side of his body, especially his elbow which took the worst of the fall, hurt him still.

"Stand up one more time, and you will get yourself killed," Kungwan warned, and Akira was afraid his uncle was right. The Archmage was much faster than him; something a stamina-boosting potion alone couldn't compensate for. *I must play on my strengths*, Akira thought, still lying on the ground to spare himself another slap. *I must strike him harder.*

Groaning, Akira slowly rolled to the right to hide the hand picking up a vial from his pocket. The instant he gulped down another dose of his potion, he summoned a lightshield that totally engulfed him before he rose to his feet.

"Come on!" Kungwan's voice betrayed his frustration as he looked for his invisible nephew. "These potions will kill you before I do!"

Theoretically, his uncle was right. Too much stamina boosting might arrest Akira's heart. Hopefully, he made the right decision when he had bet on the double dose of dandelion. He kept moving around Kungwan, but the Archmage seemed to be aware of the position of his invisible foe. *He senses my anerjy. That's how he tracks me.*

Still curtained by the invisible shield, the effect of the second dose of his potion kicked in, an immense feeling of power surging through each inch of his body. He channeled his anerjy to bind with the air trapped inside the lightshield, and in a matter of seconds, he was wielding a fireball with a five-foot diameter. *Dodge this, old man,* Akira thought, using part of his focus to hold the fireball in the air, the remaining part ready to break the shield.

And throw the massive fireball at his uncle.

For any mage, for any Red Cloak, a huge fireball this close was impossible to avoid. But one more time, Kungwan showed why he was one of the greatest Archmages in the history of Koya. Howling, he deflected the deadly fireball that missed his head by a hair. Akira struck again and again with more fireballs, each missile bigger than the previous one, but Kungwan dissipated them all with a telekinetic shield.

Not sure if that was frustration or just the rush of anerjy through his veins, Akira roared as he had never done before. *He doesn't even look tired, and I'm the one who took a booster,* Akira thought, glancing at the trees around his uncle. *Alright, then. Dodge this!*

Akira felt the bond between him and the colossal tree behind his uncle, felt the will to move it as he wished. Roaring again, he stretched out both arms and channeled his anerjy to haul the massive wooden trunk. The grassy ground cracked, ancient roots emerging from under the surface. Through the anerjy binding him with the tree, he pulled to slam Kungwan with it. Still stretching one arm toward Akira, Kungwan extended the other toward the flying tree, and just one foot away from him, the huge trunk bounced off another telekinetic shield.

"You can't hold that shield forever!" Akira didn't break the binding with the tree, and kept striking, his uncle's shield absorbing every single hit. *He looks tired, though.* Akira took note of the grimace on the Archmage's face. But how many more strikes should the old man receive before he fell? Akira had no idea, but he was sure of one thing; he would be still standing when his uncle collapsed.

Kungwan proved to be more stubborn than a mule, though. Despite his apparent weariness, he was as unmovable as a mountain, making Akira's patience grow thin. *Maybe one tree is not enough.* Without hesitation, he channeled all the anerjy he could to uproot five more trees at the same time. He knew this was reckless; he hadn't had the time to test the full impact of his experimental potion on his body. The vast quantum of anerjy he was channeling right now could be sapping him of life.

Feeling no pain or even a hint of fatigue so far, Akira drew six trees at Kungwan. The Archmage held his ground, repelling the soaring trunks with his telekinetic shield. Having no doubt that Kungwan's fall was just a matter of time, Akira maintained the ferocious attack to drain his uncle's anerjy. After blocking a few dozen hits, the Archmage roared as he spread his arms wide apart. Much to Akira's surprise, the huge trunks exploded, wooden splinters landing around the unscathed Archmage.

Did I overestimate the efficacy of my potion? Or is Kungwan much stronger than I thought? Akira was afraid it was both. At this moment, he was aware of his pounding heart, which was not a good sign, especially with the sight of the Archmage still standing in defiance despite the heavy battering against his shield.

Yes, the shield. Akira had to tear it apart first. The problem was how to bind with something that was meant to repulse any form of anerjy.

Theoretically, it was an impossible task, but Akira decided to give it a shot. This time, he didn't thrust a trunk or a telekinetic slap against his foe.

This time, he pulled. With every ounce of strength in his boosted body.

Akira felt every muscle in his body straining, his heart beating faster than normal as the surge of anerjy through him intensified. He found himself growling, the entirety of his senses consigned to nothing but the bond he was trying to establish. *This is madness, Akira. You will kill yourself before…*

And suddenly, he felt it. The bond. He could almost 'touch' it. Like for real.

So, he *pulled*. And this time, he was pulling Kungwan himself.

His uncle fell face down after a brief flight in the air toward him, and at once Akira summoned a fireball to seize the chance. The rare chance to become the one who defeated the Archmage of Sun Castle. *Every mage, every Koyan shall hear of Akira the Invincible. The Emperor himself shall know my name.*

But his curiosity took the better of him.

"WHY?" Akira bellowed, the fireball floating between his palms.

His uncle groaned as he lifted his head. "You…will…never…understand."

"Then you die with your shame. Unless you have an explanation for your treachery." Truth be told, Akira wished that Kungwan wouldn't give him a reason to finish him off before hearing that very explanation. Not because he cared about his uncle's reputation—his uncle himself didn't mind burying his own name in the mud. He wanted to guarantee that he would never ever feel a hint of remorse for killing his own blood.

With his knees on the ground, Kungwan strained to rise, a tired smile on his face. "You have always been a true believer." He gasped after coughing a few times. When he was able to breathe normally, he continued, "It was hard to convince you that the Last Day would never be what we thought."

Oh, please. Not this nonsense! "Why don't you just admit it was the Goranian coin?" Akira snarled.

"You can't be serious." Kungwan's plain exhaustion did not prevent him from chuckling. "You really believe I'm doing this for coin?"

It was a reason that might make sense to Akira. Still ready to strike his uncle with the fireball, he asked, "If the Last Day is not what we think; what is it, then?"

"Literally, a demonic delusion." Kungwan looked him in the eye. "I was like you one day; a true believer who would never buy this." After another bout of coughing, he added, "Until a seer showed me."

"Showed you what?"

"AKIRA! STOP!"

Akira turned to his cousin when he heard her voice. She emerged from the woods, sprinting toward him, her eyes wide in alarm. "What are you doing?" she yelled at Akira. "Get rid of this fireball now!"

"Stay out of this, Kim," Akira demanded, keeping an eye on Kungwan. "You are not the one I am after."

"Are you even listening to yourself?" Kim bristled. "The man you want to kill is your uncle. My father, Akira! You think I will simply let you kill him?"

The girl glowering at Akira right now was not the same gentle, lovely cousin he had liked since they were children. This furious sorceress was someone else. Someone stranger. *That's why I never wanted to involve you in this, Kim.*

"Your father is a traitor, Kim," Akira rasped. "If I don't do it, someone else will."

"I will not beg YOU!" Kim stunned Akira with a telekinetic slap that threw him off balance. When he quickly pushed to his feet, he found the fireball already dissipated. "Leave me no choice but to kill you, and I will!" She stood between him and her father, allowing her old man to slowly rise to his feet.

"*Please*, Kim!" Akira gnashed his teeth. "It's me who is begging you to step aside. Flee to Gorania if you like; I will not stop you. But your father? You can't protect him from me."

"Don't you, at least, want to hear what the seer showed me, son?" Kungwan asked from behind his daughter, groaning. "Aren't you eager to hear why, after a lifetime of service in Sun Castle, I'm leaving everything I have believed in behind?"

"We know it's of no use, Father." Kim clenched her fingers, her glowing eyes fixed on Akira. "No matter what we say, he'd always want to live in the delusion of serving the Light's cause."

Kim was not totally wrong. Akira didn't have the intention of changing his mind. He just wanted to resume the conversation his cousin had interrupted. "What did he *show* you?" he asked curtly.

Kungwan advanced, holding his daughter's shoulder. "A bleak, hellish world dominated by demons." He took another step forward, and now he was standing between his daughter and Akira. "That is Earth after the Last Day, Akira.

A haven for demons after annihilating every single human."
He lifted his fist to his mouth to suppress a cough, then he
went on, "And it will be us who invite them to our world
because we believe we can subdue them forever, but it's a
lie, Akira. An ancient delusion that we have been following
for centuries."

Akira was not that impressed. "What makes you sure that
your so-called vision is not a delusion, either?"

"It wasn't a mere vision; I was *actually* there. I was blinded
by the white sun, deafened by the demons' shrieks, burned
by the blazing air. Sooner or later, that future will be a
matter of fact unless we act today."

Akira was truly underwhelmed. How could a stupid
dream make you instantly turn on your own people?
Abandon all your core beliefs? Ruin your entire life?

"If you do believe in that vision," Akira began. "Why
don't you just share it with everyone else and 'save us all'
rather than acting like a traitor?"

Kungwan heaved a sigh. "That's not how it is going to
work."

"How do you know?" Akira couldn't help smirking. "Is
that what your seer showed you in your vision too?"

"I'm not the only one who had the same vision, Akira."
Kungwan glanced over his shoulder at Kim, who shook her
head in disapproval. "She had the same vision the same
night I had mine. A few others did. It cannot be a
coincidence."

Akira cast Kim a pitiful look. The silly girl would spend
the rest of her life in shame because she decided to follow a
father who had lost his mind.

"Alright then." Akira puffed. "Here is my best and *last*
proposal." He looked from Kungwan to Kim and back.
"You come with me to the Imperial Palace and ask for an

audience with His Radiance. I have no doubt he will listen." He leaned forward toward his uncle. "You are the head of his court after all. He wouldn't have picked you over Hanu if he didn't trust you."

Kim rolled her eyes. "I knew it was a waste of time. We must go, Father."

The instant she held her father's arm to walk him away, Akira struck both of them with a mild telekinetic slap that sent them both flying backward. "ENOUGH OF THIS!" Akira bellowed, his relatives lying on the ground, groaning. While Kim was taking her time to rise to her feet, Akira strode toward her. "Haven't you realized yet how absurd it is to fight me? Look at your father, the *great* Kungwan Sen." He swept an arm toward the old man who had finally become wise enough to stay on the ground. "He is consumed after our encounter, and I'm still as good as new. I could crush you both now if I wanted."

Standing despite her obvious pain, Kim peered at him. "Your potion. It's working, isn't it?" She nodded to herself, eyeing her defeated father. It must be devasting for her to see her old man so powerless, so helpless. "Then, I guess you are right. None of us can defeat you."

While that sign of surrender should give Akira a sense of relief, there was something he didn't like about Kim's tone. *What is she mumbling?* he wondered, staring at Kim's moving lips.

And then the ground beneath his feet quivered.

"No, Kim!" Kungwan startled Akira when he hollered, still lying on the ground. "You are not ready yet!"

"Not ready for what?" Akira asked nervously, but he didn't get an answer. Whatever that was, Kim didn't seem to be listening to her exhausted father, who was struggling to get up. Warily, Akira leaned toward her, but he couldn't comprehend what she was saying.

CRACK! CRACK! CRAAACK!

The mild trembling had grown into a horrendous earthquake that shook the woods, a dozen towering trees tumbling with a deafening clamor, a cloud of dust rising to curtain the sky. Akira wasn't sure what kind of sorcery could cause this chaos, but the real question was, if that was Kim's doing for real; what was she trying to do exactly?

"Let's get out of here, Father." Kim helped her father up. "He will be taken care of."

"The runes first!" Kungwan shouted in alarm. "The runes before…"

A horrifying shriek came from inside the huge cloud of dust. When Akira squinted, he spotted the shadow of a giant rising from the ground. *The runes first.* The statement echoed in his mind as he gazed at the twisted horns of the colossal creature, huge red eyes glowing like two small suns. That was not *just* a giant—as if a giant was supposedly a simple creature, to begin with.

Akira hadn't seen one before, but if that was not a demon in its true form, what else could it be? "What have you done, Kim?" Actually, he knew. He just couldn't believe that his cousin had never told him that she was a summoner.

"You believed that we could control thousands of demons in the War of the Last Day, right? Let's see how you fare against one." Kim turned to the demon and cried, "*Wi tek bibin!*"

The hideous demon screeched, raising his massive arms to the air. Summoning demons was not an area Akira was well acquainted with, but he presumed that Kim had just given her monstrous servant a command in *his* tongue, and obviously, that was his response.

The beginning of it.

Akira stared in awe as the demon dug his hands into the ground, wrenched a huge mass of soil, and tossed it, as if it weighed nothing, toward Akira. Channeling his anerjy, Akira pushed the gigantic projectile back, but all he could do was slow it down a bit. *I need more force,* he realized, and at once, he channeled all his anerjy, but it was too late. The landing mass of soil was too close to…

Akira felt a telekinetic force pulling him away one second before the gigantic projectile crashed into the spot he had been standing on. When he rose to his feet, he realized that his brief flight had brought him closer to Kim and his exhausted uncle.

"Why, Father?" Clearly, she was rebuking her father for saving Akira. "He was trying to kill you!"

"We need him to stop that creature you summoned," Kungwan groused then coughed. "Now stay as far away as possible from here!"

"I can confine it, Father!"

"I had enough of your foolishness," Kungwan snapped, wagging a firm finger. "Stay back, I say!"

Kim was surely offended, but she didn't answer back this time, the aversion plain in her eyes as she glowered at Akira. Her cousin ignored her and gazed at the shrieking demon that dug into the ground one more time. Another flying mass was coming soon.

"What do we do now?" Akira asked his uncle hurriedly.

"You still have some of your potion?"

Akira had one last vial in his pocket, but he felt hesitant about telling his uncle. "Why do you ask?"

"Look out, Father!" Kim yelled from behind them as she pushed telekinetically at the incoming mass. Akira pushed as well, but even their combined forces were not enough to stop such a gigantic projectile.

"Push to the side, not upward!" Kungwan instructed, both Akira and Kim acting at once. When the thrown mass swayed to the left, Akira pushed more on the left flank. A few seconds before falling, the hurled mass deviated from its path and hit the ground ten feet away from them with a thunderous noise. Before the storm of dust and debris might cover them, Kim reacted quickly and cleared the air around them.

"That thing almost killed her," Akira remarked nervously. "Isn't he supposed to obey his summoner?"

"Demons are unpredictable, especially with uninitiated summoners like my daughter," Kungwan said. "Now, I need your potion to get us out of this predicament."

Akira looked his weary uncle up and down. "How do you know it won't kill you?"

"I must get close enough to the demon to confine it."

Akira still had his doubts. "Tell me what to do, and I shall confine him myself."

"This is not the time to teach you, you damned fool!" Kungwan extended his hand. "The vial! Now!"

The demon was excavating the ground for the third time. Reluctantly, Akira handed Kungwan his last vial, and the old man drained it without hesitation, his daughter regarding him in concern. "Are you alright, Father?"

"I'm better already," Kungwan answered, although the onset of action of Akira's potion was a minute or two. Maybe he was just reassuring his daughter. "Listen," he held Akira's shoulder, "I will be vulnerable while I carve the runes around him. You must protect me, or we both die. Understood?"

Akira nodded, his eyes fixed on the huge soil mass the demon was about to throw.

"Take a deep breath, then." Kungwan barely stretched his arms, and instantly, they were inside an invisibility shield. The old man ran, and so did Akira. The demon, still carrying his next missile, shrieked as he looked for the two men who had just vanished. Obviously enraged by their disappearance, he let out another shriek before he randomly tossed the monumental mass. Akira heard the dreadful thud behind him, but he didn't dare to look back lest he get out of the mobile invisibility shield. A couple of feet away from the sprinting Kungwan could be enough to reveal Akira's position. Something you would never want, especially when you were getting closer to a colossal, mad demon trying to smash you with missiles the size of a temple.

The pace of Kungwan's recovery was impressive and also intimidating. A couple of minutes ago, the devastated Archmage could hardly utter a few words without coughing. Now he was *running* while holding a shield impermeable to air. *He can defeat an army of mages without the need to boost his stamina. With my potion, he can conquer a continent on his own.*

After evading the huge holes in the ground, Kungwan halted thirty feet away from the demon, and here the creature seemed even bigger than Akira had thought. "Be ready," Kungwan commanded him. "I must drop the shield now."

The first thing Akira did when Kungwan broke the shield was fill his lungs with fresh air. The demon spotted them and screeched as it leaned forward toward them. "Please, be quick," Akira muttered, watching his uncle carve the runes telepathically into the ground. Deflecting a monstrous missile would be hard from such a close range.

But it seemed that the demon had changed its mind about hurling things at them.

"What is *he* doing?" Akira wondered, gazing at the demon that knelt and placed his massive palms on the ground, a gust of steamy air slapping Akira's cheeks.

"Changing our habitat to something he is more accustomed to." Kungwan motioned for Akira to follow him after he was done with the first set of runes. "We need to hurry. Take a deep breath."

So, that demon was more than an enraged giant; it was also capable of wielding…magic? *Hells and demons! How many more sets of runes will suffice, Kungwan?* Akira wanted to ask, but the invisibility shield had engulfed both men already.

Their disappearance maddened the demon again. Shrieking, he shook the earth with an immense stomp, countless cracks snaking all over the ground, swallowing every tree in their way. Kungwan gripped Akira's wrist to halt him, and luckily, the cracks missed their spot. Akira wanted to ask the Archmage how they should act now, but plainly, the only thing to do was wait. Because Akira doubted there was a way to stop or evade those cracks. If you happen to be in their path, then you are simply doomed.

When the earth stopped shaking, Kungwan and Akira resumed their hurried march until they reached the edge of a bottomless crack. "Levitate me to the other side, and I shall do the same," Kungwan stated. "Be quick and precise."

The instant the shield was broken, Akira lifted Kungwan telekinetically over the crack. When Kungwan landed, he made Akira float in the air to the other side, the demon screeching upon spotting them. "Give me a minute to carve the runes," Kungwan commanded Akira, leaving him on his own to face the demon's wrath.

"Can't we just attack that thing, instead of waiting like sitting ducks?" Akira asked, and waited for an answer, his eyes fixated on the demon spreading its arms apart. *If he knew an answer, he would give me one.*

The earth was shaking one more time, and if Akira had learned something a few minutes ago, this sign did not bode well, and unfortunately, he was right. A volcano exploded at the demon's feet, and now it was raining lava and flaming stones. Wielding a wide telekinetic shield to protect himself and his uncle, Akira deflected the hellish rain, which was relatively easier to handle than the gigantic soil masses. *Please, keep it like that,* he would ask the demon, if the damned creature listened to…

Suddenly, Akira's chest ached. *A side effect of the potion?* he wondered, biting his lower lip as he drove back the showers of doom. "Hurry up!" he urged Kungwan. "I can't…" The pain became unbearable, as if a dagger had just pierced through his heart. Unable to hold the shield any longer, he fell on his back, his quivering hands gripping his chest right above his heart. Lava and flaming stones were falling on him; he was still aware of that. But he felt too helpless to save his own life.

Akira's vision started to blur, but he thought he saw the lava and flaming stones fly away from him. And then, there was Kungwan bending over him. "*Get up,*" his uncle demanded, his voice muffled, as if coming from the bottom of a deep well. "*One more…is over.*" Akira didn't hear the whole statement, his vision fading into black. He was losing his consciousness, wasn't he?

A slap on his cheek roused him, a firm hand helping him up. To his surprise, it was Kim. How long had he passed out?

"Can you still fight?" she asked in a low voice, glancing at the monstrous hellish creature that was looking the other way. "The demon is not giving Father a chance to cast the last rune."

Akira was still trying to understand the situation. The last thing he remembered was Kungwan's face. And Kim was supposed to be far behind them. While he was wondering how she had reached him, a glimpse of the rocks bridging the cracks gave him a clue. *A lot of effort to come here.*

"Answer me." Kim held his chin, not so gently at all. "Tell me you are still able to wield your anerjy."

Akira's chest pain had faded, but for some reason, moving a single muscle was now a terrible chore. Trying to ignore the exhaustion engulfing his entire body, he reached for the surrounding anerjy to bind it with his. "I...I can't," he muttered, resisting a sudden urge to cry. This weakness. This helplessness. This *uselessness* in a life-or-death moment made him wish he hadn't existed. "I'm sorry."

"You should be." Scowling, Kim turned to the demon and heaved a sigh. "Run away in case this doesn't work."

Warily, Kim walked toward the demon hurling boulders at her father on the opposite side. *You are not ready yet*, Akira recalled Kungwan's words to his daughter. "Kim, what are you up to?"

But Kim didn't heed him as she got closer to the demon facing her father. "*Beh nam prordakaar asmaan wa zameen,*" she hollered. "*Man beh shama me tokti!*"

Akira was ignorant of this cursed tongue, but he hoped his cousin was doing more than just distracting the demon from her father. Because right now, the demon was looking at her, a massive boulder in his hands.

"*Man ben shama me tokti!*" she repeated, the demon's red eyes fixed on her. Kungwan had better carve the last set of runes before the demon remembered he existed.

A horrendous shriek startled Akira. "Blast! Get out of here, Kim!" he urged his cousin. Ignoring him, she kept intoning in the demon's tongue, but that didn't deter the cursed creature from smashing her with the gigantic rock. Yes, that had just happened for real, faster than Akira could grasp. "NOOOOOOO!"

The demon was calm now, just standing next to the boulder he had just thrusted at Kim. Most probably, Kungwan was done with the damned runes, but it was too late. Kim was gone, right in front of Akira, and he had done nothing. He couldn't, even if he wanted to. Right now, he was back to his mediocre self. The aspiring mage who could never be more than a Pink Cloak.

Weak. Helpless. Useless.

Akira watched Kungwan walk around the wide perimeter the demon was confined in. The old man hadn't seen what happened to his daughter; Akira could tell from his uncle's unhurried pace. *Hells and demons!* Of all people, Akira was the one who would inform his uncle of the tragic news.

When Kungwan joined Akira, he nodded his chin toward him. "I see that your potion didn't kill you." The Archmage exhaled, gazing at the trapped *domesticated* demon. "You believe me now?" He peered at Akira judgingly. "Imagine facing an army of these cursed creatures. Because that's what will eventually happen if we unleash them upon Gorania." He leaned forward toward him, pointing to the demon ambling in his area of confinement. "They won't stop at Gorania, son. They won't stop until the last human dies."

Akira wouldn't argue anymore. Thanks to his gone cousin, he had seen for himself how hard taming such horrendous creatures could be. The shame paralyzed his tongue, though.

Kungwan cast him a studying look. "I know it's a lot to digest. Take your time to decide while we…" He craned his neck, gazing behind Akira, where he had left his daughter. "Where is Kim?"

Akira couldn't help looking at the boulder that had smashed his cousin. "She tried to wake me up so that I could aid you."

Kungwan took a moment to comprehend. "No," he muttered, his voice quivering as he stared at the boulder. "No, no, no! This didn't happen!" He seemed to be trying to levitate the boulder, but the rocky mass didn't move. Did the confining runes have something to do with that? Akira did not dare to ask the shocked father now.

"There is no need for this, Uncle." Akira warily approached Kungwan. "I saw what happened." He had better choose his next words carefully. "She didn't make it."

Kungwan fell on his knees, his eyes fixed on the largest tombstone anybody might have. For a while, he didn't say a word, and neither did Akira. *Should I say something to him?* Akira wondered, but would Kungwan accept any words of condolences from him? The Archmage must be blaming Akira for Kim's death, and Akira wouldn't dare to disagree. *Her blood is on my hands indeed.*

Tired from standing, Akira sat some distance behind Kungwan. The old man was still kneeling, staring at the huge boulder that had taken his daughter's life. To be honest, Akira found Kungwan's reaction surprising. The old man had always been firm with his daughter, sometimes even harsh. But that was nothing but a mask, it turned out. It didn't matter that you were the wisest man in Koya. No wisdom is enough to help you process such a situation.

Finally, Kungwan rose to his feet. Akira did the same, but his uncle walked past him, as if he was invisible. Knowing that he should leave Kungwan on his own, at least for a while, Akira couldn't help calling out to him. "Where are you headed to?"

His uncle halted and turned to face Akira. "Where I don't see your damned face!" he blustered, then wagged a threatening finger at Akira, slowly stepping forward toward him. "If I see you again, I shall kill you at once!"

Akira knew he should keep his mouth shut, but he couldn't do that for more than half a minute. "I want to help," he called again to Kungwan. As his uncle walked away without heeding him, Akira continued, "I want to make sure that she didn't die in vain."

Kungwan turned to Akira again, but this time, the Archmage surprised him with a telekinetic slap that threw him off balance. "She did die in vain," his uncle said, his lip curled in disdain, "when she saved your sad, worthless arse."

23. NATSU

Since Riku's safe return to her, Natsu hadn't been able to stay a single night away from him. Not like 'away from her house'—that seemed to be impossible, at least for the time being. It was more like 'within the walls of his bedchamber.' The sight of Qianfan's bastards stabbing his grandmother to death still haunted his sleep, and obviously, that would be the case every night for many nights still to come. How long would a five-year-old boy need to recover from such a traumatic experience? Because Natsu was starting to worry that it would break him instead of making him stronger.

All the way to the dock, Riku locked arms with his mother although they were trapped together in the carriage; no way could he stray far from her. Sometimes he clutched her hand so hard he almost dislocated her finger. What should she do to kill that fear in his heart?

"Excited about your first voyage across the sea?" She managed a smile at Riku. "I was six when your grandfather took me on his boat for the first time."

Riku hunched his shoulders. "Monsters dwell there, I was told."

Believe me, the reality is scarier than your fairy tales, Natsu thought, picturing the sight of Shnakar's massive hands. "They will never dare to harm us. Do you know why?" She chuckled, rubbing his head playfully, and then she pointed to Jirou, her coachman and personal guard. "Because they all fear Jirou Sen, our gallant hero."

Riku gaped at the heroic Jirou Sen. "Can he beat monsters?"

Natsu glanced at Jirou, who seemed to be amused by the conversation. "He will do whatever it takes to protect us."

Silence fell over them, and no sound was louder than the thudding hooves of the horses of her convoy. No ordinary Hokydoan was insane enough to brave the road outside the town at midnight. The only living beings they might encounter at such a late hour would be bats, flying squirrels, or raccoon dogs. There could be bandits as well—they were a fundamental part of Hokydo's natural environment—but they had some sense left to avoid intercepting the Murderous Widow.

Torches flickered on the horizon, the road becoming less quiet as they approached the docks, and the closer she was to her destination, the harder her heart pounded. Why was she anxious tonight? Was it the scale of this operation? Was it her son's presence? Or was it both? *It's better this way,* she reminded herself. *I would never be able to focus, knowing that he needs me beside him.*

Manshik was in her reception when she arrived at the docks. She took note of the look of disapproval on his face upon seeing her son clamber down the carriage alongside her. "You are not taking him with you, are you?"

One lesson Natsu had learned the hard way about this fierce business was that family could be a liability. A burden. A weak point her rivals could squeeze on. But it wasn't a weak point she could just get rid of. Fortifying it was her only possible course of action. "The earlier we teach them, the stronger they become," she said, gripping Riku's bony shoulder. She was certain that Manshik was not convinced, and she didn't bother. By all means, it sounded better than telling him that she wouldn't be able to maintain her sanity if she spent all these days away from her little boy. Yes, Manshik was a loyal man. He wouldn't betray her for that hint of softness, but he might start to question her ability to manage this dangerous business. They were living in a world where only the ruthless would survive.

Manshik leaned forward toward her, lowering his voice as he said, "You could have picked a less dangerous voyage to start teaching him."

"Less dangerous, more dangerous," she scoffed. "All voyages are dangerous, Manshik."

After giving her right-hand man her last instructions regarding the shipments of this week, she signaled Jirou to take her baggage to the ship. She walked hand-in-hand with her son across the pier toward the anchored Wraith, her men's murmurs and smirks not lost on her. The only one who received her with a genuine smile was Mushi. "It's the little boss!" she exclaimed. The Wraith's helmswoman snatched Riku from Natsu's hand and lifted the little boy up, squeezing him with both arms against her chest. "Come! Let me take you on a tour of the legendary Wraith."

Mushi's easygoingness did lift Natsu's mood, but now was not the time for slacking. "The little boss must go to bed now." Natsu took Riku back from the hands of the tall helmswoman. "In a matter of minutes, I need this vessel in the heart of the sea."

"This vessel has been ready for half an hour, boss." Mushi winked. "Once you and the little boss hop on board, we will be good to go."

Natsu wished all her crew had her helmswoman's spirit. Very few barely knew any details about this job, but somehow, they all had a clue that it could be as reckless as stealing a Turtle, if not even more. *Every job is an easy one as long as you are not caught.* And about that in particular; well, she didn't have a good feeling. And yet she had brought her son with her.

Natsu never thought this day would come, but here she was, asking the superstitious helmswoman, "Any recent visions you'd like to share with me, Mushi?"

* * *

The wind was gentle near the cliff on which the famous Sun Castle was perched. Natsu had seen it once from a distance, but she had never gotten the chance to come this close to this great fortress. Did they really need to build it this big? She would find it ironic if the answer was yes. Because who might consider attacking a place crammed with hundreds of mages?

Standing at the bow of the ship, Natsu gestured with an open palm for Mushi to stop. "You sure this is the spot, Natsu?" she asked from behind the helm, looking where a wharf should exist. "Because all I see is rocks."

Natsu had had the same concern in her last conversation with the masked mage. "He said his people would handle this. Have some faith."

Anchored just below the edge of the rocky hill, the Wraith wobbled as the hissing sea waves played with it. Not the worst of nights in the sea—Natsu had survived much worse—not the best either. But the sea itself was not her main concern tonight. It was the ships patrolling it. *The damned coastguards.* All she asked was one more night without seeing any of them. One more night, and she would be out of the Koyan waters.

One more night would do. Just one.

The sailor manning the crow's nest—the spot that used to belong to Sogeki-hei—called out to Natsu, pointing to the flickering torchlight upward. "They are here," she muttered as she spied two robed figures. She was expecting more people, to be honest, but perhaps two were enough to handle the task of loading the cargo. *One is enough sometimes*, she thought. The memory of the three sunken Turtle Ships hadn't faded yet.

Save for her sleeping son, everybody aboard the Wraith stared in awe at the crates descending from the hilltop without ropes. No, the crates were not falling; they were *landing*. Slowly, smoothly, like a feather. It was true that Natsu and her men had watched more impressive magical tricks—more horrifying, she would rather say—but who could turn his eyes away from such a display?

Crates. Boxes. Barrels. They were landing on deck, all sealed, and Natsu's men were still gawking at them. "Wake up, wake up!" She clapped as she yelled at them. "The cargo hold will not fill itself. Move your sad arses!"

Her 'gentle' command was all her men needed to remember why they were here tonight. As they started carrying the cargo away from deck, Natsu listened carefully as she paced around them. According to her conversation with the mage's contact, she expected a few *clinking* containers. Perhaps the masked mage was keeping them to the end.

The cargo hold was already full, and still it was raining crates. Were they emptying Sun Castle or what? Whoever was in charge of this fort would surely be pissed off when they woke up in the morning. *I'm meddling in dangerous people's affairs. This had better be worth it.*

The clinking boxes arrived at last, and indeed, they were the last of the cargo to land on deck. "No, not here," she commanded the men stacking the boxes next to the crates on deck. "Put them in the cargo hold."

"There is no room in the hold, boss," one of her men told her what she already knew.

"Then make room for it."

The boxes containing her reward were not the last items dropping from the hill. A cloaked woman landed on deck, and then she stretched out her hands upward, as if helping her robed fellow descend smoothly. "Tell them to pull the anchor up," demanded the lady wearing the red cloak, without even introducing herself. "We are good to go."

Natsu didn't like the tone of arrogance in the lady's voice. It took her a lot of self-composure to hold herself from reciprocating rudeness. *And a lot of golden dragons, of course. Fifty thousand, to be precise.* The beefy man accompanying the impudent lady looked younger and gentler. "As you might have been told, my colleague and I will be taking turns to boost your engine." He grinned at Natsu. "Would you please show me the—?"

"Boat!" yelled the man perched on the crow's nest. Seriously, Natsu wished that the eyes of that fool were playing tricks on him, but unfortunately, they were not.

The two cloaked mages clenched their fingers as they went to the right side of the Wraith to face the incoming boat. First of all, it wasn't a Turtle Ship, and that was a huge relief. Secondly, the boat was too small to pose a threat. Even the fishing boat of Natsu's late father was bigger than this one, but the two mages were not leaving anything to chance, it seemed. *Chance? The men on that boat must be the unluckiest people on Earth to sail here at this very moment.*

But this boat was not just passing by, or even keeping its distance. It was actually approaching the Wraith, a flapping white banner fixed on its bow. "Stand down," Natsu demanded. The beefy mage glanced over his shoulder at her, but he didn't protest. The cloaked lady obeyed as well, but it seemed that she couldn't do that without giving Natsu a derisive stare. *Yes, you whore. You might be a mage, but this is my ship. Everybody on board listens to me.*

Alerted, Natsu's men grabbed their weapons as the boat came closer. "Easy, everybody." She waved to them when she caught a glimpse of a familiar face. A face she hadn't expected to see here. "Seems that Pantu has changed his mind. Drop him a ladder."

Her former deputy stopped his boat side by side with the Wraith. Truth be told, Natsu was glad to see him ascend the ladder and rejoin her on deck, like the good old days. They started their reunion with a brief moment of awkward silence, though. And then, she began, "I thought I would never see you again." She tilted her head. "That you would go somewhere far away from me."

"I'm not here to beg for my return," he said flatly. "But for the sake of our old friendship, I've come to warn you."

Not the reunion she was expecting. "Warn me? About what?"

Pantu looked around, and at once, Natsu realized that everybody was listening to their conversation. She walked him to her cabin, and without an invitation, Mushi and the

233

two mages followed them. Curious to hear Pantu's *warning*, Natsu didn't bother dismissing them.

"You must abort this job," Pantu said to Natsu. "The Koyan Navy is going to ambush you in the heart of the sea."

While everybody in the room was processing the news, the cloaked lady asked dubiously, "How do you know that?"

Because he is the Master of Spies, Natsu almost said. "Pantu is a resourceful man." She exchanged a quick look with her former deputy. "And more importantly, a trustworthy friend. He wouldn't come to me with such news unless he was certain of it."

"It's over," Pantu stated, addressing everybody in the cabin. "Somehow, your plan has been revealed. And there is a rumor that the Archmage, the mastermind of this scheme, has been chased, but managed to escape."

The Archmage himself was involved? How could he be part of a rebellion against the regime? He *was* the regime.

Wait. Isn't that the same Archmage whom Akira claimed was his uncle?

Seriously, Natsu had graver matters to worry about than Akira's family issues. The whole situation was a big mess, and she was already part of it. If the mastermind of this operation was discovered, then everybody else involved would be. And they would be *punished*. Severely. All of them.

Now she believed that her reward was not exaggerated at all.

"If the coastguards know already, why don't they attack us here instead of waiting until we are in the middle of the sea?" the lady asked.

"I guess they would if they knew you were only two," Pantu smiled wryly. "But since they are afraid that they might be facing an army of mages, they will strike you as far away as possible from the shore to ensure that none of you survives."

Only these two? The way the masked mage had been referring to 'his people' who would join him in Gorania gave the impression that he had an army behind him indeed.

This was bad. Much worse than she had thought.

Natsu studied both mages. "Can any of you summon the sea demon?"

The lady arched an eyebrow. "What is this question about?"

With little heed to the query of his 'lovely' companion, the beefy mage shook his head.

"Hells and demons," Natsu muttered. "It was your very own Archmage whom I had been meeting with before."

The lady glared at her beefy companion, as if blaming him for giving away their master.

"Don't you realize that it doesn't matter if I know who your master is?" Natsu snapped at the stern lady. "Don't you realize that we *might* be in real danger if we don't think and act fast?"

"The only action you must consider now is sailing east to Hokydo," Pantu provided firmly. "You, your crew, and of course, the Wraith must hide there for a while."

The beefy mage shrugged. "What about us?"

"You both can handle yourselves," Pantu answered nonchalantly. "Open a portal, or whatever you call it, and go wherever you want."

"Not without our supplies." The lady peered at Pantu, and then she glanced at Natsu. "That's why we have been looking for a ship in the first place."

"Then, you are choosing between killing yourself and losing all your equipment."

"Maybe they don't have to."

After a long silence, Mushi spoke at last, and now all eyes were on her. She had better have a meaningful input to add, and not just be voicing her superstitious thoughts.

Mushi continued, "If it doesn't matter which part of Gorania you should disembark at, I suggest we head east, not west." She stared at Natsu, a strange smile on her face. "We sail to Bermania instead of Murase."

A superstitious thought would make more sense than this fatuous suggestion. Any child with a map would simply notice that a direct voyage to Bermania was impossible. More importantly, Bermania was on the *western* side of Gorania. How could they reach it by going *east*?

I shouldn't have let her join this meeting.

"I thought Botan told you, no?" Mushi was still looking at Natsu, as if Natsu was supposed to know what her delirious helmswoman was raving about. "Hells and demons! I have always known him as a secretive man, but I never expected he would hide that from you."

Now Mushi was getting on Natsu's nerves, for real. "Hide what?"

Instead of giving an answer, Mushi scanned the cabin before she grabbed a blank piece of paper and a quill. "I must show you because it could be hard to imagine." Placing the paper on a small table, she drew a crude map of Koya and the Goranian continent, then showed it to her *patient* audience. She pointed at the island on the right edge of the paper. "This is Koya." She shifted her finger toward the westmost lands on her rudimentary map. "This is Bermania." She gave them all a quick look, like a teacher making sure that all his pupils were paying attention. "As you see here, the only way to reach Bermania is to disembark anywhere at the eastern Goranian coast, then travel west through the mainland of the continent." She paused for effect before she smiled. "But that's not true. Because the world in reality doesn't *exactly* look like this flat piece of paper." To everybody's astonishment, she folded the paper and held it like a cylinder. "It's *round.*"

24. AKIRA

So, this was the end; a tiny room in a clamorous tavern.

Of all people, Akira shouldn't complain. More than once in his previous life, this was a place he wished to spend a few hours in. To take a little break from the dull routine of Sun Castle. It was a shame he had had to stick to that routine for years—years he had wasted pursuing a mirage.

Pursuing nothing.

Crying over spilled milk would not help him. Nothing would bring those lost years back. Nothing would bring Kim back. Nothing would change the fact that to the folks of Sun Castle he was a traitor, to his mother a disappointment, to his uncle a curse. A man with no place in this world; that was what Akira had become now. An outcast. Even in this tavern; once the tavern keeper learned that Akira was expelled from Sun Castle, she would kick him out of her place unless he paid for his room and his meals.

And the ale. The coin he owed the tavern keeper for the ale alone was worth a one-week stay here.

Knocks sounded on the door of his hole of a room. *Has someone told her already?* It was the first thought that crossed his mind. *Let's hope she listens to reason.* Violence was not an option he wanted to resort to; he had created enough messes already.

Akira opened the door a crack, and to his surprise, it was the teenage food server. "You are wanted downstairs, Akira Sen," the slender boy announced.

"Who wants me, boy? Your master?"

"Not her." The boy shook his small head. "It's some important customer who knows for certain that you are here."

The last trace of crapulence from last night was gone now. "What kind of important?"

"The kind that we are not used to seeing in our place. The kind who dons a purple cloak and comes in the company of guards."

Hells and demons! The little bastard should have started his announcement with *'A Purple Cloak asks for your presence.'* "His guards; do they wear the same purple color?"

The boy lifted his finger to his lip thoughtfully. "I guess two of them do. The majority wear the regular silver armor."

Only one man fitted this description. *Should I meet him or flee?* he wondered, glancing at the small window behind him. "Tell him I need a minute to change my outfit."

"He emphasized that I'm not to return to him without you."

That irksome bastard. But after a second thought, Akira started to convince himself that there was nothing to worry about. If that 'important' mage wanted him arrested, he would have sent a squad of Purple Cloaks to his door, not this clueless boy.

Akira followed the boy downstairs, and the first thing he noted was this unusual peace in the dining hall. It wasn't surprising, though, especially after knowing who Akira's eminent visitor was. Sitting at the table in the center was Wei Sen, two Purple Cloaks on their feet flanking him, two guards posted at the closed door of the tavern to prevent anybody from entering. It would be understandable if the Commander of the Imperial Guard persuaded the tavern keeper to evacuate the hall for a while. Even she was not standing in her usual spot behind the counter.

Upon seeing Akira coming, Wei thanked the little boy before he dismissed him to join his employer outside the tavern. "Have a seat, Akira." It was more of a command than an invitation from the Commander of the Imperial Guard.

Exchanging a quick look with the two Purple Cloaks guarding Wei, Akira dragged a chair and sat opposite him, stealing a glance at the canvas bag on their table. *What surprises do you have for me, Wei?* "I won't ask you how you found me. I just want to know why."

Wei furrowed his brow. "Why don't you want to be found? You are a hero, young man. You stood up to the treacherous Archmage, who is also your uncle, on your own. If that's not a heroic act, then I wonder what it is."

Akira had better pick his words about his encounter against the *treacherous* Archmage. Nobody knew that Akira was alive today because of Kungwan himself and his daughter who had saved him more than once. Nobody knew that it was Kungwan who denied Akira's wish to be part of his...rebellion.

That was why Wei had not executed him. Not yet.

"What about the demon?" Akira asked. "Still trapped, I hope?"

Wei's judging eyes were fixed on Akira. "It wasn't you who summoned it, right?"

"I'm not a summoner," Akira denied at once, not sure if that might change Wei's opinion of Akira's *heroism*. "It was my cousin Kim." Her name had never been heavier on his tongue than it was now. "She summoned it to defeat me before I might finish her father off."

"Then who cast the runes?" Wei leered at him, as if he was accused of something.

"The demon was out of control, so Kungwan confined it." Akira inhaled deeply, wearing his best impassive face. "But he was too late. The demon had already killed his daughter when he was done with the runes."

"So, it was you and him." Wei's nonchalance did vex Akira. *How dare he? He himself knew what it means to lose a child.* But maybe that was the reason. If Wei still blamed the Archmage for Lan's death, then probably, he was gloating over Kungwan's loss. "How did that end?"

Resisting the urge to spit in Wei's face was a task requiring a tremendous effort. "My potion lost its effect, so I wasn't able to stop Kungwan from walking away."

"So, after fighting him, he just let you live?"

Akira was sick of Wei's consecutive subtle accusations, and he made that feeling obvious on his face. "Perhaps he saw that I was not worth it."

"Strange." Wei chewed on his lip. "But anyway, this is not what you are going to tell His Radiance."

Akira jerked his head backward. "The Emperor?"

"After briefing him about the recent events, he demanded to meet you in person." Wei paused, as if observing Akira's reaction to this 'great' news. "I guess he wants to hear your account in your own words," he opened the canvas bag and let the item inside it slide across the table, "while wearing this."

A storm of clashing feelings overwhelmed his heart as he gaped at the red cloak before him. *His* red cloak. The ultimate prize he had been so desperate to lay hands on. The damned cloak he hated the most. He took the liberty of feeling the silky texture, which was supposed to have the same texture of his lame pink mantle, but something about this one felt different. Felt special. *It must be special. Befitting the Light's own soldiers in his holy…*

Slow down, Akira, he told himself, realizing that he had been carried away a little bit. Had he just forgotten the truth he had learned a few days ago while fighting that demon? Hadn't he realized how blinded he *and* his mother had been because of their obsession with this bloody cloak?

"Beautiful," Wei allowed himself a lopsided smile of satisfaction, "isn't it?"

This beautiful piece of silk was the root of Akira's misery. "Am I to return it after the meeting?"

Wei chuckled. "It's all yours." His smile faded as he added, "But first, we must rehearse your account before you stand before the Emperor."

Akira didn't like the sound of this. "Is there something in particular you don't want the Emperor to hear?"

Wei's lopsided smile was back, as if appreciating Akira's understanding. "You see, Akira; the Emperor is the Light's shadow on this Earth, a holy man burdened by the glorious mission of leading us through the dark. Such a holy being does not like to be bothered by too many details. He is more into the big picture, leaving the details for our humble selves to take care of."

Wei was either too eloquent or too nonsensical. "Meaning?" Akira tilted his head.

"You are a hero. Your uncle is a traitor. That's all His Radiance must hear, in case he allowed you to talk, of course." When Akira squinted at him in confusion, Wei continued, "Don't give me that look; His Radiance might just summon you to thank you for your heroic endeavor. But in case he grants you the chance to talk, remember; stick to the main events that serve the story of your heroism. How you survived, how Kungwan confined the demon, how his daughter died; all of this is irrelevant." Wei leaned back in his seat. "Have I made myself clear?"

Akira found himself balling his fists beneath the table. *You bastard! Kim's death is not irrelevant, you bastard!* "It's all clear to me, Commander," Akira hissed curtly. "This is all about you and Hanu Sen covering up your failure in stopping my uncle."

Akira might have gone a bit too far, but he would do it again if he had the chance. It was the least he could say to this sad being.

Wei's reaction was not what Akira expected, though. "How do you define failure, boy?" The commander smirked. "Because I don't think that Kungwan himself would consider the half-dozen mages who followed him to Gorania a success."

Only six? For a legend like Kungwan, the number was too low indeed. "What about the supplies, Commander? You caught the ship, right?"

Wei took a breath, obviously exerting some effort to appear reserved. "It is just a matter of time."

"What?" Akira didn't bother concealing his gloating smile. "You haven't caught it yet?"

"Son, we have an armada *and* a sea demon that cover the entire Koyan Sea," Wei forced the words through gritted teeth. "There is no way for them to make it to Gorania without us spotting them."

You know nothing about the Wraith, Commander. Not that Akira complained, but the Emperor's fools were too cautious to act upon Akira's first warning. Another reason for Akira to celebrate Wei and Hanu's failure.

"Just a hypothetical question." Knowing how dangerous the likes of Wei could be, Akira didn't wish to deprive himself of the joy of teasing this rascal. "What will happen if Kungwan's ship sneaks past your armada *and* your sea demon?"

"You had better wish this doesn't happen, young man." Wei sounded menacing as he leaned forward, his jaws clenched. "Because regardless of what you might say in your defense, it will always be on you." He pointed his finger accusingly at Akira. "*You;* the one who misguided us with his false information."

You can't hear such a threat from the Commander of the Imperial Guard and take it lightly. "You will blame me for *your* slow reaction?"

Wei slammed his palm across the table. "Talk to me in a way I don't like, and I will make sure you are tortured before being executed for all the crimes you committed *and* even those you didn't."

Akira should have known better than to provoke a man so close to the Emperor. *I must get out of here.* And by here, Akira was considering places beyond this tavern.

"I would never dare to offend you, Commander." Hopefully, it wasn't too late for Akira to play nice. "When is the meeting with His Radiance?"

Akira's sudden apologetic tone seemed to please the commander. "Tomorrow, after we have captured Kungwan's ship. A good moment to stand before the Emperor, if you ask me." Wei curled his lip in disdain, as if saying, '*You don't deserve the honor, boy.*' "Until then, you must clear your head and think of every word you are going to say to His Radiance."

"In case he allows me to talk, of course." Akira echoed Wei's statement, and surprisingly, the commander's grim expression relaxed a little upon hearing this.

Wei rose to his feet, staring judgingly at Akira. "Regardless of your upcoming meeting with the Emperor; you did the unthinkable when you decided to face someone like Kungwan on your own." The commander leaned toward Akira as he added, "You can be the next champion of Sun Castle. Don't let your foolishness take that from you."

The next champion of Sun Castle, the words echoed in Akira's mind, even after Wei and his men left the tavern. *I can be the next Minjun.* The tavern keeper and her customers were back, and Akira was still sitting at his table, stuck in his thoughts, his hollow eyes fixed on the red, silky prize.

Maybe there was still a place for him in this world.

* * *

Akira would be surprised if Wei hadn't assigned one of his men to tail him. *Those honeyed words about the next hero wouldn't fool a child. Wei and Hanu would never trust the likes of me.* Until further notice, they would keep him under their watch, counting every breath he took if they must. What should he do to win their trust? He had no idea, and he was not even trying to figure it out. All that preoccupied his mind right now was the visit he felt compelled to pay today.

Now clad in his Red Cloak, Akira didn't have to pay the coachman who had taken him to his destination—not to mention how grateful the coachman must have felt for serving one of the Light's holy soldiers. After the carriage had left, Akira stood in front of the door of the house he hadn't thought he might voluntarily return to anytime soon. For a second, he felt that coming here wasn't worth it because simply, it wouldn't change anything.

Would it?

Akira drew in a deep breath before he knocked on the door. Deep inside, he hoped that his mother wouldn't answer, not because he was worried about her endless ridiculing. *No, not this time.* He just didn't like the sight of her face. The face that reminded him of a lifetime of shame. Of worthlessness.

Of delusions.

The door was opened. First, there was that blank expression on her face, as if she was unable to process the picture her eyes had just captured. Two seconds later, the eyes widened, the eyebrows rising, the forehead wrinkled. Now she knew what she was looking at. The thing she surely had trouble with was: how?

Akira smiled crookedly. "You are not letting me in or what?"

Chiaki took him off guard when she lunged toward him—a move he didn't expect from a lady her age—and…hugged him? Yes, this was a hug indeed. It felt strange for someone whose last hug had been ten years ago. And it was not from this lady even.

His mother held his hand as she walked him inside, and Akira didn't protest. Once the door was closed, she began,

"So, the rumor from Sun Castle is true." She didn't utter a word for a moment as she got busy contemplating her son, a rare smile plastered on her face. Akira didn't remember he had seen that joy in her eyes before, not since his father's shameful execution. *No, not just joy.* It took Akira a moment to realize that there was something else in her beaming eyes. *Pride.*

"What rumors came from there?"

"Your uncle's treachery." Her hatred for Kungwan was no secret to Akira. "Yesterday, I found everybody in the school talking about the letters he left." She pressed her lips together, and a few seconds later, he realized she was trying to stop the tears from welling up in her eyes, but to no avail. Gently, she laid one hand on his cheek. "And the fearless lad who made a stand against him."

Akira couldn't deny the satisfaction he was feeling right now. Fame and respect had never been more than two alien words to him, but that was something from the past, it seemed. Wei was not messing with him; Akira was already the new champion of Sun Castle.

Elated, and also curious, he asked his mother, "Do you have any idea what those letters were about?"

"Lies of a demented old man. One of my fellow teachers has a daughter in Sun Castle, so she got a copy. Can you believe the desperate bastard? He wrote a letter to every single mage in Sun Castle." She scoffed when she added, "The audacity! The coward doesn't only justify his treachery with mere delusions; he begs us not to fight him."

Let me guess? You never read the letter, Chiaki. Because I believe the demented old man is trying to say that he has left Koya to prevent a war, not to start one. A war that will pave the way for the invincible demons to take over our world after annihilating all of us; Koyans and Goranians alike.

"You think anybody would fall for his lies?" Akira feigned a smile. "I heard he had some followers."

Chiaki waved dismissively. "You mean those fourteen mages? Let them all burn in hell. We don't want them. They will regret it when the next Archmage leads us in the Third Crossing and vanquishes them with the Goranian scum they belong to."

Fourteen? Wei was talking this morning about six 'traitors.' Either Wei lied (How surprising!), or the traitors were growing in numbers by the hour.

"If all Koyans are as faithful as you are, Mother, then make no mistake," Akira took off his red cloak and tossed it toward the nearest chair, "we are all doomed."

Akira headed to the door, leaving his speechless mother behind him. His last statement must have taken her by surprise.

"Akira!" His mother picked up the cloak and strode after him. "What is the meaning of this?"

"You have always wanted that cloak. It's all yours." Akira took a vial of his experimental potion out of his pocket and inspected it. It was almost but not *completely* empty, and that was all he needed. Two drops would do to help him wield an invisibility shield for a minute. And he could make good use of this minute to lose whoever was keeping an eye on him. "You can take it and show it to the folks in your school to avenge your hurt pride."

This did not amuse his mother, and he knew that. "Is that a stupid joke? You can't leave your cloak here and go outside just like that."

"I don't think I will need it where I am headed." Akira was now invisible as he summoned the shield. "Took me long enough to realize that you need the red cloak more than I do."

25. NATSU

To all Koyans, this was the edge of the world. To her late husband, it was just a passage to the other edge of the world.

The last time Natsu saw land was ten weeks ago, when they had briefly stopped by Hokydo to triple their food supplies before setting out for the longest voyage a man would ever make.

The engines never stopped thanks to Jihoon and Tashihara, the two mages who kept taking turns. But the fire they produced to feed the engine seemed to be consuming their bodies. Starting from the third week of the voyage, their 'sessions' made them dizzy, and that urged Natsu to give each one of them an extra snack that included an apple, two eggs, and three spoons of honey. According to the mages' themselves, that snack was enough to replenish their anerjy. In return, Natsu had to reduce the food and water rations of the rest of her crew, Natsu herself included, to the bare minimum. Though Mushi didn't stop promising her that the voyage would be over soon, Natsu didn't wish to leave anything to chance. "I need to hear something a bit more specific than *soon*," Natsu told Mushi, but the helmswoman of the Wraith never gave her a better answer.

The seventy-seventh day brought the answer Natsu and everybody else had been waiting for. From the crow's nest, came the call that urged all men and women on deck to gaze in anticipation eastward, where the sun had risen a couple of hours ago. "Land!"

One word was enough to change the mood on deck. The crew cheered and roared in excitement upon spotting the distant coast. A sailor started singing, the rest dancing around him in a big circle. Mushi raised her hands in the air, but probably, she was just muttering prayers of gratitude to the Light. Even Riku, who was too young to totally understand the situation, was giggling at the dancing crew.

The clamor must have awakened Tashihara, who was taking a nap during Jihoon's turn, and for the first time, Natsu caught a glimpse of a smile on the face of the stern mage.

"Are we sure this is the western Goranian coast?" asked Tashihara.

"Let's hope so." Natsu glanced at Mushi. "She is the one who made this voyage before."

"Not *this* voyage." Mushi lifted a finger. "I only went to the port of Inabol in Byzonta with Botan." She nodded her chin pointedly toward the coast on the horizon. "This will be my first time to visit Paril, the capital of the Bermanian Kingdom."

Tashihara's rare smile faded as she asked dubiously, "Why are we headed to a venue you never went to before?"

"Because it is the nearest Goranian port to us. We have no reason to risk a longer voyage to Byzonta."

"What could be the reason to take that risk, may I ask?" Natsu scoffed.

"Coin, boss." Mushi grinned. "Byzonts never had a problem trading with us, even before the Inabol Treaty."

If the news Natsu heard about that treaty was true, then disembarking at Paril shouldn't be a problem. There was no reason for the Bermanians to be hostile, right?

To reach the port of Paril, the Wraith would have to sail through a gulf defended by a dozen guard towers on both flanks. "Raise a white banner. Quickly," Natsu urged the nearest man to her, before any of the Bermanian archers manning the towers might decide that the Wraith was a threat. One fire arrow could be the spark of a deadly fire shower. Shame if her impossible voyage ended a couple of miles away from her destination.

So far, the Bermanians didn't show any hostile reaction toward the ship that had just docked at their port. A squad of armored footmen was waiting for them at the piers, but none of them interfered with Natsu and her crew as they disembarked. Keeping her son behind her, Natsu studied the Bermanian soldiers standing in her way. "You speak Goranian?" she asked the two mages standing behind her, but to her surprise, they shook their heads. *Very well, honorable mages. Let a simple man from Hokydo handle this.* "Pantu," she called to the most fluent Goranian speaker here, nodding her chin toward the Bermanian soldiers. "We are going to need your services in translation."

"No, you won't," came a voice from behind the Bermanians, who made way for a black-bearded Koyan mage donning the red cloak. Before Natsu could ask who this Koyan was, Jihoon and Tashihara hurried to him excitedly, calling him by the name Kyong. They showered him with questions about how and *why* he had come here,

251

but he gestured for them to slow down. "We will have all the time to talk soon." He told his peers, and then he smiled at Natsu as he approached her. "You must be Natsu."

Natsu never saw this face nor heard this voice. "Have we met?"

"No." Kyong grinned. "But you met our Archmage, Kungwan Sen. He told me you were worth a thousand men. He had no doubt you would make it here safely."

The Archmage with the mask. "How did he know I would make it *here*? We are hundreds of miles away from the original destination we agreed upon."

Kyong's smile widened. "Your agreement won't matter if a seer says otherwise. The seers are always right, Natsu."

Natsu never had much faith in seers, but this voyage between the two edges of the world had already shaken one or two of her core beliefs.

The brawny Bermanian soldier who seemed in charge leaned toward Kyong, and the two talked briefly in Goranian. "Alright," Kyong said to Natsu. "This is Blade, Captain of King Masolon's Royal Guard. His men will escort you and your men to your lodgings. You surely need some rest."

A lot of rest. A warm meal. And a bath. "What about you?" she asked Kyong, glancing at Jihoon and Tashihara who flanked him.

"We have a lot to discuss with the Bermanian court," Kyong said. "The start of a new era."

* * *

"When will we go back home, Mom?"

Natsu wasn't sure if she was ready to have this conversation with a five-year-old child. How could she explain to him that there was nothing left for them back home? That *home* was no longer a safe place?

"Don't you like it here? Look." Natsu opened the window of their new room, pointing to the colossal towers of the royal palace in the distance. "Have you ever seen anything like this before?"

Her son didn't seem impressed as he gazed at the magnificent building. He looked back at her. "I want to go home."

Natsu heaved a deep sigh before she took Riku into her arms and laid a kiss on his forehead. "This is our home now, Riku. You will love it." And she would have to love it too. Her first encounter with Bermanian food was not the most pleasant experience to start her stay in her new home with. The tavern they were staying at was serving charcoaled meat and cooked vegetables today, and she and her son had barely touched their meals. The only food they were able to eat was the apples, and fortunately the Bermanians did not cook them.

There were knocks on her door. *Probably, it's Pantu, and he's just picked the right moment to show up.* Natsu was thinking of sending him to fetch her and her son some raw fish.

Riku opened the door, but it was neither Pantu nor any of her men. "May I come in, Natsu?" the bald Koyan stranger donning the red cloak asked flatly.

"Kungwan Sen?" Natsu recognized the voice of the mage who finally came to her without his mask. The great Archmage of Koya. *The former Archmage.*

"Can we talk here?" Kungwan scanned the room quickly. As a venue, it was too underwhelming for such a meeting, but a wooden chair and a bed would do.

"If you have something to discuss in private, then I don't have a better place in mind at the moment." Natsu gave him an inviting gesture.

"I will be brief." Kungwan stepped inside and closed the door behind him. Instinctively, Riku backed to his mother's legs, as if seeking safety in her proximity. Or was he trying to shield her from that stranger?

"First of all," Kungwan began, still standing, "I've come here myself to say thank you. My folks and I will forever be in your debt."

Natsu shrugged, holding her son's shoulders. "It was a business deal after all. You kept your end, and I kept mine."

Kungwan cast her a pale smile that was short-lived. "It was way more than that, Natsu. That cargo you bravely transported across the Endless Sea might help us prevent the extinction of our kind. You and your men deserve to be remembered in history for your heroic mission."

Truth be told, Natsu didn't care that much about the myths of the Last Day. All that concerned her was her insanely huge payment that would secure her and her son for the rest of their lives.

"My men and I appreciate your respect." Natsu inclined her head toward him.

"Having said that, I'm afraid I bear some news that you might not like." Kungwan pressed his lips together. "It's not the end of the world, though. And that's why I have insisted on informing you myself to discuss together how we can figure this out."

Natsu should have sensed the bad news earlier. "What is it, Kungwan Sen?" she asked, tightening her embrace around her son absent-mindedly.

"Listen. Queen Rona does appreciate what you did." Kungwan smacked his lips then sighed. "But I don't think she is ready to accommodate too many Koyans in her kingdom. Not for the time being, to say the least."

Natsu was more confused than irked. "*Queen* Rona? I thought this kingdom was ruled by some king."

Kungwan winced. "I know it's different from what we are used to in our country, but the queen here is as powerful as the king. Anyway, she has given you three days to arrange for your departure."

"What is the meaning of this?" Her dream of a peaceful life had suddenly turned into a nightmare.

"I'm not saying this is right, Natsu, but until only a few months ago, Koyans were never allowed to set foot on any Goranian soil. The people here need time to get used to seeing us living among them."

Something did not add up. How were the Koyans supposed to help a faction that did not tolerate their co-existence, to begin with?

No, this is not only about us being Koyans, she thought. "You and your folks from Sun Castle," she started. "You are not included in that three-day time limit."

Clenching his jaw, Kungwan said, "They need us, Natsu. Raising an army of mages in Gorania is a priority now."

"Right." Natsu smirked. "But raising an army of smugglers? I guess that will be frowned upon."

Kungwan's silence confirmed Natsu's suspicions.

"I understand your frustration," he said apologetically. "But trust me, that will change over time. Mages have been flocking to Gorania since I came here. Some have brought their families even. It won't be long before we become part of the Goranian community."

"And what am I supposed to do until then?" she snapped. "Go back to Koya and surrender myself to the coastguards?"

It wasn't Kungwan's fault, she knew, and yet he didn't react to her fury. All the Archmage did was take a deep breath and say, "The people of Byzonta are more hospitable, I hear. I'd go there if I were you."

That coincided with Mushi's brief account of the Byzonts. *I need to talk to her and Pantu right now.* "Best of luck in your war, Kungwan Sen," Natsu curtly said, to conclude this disastrous meeting.

"Believe me; my priority is to prevent it." Kungwan opened the door, and before stepping outside, he added, "But if it happens, it will be your war too."

* * *

While Jirou was keeping an eye on Riku in the tavern, Natsu took Pantu and Mushi for a walk in the streets to breathe some fresh air. The instant they stepped outside the tavern, she became aware of the stares of every passerby. Some were staring in curiosity, others in disapproval and even disgust, but so far, no Bermanian actually harassed them.

To make use of her time, Natsu headed to the marketplace, hoping she might find some raw fish for herself and her starving son. On their way, she recounted her conversation with Kungwan to them and waited for their reaction. After a moment of awkward silence, she halted and faced them both. "What is it? You don't think we can settle in Byzonta?"

Both Mushi and Pantu exchanged a look. "Byzonta is fine." The helmswoman turned to Natsu. "But who said anything about settling in the first place?"

Only now did Natsu realize that she had never discussed the subject openly with them. "I thought it was the logical

256

consequence for helping those mages. In the eyes of our people, we are traitors now."

Pantu shrugged. "Traitors, thieves; we have always been outlaws. What has changed now?"

Natsu found herself chuckling. *We are outlaws here. We are outlaws there.* But no, there could be a chance for her and her son to start a new life in Byzonta. "You know what has changed, Pantu? We don't have to be on the run until we die. With the commission we have earned from this job, we can all live like kings here."

Giving her a lopsided smile, Pantu swept an arm toward the royal palace, whose towers were visible from any corner of the city. "We don't need this to live like kings, Natsu. All we need is a boat."

Mushi nodded in approval. "The Wraith is our throne, the sea our kingdom."

Maybe Natsu shouldn't have assumed that her entire crew would follow her in her retirement plan. Not everybody sought peace; she should know better. Some would never feel alive unless life kept them on their toes. Natsu herself had been this person one day, but that person was gone.

For good, may I ask?

"Very well." Natsu put her hands on her waist. "Gather the crew in the dining hall tonight. We shall inform everybody of their share of the prize, and then we will let them decide."

"Sounds fair." Pantu paused thoughtfully. "But if you are going to settle in Byzonta, what shall happen to the Wraith?"

The Wraith was more than a ship to Natsu. It was the child of her late husband. A token of the most glorious and most humbling days of her life. It wasn't fair to keep this masterpiece idle, though. "Waive your share of coin to me, and she is yours."

Pantu's eyes widened, his jaw dropped. "I can never say no to this, but are you sure this is what you want, Natsu? I can't picture you spending the rest of your life away from deck."

Of course, it wasn't the life she wanted, but it was the life her son *needed*. "I believe I have a role to play for the Koyan community that Kungwan wants to establish in this part of the world." Natsu folded her arms across her chest, grinning at Pantu, the new captain of the Wraith, and Mushi, who was still digesting the fact that he had just become her new boss. "This continent is already in dire need of a tavern that serves Koyan food."

EPILOGUE

Seventeen years later,

Why would anybody knock on the door of an abandoned house in these dark times? If it was someone in desperate need of shelter, they should pound the door harder. A thief would be quieter, though. *This is the knock of someone who knows that this house is not abandoned.*

"*Open, Akira. I know you are in there.*"

Alright then. That was not someone who *only* knew that the house was not abandoned. The voice didn't sound familiar, though. "Who is it?"

"*I'm sure you heard once about Wang the Seer.*"

Wang the Seer? There had been no word about him since the Inabol Treaty. Some believed he was dead.

Akira opened the door a crack, dubiously studying his uninvited visitor. A sweaty, bald Koyan wearing a ragged tunic. He could be a seer. He could be a bandit. He could be anybody. "How do I know you are who you claim to be?"

The rugged visitor smiled wryly. "Isn't it enough that I found you?"

Akira had been living in these Goranian wastelands for years. The only people he met were either travelers who needed his help or raiders who deserved his deadly jumuns. "What do you want from me, Wang Sen? You have a reputation of being associated with bad news."

"I do what I must," Wang said. "About time you did the same. Your people need you."

Seventeen years had passed, and yet the nightmares never stopped. The sight of the demon smashing his cousin had been haunting his sleep and sometimes his waking hours too. "If you are really a seer, you will know that I'm not the person my people would welcome."

"A lot has happened while you were rotting in your solitude." Wang gave him a dismissive gesture. "Now gather your things and ready your horse. You have a long ride ahead of you. Let's hope you are not late already."

Want to know what happens next?

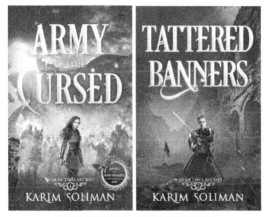

Bonus Content

Gorania

The continent named after Emperor Goran the Great used to be the Koyans' homeland until their crushing defeat against the barbarian hordes living beyond the Great Desert. Since that glorious war, which is also known as the Second Crossing, the continent has belonged to its new kings who founded the first five realms of Gorania, marking the birth of *Age of the Five Kings*. Later the Goranian realms became six after Byzonta fought for its independence from Bermania.

As the early Goranian ancestors were not fond of writing their history, it is not known if Goran was born decades or centuries after the Age of the Five Kings, but it is recorded that he was the one who united the Goranian factions under his rule. The unity didn't last for more than six decades, but it left one major outcome: the Common Goranian Tongue.

The Goranian factions were back to their clashes after the fall of the short-lived Goranian Empire. That said, the Goranians have been sticking to one rule despite their differences: no Koyans are allowed to live on Goranian soil. Only Mankola and sometimes Rusakia allow naval trade with Koya, but the Koyan merchants are never allowed to go past any Goranian port.

Don't miss

ARMY OF THE CURSED

BOOK ONE OF
WAR OF THE LAST DAY

KARIM SOLIMAN

KARIM SOLIMAN

PROLOGUE

Something was wrong with his mare.

Yukan pressed his thighs on Thunder, urging her to keep up with his mounted clansmen headed to Si'oli. The mare was not in a responsive mood, though. With every attempt to hurry her, Thunder did the opposite until she eventually halted. Why did she resist him today? Did she share his worries about their cursed destination?

"What is it, Yukan?" Dogo stopped his brown stallion next to Thunder. Though he was a decade older than Yukan, the muscular fiftyish man's beard had fewer strands of white hair.

Yukan breathed in slowly as he petted Thunder. "She could just be thirsty."

Dogo pinched Thunder's neck and released her, but the mare's skin took a while to retract. "*Just* thirsty, you say?" Lithely, he swung down off his stallion and felt Thunder's pulse below her jawbones. "She is dying, Yukan. When was the last time you gave her water?"

"She drank just before we moved."

"By Si'oli, Yukan!" Dogo grabbed one of the six waterskins strapped to Thunder, three on each side. "When were you intending to use these? You could have wetted her parched throat, to say the least."

Yukan was about to stop Dogo from wasting one precious waterskin, but in the end, he took pity on his poor mare. "I thought we should use our water wisely. The sun is killing us, and we haven't even made it to Si'oli yet." Which would surely be much hotter than here. Only the Light knew how hellish that cursed desert could be.

After Thunder drained half of the waterskin, Dogo rubbed her neck and pulled the waterskin away. "Skeptical, like you have always been." He strapped the waterskin back to Thunder again. "Weren't you listening to the Mages?"

Yukan had been, like the rest of the hundred thousand horsemen riding to Si'oli. By order of the damned Mages, every able man and youth from all the clans of Ogono was headed to the cursed desert, hoping that would bring the Light's mercy on the poor women and children trapped in their hunger-stricken homes. The Doom had reduced their villages into scorched lands, as a fair punishment from the Light for all those past years of bloodshed and oath-breaking. While it could be true that Yukan's clan, the Korigaidis, should be the one to blame—for starting that endless cycle of blood and betrayal—no clan was excepted from the wrath of the Light. Everybody in Ogono—men, women, children, elders, even the cattle and the horses— were paying for it. When the Mages commanded them to shed their blood in the promised lands of Gorania to earn their salvation, no one dared to question their order. Even if that order implied braving the cursed desert haunted by the demons.

"We are the Sacred Army, Yukan," Dogo went on. Probably he thought that Yukan had missed something from the Mages' speech before their *glorious* march. "Protected by the word of the Light, none of us shall suffer in Si'oli."

"I believe they were talking about the Light's protection from demons. They said nothing about thirst."

Dogo stared at him, and then he laughed. "We had better move, old man." He nodded his chin toward the vast horde sprawling across the desert valley behind them. "Unless you want to join the lesser clans at the back."

They were still on their way to start their *sacred* war, and still Yukan's people believed they were above the other clans in Ogono. When would the Korigaidis realize that placing them at the front lines of the Sacred Army had nothing to do with honoring them? While one might argue it was their prowess in battle that earned them their place, Yukan saw it as a higher share of suffering for his very clan. The fearless Korigaidis, who always boasted that their name was a synonym for death to their enemies, were about to test the most tormenting way to die.

"Don't wait for me, Dogo." Yukan dismounted and rubbed Thunder's shoulder. "I don't think she is ready now."

Dogo peered at him. "Do not underestimate the Mages' words, Yukan. All it takes to doom us all is one deserter."

Kill the deserters. Otherwise, they will kill you, Yukan remembered the Mages' warning. While he wondered why the entire army would suffer the Light's wrath because of one deserter, he couldn't see the point of deserting, to begin with. Either you flee to the scorched lands to die alone, or you return to your family to perish together.

Maybe that explained why it never crossed anybody's mind to question or even ponder the Mages' order. To put it simply, nobody had anything to lose.

To give his mare a chance to replenish her strength, Yukan walked her for an hour, his head and tunic soaked in his own sweat. As the midday sun was becoming harsher by the minute, he resisted the urge to quench his thirst or even glance at the waterskins. *Not now, Yukan. You will need them later,* he kept telling himself whenever he couldn't take it anymore. *Dogo knows nothing. Our ancestors called Si'oli the cursed desert for a reason. Those Mages are not telling us everything.*

And speaking of the Mages; where were they now? Shouldn't they be marching with their 'Sacred Army'?

The thought did alarm Yukan. Now lagging behind his clansmen because of his exhausted mare, he was marching alongside the *lesser clans* at the rearguard of this damned Sacred Army. "Where are the Mages?" he asked more than one horseman passing by him. A few told him they didn't know, but the majority didn't bother to even answer him, and he wasn't sure why. Did they loathe him because it was obvious he was a Korigaidi? Or did they find his question too silly to take seriously?

Yukan stopped walking his mare and waited until he could see the last horseman in the horde. "What is your problem, Korigaidi?" A lean, dark-skinned spearman approached Yukan, and a few of his kin followed him. *Xantis,* Yukan recognized the best spearmen in Ogono. From their suspicious looks, he could tell they had mistaken him for a deserter. He must be lucky those Xantis took the trouble to ask him, instead of thrusting a spear into his back. Killing a deserter would be a glorious act today.

"I'm looking for the Mages." Yukan was outnumbered one to six, but he did his best to keep his calm. He was still a

Korigaidi. And a Korigaidi was a dangerous being to mess with. "You know where they are?"

"A smart Korigaidi." The Xanti glanced at his fellows, some of them chuckling. "That's a first."

Twenty years ago, those Xantis wouldn't have dared to intimidate him. At that time, Yukan would have slayed all six of them with his sword while they were still dancing with their spears. Those young cocky bastards were clueless about one important fact: The forty-seven-year-old Korigaidi standing in front of them was *still* capable of slaying them. He might get a scratch or two, but eventually, he wouldn't be the one lying on the ground in a pond of his own blood.

"Listen, *boys*." Yukan glared at the six Xantis. "If you have no answer to my simple question, then I suggest you get out of the way of that smart Korigaidi."

"We have been marching for weeks across the scorched lands to make it this far." The young Xanti gnashed his teeth. "We will never let all of that go in vain because of one coward."

The last word was enough to make Yukan's blood boil. Without thinking twice, he reached for the sword strapped to his back and...

"*STOP! Stop this farce at once!*"

The seven quarreling men turned to the balding, fair-skinned horseman yelling at them. He was a Quashtran; Yukan could tell from his looks and, more importantly, his long bow. And he wasn't alone. A dozen mounted Quashtran archers flanked him, their faces grim, their eyes scanning their *potential* opponents. One wrong word, and Yukan would die with those foolish Xantis.

The furious Quashtran and his clansmen approached measuredly, yet still keeping their distance. "Haven't you had enough blood yet? Our women and children are already suffering because of our sins."

"We caught him trying to abandon the army," the Xanti told the Quashtran.

"That's a lie!" Yukan barked. "I was looking for the Mages."

"What's your business with the Mages, Korigaidi?" the balding Quashtran asked suspiciously.

Yukan could tell him to mind his own business, but that answer wouldn't take him anywhere. "Just tell me where they are. I must talk to them."

"You see?" The Xanti swept an arm toward Yukan as he faced the Quashtran. "He is taking us for a bunch of fools."

"We will take it from here, brothers," the balding Quashtran firmly said to the Xantis. "Be on your way. We will see you in Gorania."

The Xantis looked from the Quashtrans to Yukan and back. Surprisingly, they made no stupid move and abided by the Quashtran's *gentle* command. When nobody was standing between Yukan and the mounted archers, the balding Quashtran said, "You should pull yourself together, wise man. Whatever the pressing business you have with the Mages is, no one will allow you to go back to Ogono. It's too late now."

Back to Ogono? Too late? *We will see you in Gorania*, Yukan recalled the Quashtran's words to the Xantis. "May the Light have mercy on my soul," Yukan muttered, gazing at the endless desert around him. It resembled the desolate sandy lands at the northern borders of Ogono except for one missing feature. *When you see sand but no hills, turn around and race the wind until you spot the first rock.* For generations, the Korigaidis had passed that piece of advice to their descendants to prevent them from being *swallowed* by Si'oli.

But today, Yukan was not swallowed. He was here in Si'oli out of his own will.

"So, you say the Mages are not marching through Si'oli with us?" Though Yukan was almost certain of the answer, he asked the Quashtran, hoping he might hear something surprising.

"Why should they? They did their job by showing us the path. Now it's our turn to do ours."

Those Mages did not need to be warriors to join this horde. If this Sacred Army was *sacred* as they claimed, they could just accompany them on this march through Si'oli, at least to embolden any wavering hearts, like his. But they knew the truth of this place. They knew they couldn't protect themselves, let alone a hundred thousand men.

"I must warn them," Yukan said as he jumped on his mare.

"You understand we will shoot you in the head once you make one step toward Ogono?"

"I'm not going back to Ogono on my own, Quashtran," Yukan said. "You had better urge your people to come back while they still..."

Yukan paused when he noticed that eerie silence reigning over the desert. The Quashtrans noticed it too, all of them gaping at the huge horde that suddenly stopped its march. What would make a hundred thousand men suddenly hush, all at the same time?

And then Yukan could hear it. A faint screech echoing in the desert.

From Yukan's spot, he couldn't see the front-most riders of the Sacred Army, but he could tell for certain they were not silent anymore. With more dreadful screeches ringing all over the place, the nervous hubbub was getting louder. Even the horses became edgy and started neighing in unison.

Thunder, who was no exception, joined the restless chorus. While looking around to see where those screeches were coming from—because they sounded as if they were coming from everywhere, even from the ground underneath their feet—Yukan petted his mare in a desperate attempt to calm her down. But how could he do that while she could sense his own anxiety?

"*The sky!*" the riders in front of Yukan repeated the word more than a dozen times. Thunder raised her forelimbs as countless stars appeared in the bright sky. A few seconds later, Yukan noticed they were actually moving. *Those are not stars. They are comets.*

And they were descending. With piercing, horrifying cries that didn't belong to any creature known to this world.

"May the Light have..." Yukan didn't continue his prayers as he realized what those *comets* really were. Without thinking twice, he wheeled Thunder and spurred her to gallop back toward Ogono. The Quashtran, who had been embracing the Mages' words a few minutes ago, was not seen anywhere in this havoc.

Yukan didn't look back to see why the men behind him were shrieking. "Just fly, Thunder! Fly! Fly!" he urged his mare, though she didn't seem in need of his commands any longer. The mare was following her own survival instinct right now. As the shrieks were getting closer and the screeches were growing louder, Yukan's instinct told him he was a dead man. The last thing he remembered was a horrendous cry piercing his ear as a column of fire engulfed him.

About the Author

Karim Soliman earned his first writing commission through his contribution in the first and last issue of his school magazine. Twenty years later, he earned his next commission from Sony Pictures.

While he holds a bachelor's degree in pharmacy and a master's in business administration, Karim finds his groove in building worlds and messing with his characters. His debut "The Warrior's Path" was a #1 bestseller on several fantasy subgenres on Amazon, and his book "Army of the Cursed" was an SPFBO semi-finalist.

When Karim is away from writing, he struggles with his insomnia and continues his search for his next favorite dessert.

To reach out to him and hear the latest news about his work, check his website:

https://writerkarimsoliman.com

Want to know how it all began? Check the Tales of Gorania series.

Or binge-read the boxed set.

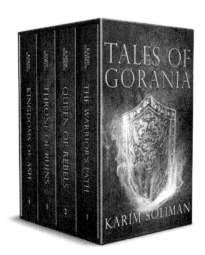

Printed in Great Britain
by Amazon

22826735R00162